5/12   FC   4-

D0430333

PRAISE FOR CHRISTOPHER BELTON AND *ISOLATION*!

"Engaging and hard to put down, with underdog characters to root for—big!"

—*Booklist*

"Belton delivers a fast-paced and exciting suspense thriller with a doomsday premise that is frightening and fascinating. It's one of the best novels I've read in a while."

—Raymond Benson, author of
The Man with the Red Tattoo

"Belton's Crichton-esque pacing . . . is brisk and readable."

—*Publishers Weekly*

THE EXECUTION

Hisamitsu was not sure what was in store for him, but he knew it would not be pleasant. At the very least he was in for a beating. He was not scared for his life. The Yakuza sometimes polished each other off during gang wars, but their activities rarely resulted in the death of non-related people.

The car finally came to a stop concealed from the road by a clump of bushes and assorted foliage. The driver turned on the interior light before killing the engine, extinguishing the headlights and climbing out of the car. The man in the back covered him while his colleague in the passenger seat got out, still clutching Hisamitsu's bag, before backing out of the car himself. The driver opened the door of the back seat and pointed the gun at Hisamitsu's head. Something in the driver's eyes—a slight squint as if waiting for a balloon to pop—warned Hisamitsu that he was witnessing his own execution. Why? The word rattled around inside his head as pressure was increased on the trigger. . . .

Other *Leisure* books by Christopher Belton:

ISOLATION

NOWHERE TO RUN

CHRISTOPHER BELTON

LEISURE BOOKS   NEW YORK CITY

To Michiyo, Jamie, Shane, Akiko and Liam
Thank you all for being there.

LEISURE BOOKS ®

August 2004

Published by

Dorchester Publishing Co., Inc.
200 Madison Avenue
New York, NY 10016

This book was originally published under the title *Crime Sans Frontiéres*.

ISBN 0-8439-5380-2

Visit us on the web at www.dorchesterpub.com.

NOWHERE TO RUN

Chapter One

Japan (Tokyo)

It was raining as she left the subway station and turned right along the Showa Dori, but apart from bunching her shoulders lower into her light raincoat, she gave no sign of having noticed. Her black hair quickly absorbed the drizzly moisture and shone in the glare from the overhead streetlights, and the shoulders of her beige raincoat darkened quickly. Her hands, jammed deep into her pockets, fiddled nervously with two keys, but this was the only sign of agitation she allowed herself.

Less than three minutes after leaving the subway, she pushed open the glass door of the Ishihara Building, walked silently over the dull and yellowing linoleum, past the single elevator, and turned into the stairwell. Taking care to prevent the swinging buckle of her raincoat from coming into contact with the stair rails, she swiftly climbed to the fourth floor. The only light

1

source on the fourth floor came from a red lamp located above a fire hose, but it was sufficient to illuminate the legend "Sunset Travel Bureau, Co. Ltd." blazoned in both Japanese and English across two glass doors opposite the elevator. The office was dark and obviously empty, but she knocked twice and waited in the silence. As expected, there was no answer. Taking the keys from her pocket, she held them up to the red glow and, selecting one, inserted it into the single lock at the very bottom of the door. Taking a deep breath, she turned the key and pushed, half expecting the door to stay locked. It opened. She now had thirty seconds to locate and turn off the alarm with the other key before bells started ringing in the security maintenance office three blocks away. She found the alarm control box where she had been told it would be—ten paces along the wall to the left—and swiftly disarmed it.

Stepping carefully, she moved across the dim office toward the pinprick of light that shone through a frosted glass door panel over to the right. The humming noise became perceptibly louder as she neared it. She had noticed the low-pitched hum as she entered the office and had breathed a sigh of relief. Her biggest worry had been that she would find the computer powered down and have to waste twenty minutes while the IPL ran—time she could ill afford.

She opened the door, stepped inside, and switched on the light. The small windowless room had only just enough space for the three towers of the IBM computer, two monitors on stands, two printers, a small, gray metal desk, and a rack of metallic tapes. She glanced at the clock over the desk and checked it against her watch.

21:10. Fifty minutes in which to get the job done and leave the building before it was locked up for the night.

She unbuttoned her coat, sat down at the main console, and removed a single sheet of paper from her inside pocket. Smoothing it out on the area beside the keyboard, she turned her attention to the sign-on screen displayed in yellow against a black background on the VDU. She tapped in "ANPANMAN" twice for sign-on code and password, and after a second's pause the screen displayed a menu. Ignoring the menu, she typed in the command to display the print queue, only to trigger a nonauthorization error. She clicked her tongue in exasperation and signed off. She might have known that any staff member who used a cartoon character's name for a sign-on code would not have system authority, but it irked her to realize that the information she had been given was flawed. Surely they must have realized that the machine would not let anybody—let alone Anpanman—mess around in its interior.

She sat back and considered the situation. She would now have to guess her way into the system. She turned back to the keyboard and typed in "TEST" twice, but access was denied. At the time of system installation the most common sign-on code was TEST, and it usually carried full system authority, but if this system had ever used this code, it had been erased. She dismissed the other most common code, GUEST, as having too low an authority status, and tried AS400, IBM, EDP, MANAGER, CPU, and SE, all of which failed. In desperation she tapped in "QSECOFR"—the password that is set in the factory and comes with the machine—and was surprised when the computer's system menu flashed onto the screen. She suppressed a grin. Nobody, but nobody, leaves QSECOFR in the user profile—at least, almost nobody.

Having gained access to the system, she checked the active job list to make sure she would not interfere with any batch jobs, swiftly called up the print queue, put all subsequent jobs on hold to prevent the printer from spewing out reams of paper while she worked, noted the final queue entry, and amended the priority parameter to ensure that any lists she did generate would join the back of the queue.

Although she was now into the system, she had no idea of the program codes to run the customized system she needed to work on. She typed in "DSPUSRPRF" and scrolled through the list of user profiles to find a code that would give her high-authority access. It amused her to discover that most of the staff codes were cartoon or famous TV characters. She finally selected SAZAESAN, signed off, and punched in the new code.

Once again the main operation menu was displayed. This time she input the number 3 and the AMEND ITIN-ERARY screen appeared. The screen prompted her to input a tour number, and referring to the sheet of paper beside the keyboard she typed in a ten-digit number. The screen changed once again to display a full page of tour movements. She glanced at the top of the screen to double-check the tour name against the piece of paper, and was satisfied to note they matched exactly: FIT MR. KITAZAWA.

Using the roll-down key, she scrolled through the data until APRIL 07 was displayed at the top of the screen. Halfway down the page of data was an entry that had Mr. Kitazawa arriving in Madrid at 11:15

aboard the BA458 flight from London, status on request. She moved the cursor to this entry and quickly typed IB5163 over the flight number, 14:55 over the arrival time, and changed the status from RQ to OK. When she updated the amendment, an A was also logged in the file record to indicate that a change had been made.

Back in the main menu, she selected "14" for data sending and hit the Enter button to reconfirm her choice. The machine started to work. Record by record it worked its way through all of the system's main data files, hunting for records with the A flag. Coming across the entry she had amended, it paused long enough to open an intermediate holding file, copy the whole record into it, and then erase the indicator in the original file. Continuing its search, it came up with three other records, each of which it also copied into the now-open file. Having reached the end of the file, it went on to the next main data file, repeating the process until it had made a total of five temporary files—one each for basic tour data, tour itinerary data, rooming list data, invoicing data, and tour message data.

The machine then went to work on the temporary files. It double-checked each piece of data several times against other files to establish if the record was a valid contender for sending and, having satisfied itself, realigned the data to contain certain control flags and set the address for its destination before "packing" it into the most economical form for transmission and copying it across to the sending file.

The machine then connected itself to Nippon Dentsu's digital cable network and the data began to flow. Moments later, the data record she had amended arrived in the computer located in the Sunset Travel

Bureau's Madrid office on Calle de la Palma, was "unpacked," duly processed, and written over the top of the existing record, effectively erasing the original data from memory.

Having received signals back from all destinations that data had been accepted without error, the machine in Tokyo cut itself off from the rest of the world, deleted the temporary files, and returned to the main menu. The complete process from start to finish had taken two minutes eighteen seconds.

A slight smirk of satisfaction creased her face as she typed in the command to allow edit of the print queue. She noted that the machine had generated four checklists throughout the whole procedure—none of which had been passed across to the printer owing to the hold command. She deleted them, took the machine off hold, and signed off. Her job was nearly finished.

Replacing the sheet of paper back into her pocket, she double-checked that the computer room showed no signs of her entry before switching off the light and stepping outside. She waited for her eyesight to readjust to the gloom and then began walking slowly up and down the rows of desks, searching for a desktop calendar open at October 4. She found it on the third row. She flipped the pages to November 16 and found the prearranged confirmation she sought in the three Chinese characters that said "birthday." She slipped a plain white envelope from her inside pocket and placed it quietly into the top left-hand drawer of the desk. The owner of the desk had received an early birthday present of ten crispy ten-thousand-yen notes.

Tracing her feet back to the front entrance, she reset the alarm, left the office, locked the door, and proceeded down the stairs as quietly as she had mounted them.

The rain had stopped by the time she reached the street, but the slick roads glistened wetly. She made her way down the street to the bright lights surrounding JR's Kanda Station, pausing only to remove a cell phone from her inside pocket beneath the illumination of a streetlamp. She dialed a local number and waited.

"Hello?"

"It's me," she said. "The work has been completed."

The phone clicked and went dead.

Replacing the cell phone in her pocket, she made her way to a self-service coffee bar just in front of the station, where she ordered a coffee. She relished the hot liquid as it burned a track down her parched throat. A glance at her watch told her she had made it with plenty of time to spare; it was still only 21:47. Finishing the coffee, she placed her empty cup on the back of the service counter and threw the crumpled napkin she had used to wipe her lips into the waste bin. Within it were two keys and a tightly balled sheet of paper.

England (Sunderland)

The sound of the production line was slightly muffled inside the computer room, but not enough to allow the gentle hum of the air-conditioning to be heard. The plant worked on downgraded production during the graveyard shift, so only seven of the sixteen personal computers that controlled the production robots continued to transmit their signals. The computers were left mostly unattended, but it was not unusual for a foreman to occasionally enter the room to check production figures.

Yamada Motors had established the plant in the north of England during the late eighties in order to produce its Carolina hatchback, but production had been extended to cover a number of engine parts for four other models produced in similar plants across Europe.

The graveyard shift—stretching between one o'clock and eight o'clock in the morning—was manned by only twenty-eight workers, whose basic job was to check that the quality of work turned out by the seven tireless robots that were not afforded nights off was flawless. The job was boring but well paid, and most of the checks were cursory anyway. After all, robots didn't make mistakes.

It was approaching three o'clock when the door of the computer room opened and a figure in a gray, one-piece overall with the bright yellow Yamada logo attached to the top left-hand pocket entered. He carried a clipboard and began to make a slow circuit of all sixteen workstations, stopping momentarily before each to jot down a comment. Arriving at workstation No. 9, he affected a dramatic double-take, in case anyone was watching, and settled down in the swivel chair positioned directly in front of it.

Turning his back on the window that looked out onto the shop floor, he removed a single CD-ROM disk from the pocket adorned with the company logo and, using his clipboard to conceal the motion, surreptitiously inserted it into the disk drive.

The drive hummed into action, and the screen saver, displaying a swirling geometric pattern to prevent the image of a static panel being burnt onto the surface of the screen, was replaced with the main menu. The phrase "Off-line—Stand by" was displayed on the top right-hand corner of the screen, and having checked this to assure himself that the machine was not actively linked to one of the robots, he selected "Parameters" by hitting the f.4 key and waited while the new display scrolled onto the screen. The new screen flashed a warning stating that all prior parameters would be erased if he continued, but that the procedure could be aborted by pressing the ESC key.

He pressed the carriage return key.

The indicator beside the disk drive flashed momentarily and the computer asked him to type in his authorization code. Checking his clipboard, he tapped out J03GH472 and hit the return key again. The legend "Parameter Loading in Progress" began to flash on the screen and the disk drive whirred into life. It took just under fourteen seconds for the parameter files to be copied from the CD-ROM and written over the original files on the computer's hard disk, and when this was complete the screen returned to the original menu. He leaned forward as if studying something on screen, pressed the button to eject the disk from the drive, slipped it into his pocket, and leaned back as if satisfied. He made a short note on his clipboard, glanced out of the window to see if anybody had observed the entire process, and, confident that nobody had, continued with his rounds of the remaining workstations.

Ten minutes later, he was back in the canteen sipping a cup of hot Nescafé from the vending machine. He waved cheerfully at a couple of fellow workers who arrived for a break, and found it difficult to wipe the smile off his face after they had sat at another table and begun to open packs of sandwiches.

He had worked for the company for six years, and although they paid well and treated him well, six thousand quid was a lot of lolly for a ten-minute job. His wife was going to be over the moon when she discovered that they could actually afford that holiday on the Island of Rhodes that he had promised her just about every year of their seventeen years of marriage. Yes, there was no doubt about it; he was only four and a half hours away from completing the most profitable shift of his entire career.

France (Paris)

The Rue du Faubourg St. Honoré runs parallel with the Avenue des Champs-Elysées and is filled with droves of fashion-conscious shoppers and tourists during the day. At night, however, it empties out to reveal a narrow street lined with an impressive mixture of timeworn and modern architecture.

The head office of Coppens Industrial Construction S.A. occupied four floors of a semimodern building not one hundred meters from the intersection with the Bd. Haussmann, and, as was usual for nine o'clock on a Friday evening, lights still blazed on the third floor.

Muffled voices speckled with intermittent laughter could be heard as the man carefully pushed open the swing doors to the third-floor office and silently slid inside. He padded gently over the open-plan office to a desk at the far side and crouched down behind it before looking over at the door of the general manager's office, which opened out into the office. Confident that he had been neither seen nor heard, he leaned back against the wall, stretched his legs out under the desk, and glanced at his watch. He had about one hour to wait, and he wanted to be as comfortable as possible.

He knew from six weeks of keeping a close watch on the office—especially at night—that the four or five managers invited into the general manager's office for the regular Friday-night drink would begin to make moving noises at around 21:30 and that the general manager would wave away their protests and open another bottle of wine or ply them with refills from the ever-present brandy bottle. The managers would laugh, make dramatic gestures, and accept the final drink, but its consumption would be punctuated with loud exclamations as each in turn made emphatic shows of realizing the time, followed by derogatory remarks about their wives and the punishment they could expect if they stayed any longer. The ritual played through, the empty glasses would be placed on a tray for the cleaner the next morning, and they would collect their coats and briefcases, then leave the office together. The general manager would have a last snifter of brandy for the road, telephone for a taxi, and leave about ten minutes later.

True to expectations, the door to the general manager's office opened at a few minutes before ten and five men filed out, still talking and laughing bawdily about one of the office girls. The man concealed behind the desk held his breath while each man collected his jacket and bag from a line of narrow lockers located beside the rest rooms and shouted out a final farewell to the general manager, still seated in his office, cradling a brandy balloon in both hands. When the office was finally quiet, the general manager heaved himself up from his chair and refilled his brandy glass. Back in his seat, he telephoned for a taxi and then began to flick through the pages of his desktop diary in a bored manner while taking an occasional sip from the glass. Tiring of this, he finished off the brandy, placed the glass on the tray with the other empties, and collected his jacket from a stand behind the door. The man behind the desk watched him set the alarm, turn the lights off, and lock the office, but refrained from breathing a sigh of relief until he had heard a car stop outside, a door slam, and the racing of a motor as it pulled away again.

He was in. All he had to worry about now was getting out, but as that problem would not loom for another nine hours, he dismissed it from his mind and adjusted his position on the floor. Although he knew security staff did not patrol the building, he had decided that he would remain hidden for at least one hour before starting work, just in case the general manager had forgotten something and returned.

The hour passed slowly, but he was no stranger to boredom and found much to occupy his thoughts. He checked his watch regularly with the light from the street, but did not move until the second hand had actually passed the top of the dial to indicate that it was eleven o'clock exactly. His first action was to remove a 300ml bottle of mineral water from a small sports bag he had brought with him and take a swig to quench his thirst. Replacing the bottle, he quietly got to his feet and walked toward an area of the office that was partitioned off with gray screens to create a small meeting room. The streetlights provided sufficient illumination for him to navigate across the office, but visibility was drastically reduced behind the screens, so he fumbled in the bag and withdrew a penlight. The thin beam revealed the screened-off area to hold a long cream-colored table, eight chairs, and an electronic whiteboard. The top of the table was piled high with folders, loose papers, two telephones, and a personal computer, and the whiteboard displayed a mass of scribbled comments and free-hand diagrams.

Clearing a space beside the computer, he pulled up a chair, placed the sports bag on the floor beside him, and switched on the main power to the machine. While the computer fired up and loaded the OS, he leaned over to the bag and removed a notepad, a pen, a plastic case containing a single blank CD-R disk, and a small laptop computer. Arranging these items in convenient locations around the computer, he snapped off the penlight and turned back to the computer screen that now displayed the Coppens's logo on the wallpaper of the desktop. Selecting the file manager with the mouse, he began to browse through the system directories to get an idea of the layout. It took him only twenty seconds to discover that the system contained two hard-drive spindles, C: and D:, and that the C: drive was used specifically for applications and programs while the D: drive contained only data files. Concentrating on the D: drive, he began to browse through the various directories contained therein. A closer inspection revealed that the data that interested him was stored within a subdirectory titled TENDER.

The TENDER subdirectory contained a total of thirty-seven files, and he began to scroll through these to find the names of the fourteen files that were neatly written down on his notepad. Having found the first, he scrutinized the screen and wrote down the date and time of the last update beside the entry on his pad before moving on to the next. Within a few moments, he had logged all fourteen files and grunted softly in satisfaction. Things were going better than he had expected.

Next, he leaned over and hit the power switch on the laptop he had brought with him. When it had powered up, he shifted his position slightly until he was comfortably facing the screen, then clicked on the DOS prompt and typed in the "Date" command. Referring to his notepad, he tapped in the date of the first file on his list and pressed the carriage return key. He then typed in the "Time" command and amended the system clock to one minute earlier than the time written beside the same entry in the desktop computer. He knew he was probably going too far—for who ever checked the date and time of file update?—but he was a perfectionist and was at his happiest when he knew he was doing a good job.

Starting up the same word-processing software as the Coppens' computer, he called out the first of the fourteen files that resided in a directory on his own laptop and hit the Save button when his system clock corresponded to the time logged in the notebook. He closed the file and then checked to ensure that the revised information had been logged against the file name. Satisfied, he returned to the DOS prompt to repeat the same procedure for the next file.

It took nearly twenty minutes for him to modify all file times, but he would not have overlooked this if it had taken five hours.

He then burned all fourteen of the updated files onto the CD-R disk, switched off the laptop, and turned back to the Coppens's desktop computer. Once again using the file manager, he copied the files from the CD-R disk onto the TENDER subdirectory, overwriting the original data and replacing it with the data he had brought with him. He then deactivated the "Read Only" flags on the new files, removed the disk from the drive, ended the file manager, and switched off the computer.

He ran the entire procedure over in his mind once again to assure himself that nothing had been overlooked, then began to replace all of his belongings into the sports bag. His work was finished.

Ten minutes later, he was laid out on the sofa in the general manager's office. He drank some more water and ate a bar of chocolate, checked to ensure that the alarm on his wristwatch was set at six A.M., and then closed his eyes.

The buzzer on his watch woke him at exactly six o'clock, and he was instantly alert. Having established his bearings, he visited the toilet to pee and rinse the sleep out of his mouth, then revisited the screened-off meeting room to make sure he had left no evidence of his night's labors. Satisfied that no trace of his presence remained, he returned to the desk at the back of the office and resumed the position on the floor that he had maintained the night before.

It was a little after seven when he heard the noise of keys turning in the lock of the main door. He pressed himself harder into his hiding place to avoid detection and was relieved when the door did not open. His previous studies of the building had indicated that the janitor unlocked all doors from bottom to top to provide access to the cleaners, but the cleaners did not begin work until seven-thirty. This gave him approximately twenty-five minutes to get out of the building, and as the janitor had taken the elevator to the next floor up, now was his best chance.

He peeped over the top of the desk, grabbed his bag, and crept silently across the carpeting to the door. Nobody was in sight, and with his heart pounding in his chest, he sprinted down the stairs and managed to gain the street without being noticed.

He whistled jauntily as he strolled down the street to the Place de la Concorde, where he would catch his train home.

Chapter Two

Switzerland (Geneva)

Armin Marceillac leaned back in his chair and tapped his front tooth thoughtfully with the end of a pencil. The six files laid out on his desk were puzzling him. The contents of each described what was deemed to be a computer-related crime, but apart from that they seemed to have absolutely nothing in common. Except the word "Japan."

"Sylvie, is the boss in yet?"

Sylvie Keppler looked up from her computer screen and nodded her answer, eliciting an exaggerated look of surprise from Marceillac. Jasper Hewes was not a bad boss to work for, for a Brit, but his working hours were well-known for their eccentricity. It was unusual to catch him in the office before eleven o'clock in the morning, but he could usually be found at his desk at midnight, unless he was forced to attend a function that he had been unable to wriggle out of.

Marceillac picked up the phone and jabbed a finger at the keys. "Morning, sir. I have something I would like to discuss with you if you have a moment." He raised his eyes to the ceiling for Sylvie's benefit and was rewarded with a grin. "Yes, sir. I'll be right in."

Collecting the files on his desk, Marceillac looked across at Sylvie. "Maybe you ought to join in on this. I think I have something that might affect us both."

"Sure," said Sylvie. "Anything interesting?"

"Mm, difficult to say for sure, but I might need you for a sounding board. Any objections?" Sylvie grinned again, picked up a spiral-bound pad of notepaper, and walked around the desk toward him. Marceillac whistled in approval only to receive a playful slap on the arm.

"Come on, animal." Sylvie linked her arm through his. "I am a sounding board and nothing more. Remember that," she said, wagging her finger at him like a schoolmistress admonishing a naughty child.

Jasper Hewes's office was wood-paneled, cozy, and redolent of cigar smoke. An antique desk stood at right angles to the far left-hand corner, providing Hewes with a view out onto the Chemin des Colombettes during his not-infrequent lapses into contemplatory thought. A laptop computer occupied one corner of the desk, but this was the only indication of the modern age, and seemed slightly out of place in an office that could have been lifted straight out of an old and venerated place of learning.

The International Organization for Computer Crime (IOCC) was established in 1993 to collect and correlate information and to act as a liaison between the rapidly increasing number of agencies set up in advanced nations to combat the burgeoning problem of computer crime. An offshoot of the Commission on Crime Prevention and Criminal Justice—which is solely answerable to the General Assembly of the United Nations—the IOCC also maintained close links with the World Intellectual Property Organization, hence its location on the Chemin des Colombettes in Geneva. Despite its rather grand title, the IOCC was mostly engaged in passing information between the agencies in different countries and generally policing the mass of on-line servers connected to the Internet for flagrant transgressions of property rights.

Hewes was already seated on the sofa when Marceillac and Keppler arrived, and he waved them to the two armchairs facing him across an oak coffee table.

"Now, what can I do for you, Armin? Not trouble, I hope."

"I am not sure, sir," said Marceillac in heavily accented English. Despite the fact that the IOCC was located in Geneva and staffed almost entirely by a workforce of Swiss nationals, Hewes's French was painfully labored and everybody spoke to him in English. "Maybe I am chasing shadows, but I have found six nonrelated cases that all seem to have a common link with Japan. It could be coincidence, but I thought I should bring it to your attention."

"And so you should, my boy, so you should. Fire away."

Marceillac placed five of the files on the coffee table and opened the sixth on his lap. "This report came from Madrid," he said. "The president of a Japanese construction company went missing and was discovered three days later with his throat cut in the rose garden of the Parque del Retiro. The Madrid office of the travel agency who had arranged all of his movements sent a representative to the airport to meet his scheduled flight, but he was not on it. It was later discovered that the information regarding his flight status was tampered with in the Tokyo office and false information sent through to Madrid on-line. Presumably somebody else met his real flight, pretended to be the agency rep, and spirited him away to his death."

Sylvie looked up from the notes she was furiously writing. "Has the tampering in Tokyo been confirmed?"

"Yes, but the culprit has yet to be found. A time stamp revealed the fact that the data was transmitted from the Tokyo office to Madrid at 21:26 local time, but there was nobody in the office at that time. Also, the office makes only one transmission per day between 17:30 and 18:00, and it has been verified that this transmission was carried out as usual."

Hewes nodded sagely and motioned for Marceillac to continue.

"Coincidence number two." He picked up the next file. "Yamada Motors, a Japanese automobile manufacturer, was forced to recall nearly eighteen thousand Carolinas produced in England owing to faulty engine mountings. It appears that the parameters for the assembly robot were changed to reduce the amount of spot welds from fourteen to nine on a certain area of the mounting, but nobody noticed until one of the vehicles was returned to the factory for inspection following an unrelated problem. It has still not been established when the parameters were actually changed, so all vehicles have to be recalled. Fortunately, no accidents have been reported, but the cost of the recall will certainly jeopardize the future of the plant."

Hewes, leaning back with his eyes closed and hands steepled before him, said, "How were the parameters changed? Is that an easy thing to do?"

"In this case, no." Marceillac flipped over a page in the file and traced his finger down until he reached the spot he wanted. "The computers that control the robots are imported from Japan already set up and do not contain any applications with which to amend the internal settings. All modifications are sent across from Japan and can only be loaded into the machine from a CD-ROM with the use of an authorization code. The system security also cancels out the possibility of the parameter files being copied from the disks and amended in a different machine."

"So how was it done?"

"So far nobody knows."

Hewes grunted, and Marceillac picked up the next file.

"Coincidence number three. A French construction company submitted a tender for a large-scale dam project in Zaire, but the actual document itself was severely tampered with. Several important areas contained ludicrous figures, and there were even some highly racial remarks about Africans in general and Zairians in particular. This must have been carried out right at the last minute, as all of the documents were checked and rechecked several times before the final printout and subsequent submission. Needless to say, the French company lost the project, and have even been threatened with reprisals."

"I don't see the relationship," said Sylvie.

"The only other contender for the project happened to be a Japanese company."

Hewes heaved himself forward in his seat and reached out for the three files covered so far. The lines on his forehead became pronounced as he flipped through them one by one. "And the others?" he prompted.

"The other three don't appear to have the same massive implications as the first three, but still manage to poke a finger at Japan. A virus was released in the computer of a software company in Seoul, Korea, and the disk was wiped clean, effectively destroying four months' worth of development work. The backup machine was also wiped clean. Fortunately, they still have all printed documentation, but the project has been delayed for a minimum of six weeks. So far a motive has yet to be discovered."

"And the link with Japan?" asked Sylvie.

"The virus resided in the main memory, so it failed to destroy itself when the disk crashed. An investigation of the program came up with some unprintable characters that were finally discovered to be Japanese double-byte Kanji."

"Did these characters provide any leads?" Hewes was once again sitting back on the sofa holding the files on his lap.

"No, they simply gave a name that is presumed to be the name of the programmer—Suzuki, a very common name in Japan." Marceillac pulled another file. "The next concerns a London-based law firm," he continued. "The company handles the interests of several Japanese clients within Britain, and it was discovered that a line of code had been added to their on-line software so that all e-mail sent out from the office was duplicated and automatically sent to a server account in Japan. We had the Tokyo office check up on the account, but the holder professed innocence and they believe him. It seems as if somebody had managed to get hold of his account number and password and was using it on a daily basis."

Marceillac drew a breath and waited while Sylvie finished scribbling her notes. Opening the last file, he glanced over at Hewes and was glad to note the look of concern on his face reflecting his own worries. He had been slightly reluctant to approach Hewes with the problem in case he had waved it away and accused him of clutching at straws. In fact, he discovered that reading each file out loud had enforced his conviction that at least some of the six cases were linked.

"And the last one," he continued, "is a simple case of breaking and entering. An unemployed systems engineer was caught in the office of the mayor of Greensboro, North Carolina, in the process of copying everything from the mayor's personal computer onto floppy disks. During questioning he revealed that he had been approached by two Japanese men who offered him five thousand dollars for the data, but he knew neither their names nor how to contact them. So far that is all the information we have, but the local authorities have more or less given up on the idea of catching the instigators and appear to be satisfied with simply charging the man with illegal entry and attempted burglary."

Having finished his monologue, Marceillac replaced the files on the table and sat back expectantly.

"What do you think, Sylvie?" asked Hewes.

Sylvie looked backed through her notes. "Well," she

said, turning her deep brown eyes onto Hewes, "I think we have the cause for an investigation, but first I would like to know the general percentage of computer-related crime with any links to Japan over the past several years. Six cases is not a lot considering the volume of crime we have coming out of America and Europe."

"Armin?"

Marceillac cleared his throat. "I have already run some checks and discovered that there were a total of two computer-related deceptions coming out of Japan last year, none for the year before, and only one for the year before that. This is, of course, ignoring the run-of-the-mill viruses that pop up every now and then. Also, all six of these cases occurred within the past two months, which seems just a bit too coincidental."

Hewes stood up, walked over to his desk, pressed the intercom button, and ordered three cups of coffee. Back in his seat, he rubbed his chin with a gnarled hand. "Have you been in touch with the Electronic Crime Bureau in Tokyo about this?"

"Not officially. But I did send a message requesting figures for domestic computer crimes over the past few years. I wanted to see if a similar increase was prevalent within Japan. I should get a reply sometime tomorrow."

"I think we need that reply a bit sooner." Hewes walked over to his desk again, seated himself, and flipped open a desk diary. Having found the number, he punched it out and waited for the connection.

"Ah, yes. Good evening. This is Jasper Hewes calling from Geneva. Could I speak to Mr. Hirata, please?"

The coffee was delivered while he waited. He was stirring in the second spoonful of sugar when a voice came on the other end of the line.

"Good morning, Jasper. I trust you are in good health."

"Tsutomu, my friend. Good to hear your voice. And, pray tell me, what are you doing in the office at this time of night?" said Hewes, glancing at his watch and adding the seven-hour time difference. "Don't you have a home to go to?"

"I simply follow in your footsteps, Jasper. My work is an all-consuming passion, and I would rather spend time with it than sit alone at home." Hewes laughed dutifully and took a sip of coffee. "Listen, Tsutomu. One of my colleagues in the office here sent a message to"— he looked across at Marceillac, who mouthed "Hisamitsu" in reply—"Mr. Hisamitsu requesting some data. I wonder if you could push it through and get it to us within today."

"I'll check. Hold the line." Hewes could hear Hirata speaking to somebody in the background. "Hisamitsu has all the data ready and can send it off to you in about ten minutes."

"What? Your staff are also at their desks?" asked Hewes in surprise.

"Most, but they are simply killing time until their favorite bar opens."

Hewes expressed his thanks and replaced the receiver. He then pressed the intercom and kept his finger on the button while he spoke to his secretary. "Lutgard, I am expecting some e-mail addressed to either myself or Armin from Tokyo in the next few minutes. Could you print it out and let me have three copies, please?"

While they waited for the data, they reviewed what they had so far. Although six seemingly coincidental cases was a poor basis for initiating further action, they all felt that it at least warranted a low-level investigation of some form. Neither would have admitted it, but both Marceillac and Keppler were hoping that an investigation would be sanctioned. Despite the fact that the staff of the IOCC liked to romanticize their work by giving the impression that they were involved in eradicating *crime sans frontieres*—crime without borders—their daily working lives followed routine to an almost boring degree, and anything to get their teeth into would come as a welcome break. Marceillac's most recent taste of excitement had been his involvement in coordinating the capture of two students from Sweden's Royal Institute of Technology who had had the temerity to provide popular software free of charge on the Internet at a cost of one point seven million dollars to the publishers, but his part in the operation had simply been to pass messages between the Office of International Criminal Justice in Chicago and the Stockholm office of Europe's Business Software Alliance. Sylvie Keppler's track record was even more mundane, so a case that included murder and intrigue had them both licking their lips in anticipation.

Twenty minutes later, the secretary arrived with the copies of the data from Tokyo and they relapsed into silence as they scanned the pages.

"Interesting," said Sylvie after a moment. "I do believe you are onto something, Armin."

The first page contained a short message from Hisamitsu expressing his hope that the figures would be useful and not to hesitate to contact him should further information be required, but it was the second page that held everybody's attention. It contained a table of figures broken down by month and covered the number of computer-related crimes within Japan over the past three years and the first five months of the current year. It was obvious at a glance that computer crime had skyrocketed in Japan.

Hewes was the first to look up from the sheet. "The figures took a threefold jump in March and have stayed stable at this inflated rate ever since. Remarkable."

Hewes fumbled in his pocket for his cigar case. He tried to avoid smoking when in the company of others, but he was capable of conveniently forgetting this self-imposed regulation when it suited him.

"This certainly cannot be put down to a warm spring." It was a well-known fact that crime figures surged during warm weather. "Well, Armin, my boy, you have convinced me that something is afoot. How do you wish to proceed with it?"

Marceillac leaned forward and placed his elbows on his knees. The question had caught him unprepared, for he had not expected his boss to be won over so easily and had yet to really formulate any firm plan of action. His mind racing, he began to tentatively voice his thoughts as they occurred to him.

"First of all, we shall need to give a complete report of our suspicions to the ECB in Tokyo and ask them to add any comments they might have. I would also want them to send me all reports on the computer crimes that were carried out in Japan since the beginning of March. There is a chance that we might find some similarities there."

"Would it be possible to gain access to the Interpol files?" asked Sylvie. "There are a lot of computer-related crimes that never arrive on our desks because they are not recognized as such. Maybe we could find a few more links."

"I will also contact the agencies handling these cases for updates." Marceillac slapped the pile of files on the table with the flat of his hand. "Maybe there have been some developments."

"Right!" said Hewes, getting to his feet. "That should be sufficient to start with. I'll arrange for the Interpol files to be sent to you, Armin. All files in which the word 'Japan' appears since the beginning of the year should do it. I'll also contact Hirata in Tokyo and set up a tele-conference for eleven o'clock tomorrow morning. I'll want you both to join in. In the meantime, see if you can get somebody else to handle your work, Sylvie, and join forces with Armin. Your first job will be to draft a report of everything you have told me this morning and prepare it for sending to Tokyo. Let me see it before you send it, and I'll add my own footnotes. And now, I think it is time for lunch. You are both invited and would conceivably incur my everlasting displeasure if you refuse."

Japan (Tokyo)

The Electronic Crime Bureau occupied three hundred and forty square meters of space on the fourth floor of a gray and monolithic building in Kasumigaseki, a business area of Tokyo famous for its vast number of government offices and the sarin poison-gas attack carried out by a religious cult in March 1995. The ECB was set up in April 1994—not because Japan had an uncontrollable volume of computer-related crimes but because most other UN-member countries already had similar agencies and the Prime Minister's Office did not want to feel left out. Administered by bureaucrats, the ECB had only four plainclothes detectives in residence. The remainder of the twenty-eight-strong staff were civil servants who had a natural penchant for working with computers.

Tsutomu Hirata was the director general of the ECB. A fifty-two-year-old career bureaucrat, he had graduated from Waseda University with honors some thirty years previously and had worked for the government ever since in a wide array of positions that had taken him through various agencies, including the Telecommunications Division of the Ministry of Foreign Affairs, the Meteorological Satellite Center in the Meteorological Agency, and the Security Bureau in the National Police Agency.

Hirata settled himself in front of the computer screen in one of the meeting rooms and reread the file received earlier from Geneva while he waited for the teleconference connection. He was impressed with the concise way in which the report had been laid out and reminded himself to commend Jasper Hewes on his thoroughness.

The computer beeped and the light under the small camera located above the monitor flashed red to indicate it was operating. He crossed one leg over the other and watched Jasper Hewes's face materialize on the left-hand side of the screen. A moment later, the image was reduced in size and transferred to the top of the screen as two other faces emerged in equal-sized windows directly below it. The teleconferencing system could handle a maximum of sixteen connections simultaneously, but the size of each image was reduced in proportion to the number of people on-line at any given moment. The right-hand side of the screen was reserved for documents, and as he watched, the first page of the file he had received appeared. With the use of the mouse he scrolled to the end of the document to see if any further information had been added. It hadn't.

"Good evening, Tsutomu," said Hewes. "Sorry to drag you away from your desk."

"Think nothing of it, Jasper. My time is your time," replied Hirata graciously. He felt a slight flush of embarrassment as his voice rang through the otherwise unoccupied room. He wondered what his daughter would say if she could see him sitting alone in a room holding a conversation with twenty kilograms of electronic components.

"Let me introduce you to two of my colleagues," continued Hewes, "Armin Marceillac and Sylvie Keppler." Both inclined their heads slightly, and Hirata returned the bow.

The introductions over, Marceillac launched into a brief recap of events so far.

"Yes, I've read the report, Mr. Marceillac, and I must praise you for some excellent investigative work," said Hirata, attempting to get over the slight feeling of annoyance that none of the three people on screen would look him in the eye. Their cameras were obviously positioned too high over the monitors, with the result that it seemed as if they were addressing his tiepin. He wondered at which portion of their anatomies he was directing his remarks. "We have certainly noted the increase in domestic computer crime here, but we had no idea things had spread so far across the globe. However, I find it difficult to believe that this is the result of an organized syndication, as you seem to suggest. I am sure that if we analyze the past three months' figures for computer sales and on-line account holders in Japan, we will find similar rates of increase—"

"Actually, sir," interrupted Sylvie, "we were comparing those figures this morning, and the percentages were totally disproportionate with the crime rates. Also, the level of knowledge and the logistics involved in these crimes are of such a degree that it couldn't possibly be a case of junior with a new PC."

Hirata nodded his agreement. He had, in fact, read the same conclusion into the issue himself. "I understand you want copies of all files for the past three months. May I ask what you intend to do with them?"

Hewes answered this one. "We wish to go through them and see if we can find any further links, something that you may have overlooked."

"Well, I can understand your interest, but I have yet to be convinced that this is a job for the IOCC. Six cases relating to Japan hardly seem to call for an international investigation, and the data you are requesting is strictly domestic in quality. As you know, I am under no obligation to provide you with information on domestic issues."

"You are, of course, perfectly within your rights to refuse me this, Tsutomu, but we are convinced we are onto something and your cooperation would be invaluable. A personal favor, maybe . . ."

"Aha . . ." Hirata laughed. "You certainly know my weaknesses, Jasper. Well, all right. Let's call it a personal favor. One, I might add, of which you will be reminded the next time you are in Japan round about the hour of the evening meal. I have been informed of a rather exclusive restaurant in Akasaka, but my meager salary prevents me from putting it to the test."

"Thank you, Tsutomu. I appreciate this very much."

"You will have to let me have a few days, as the files must be translated into English."

"There is one more favor we wish to ask, Mr. Hirata." Merceillac's eyes were still firmly fixed at a point approximately ten centimeters below Hirata's chin, but he was getting used to it. "Go ahead, Mr. Marceillac."

"Could you possibly assign one of your detectives to work with us on this? I would be willing to brief him or her myself. We are certain to have many questions as the investigation progresses, and we do not wish to trouble you any more than necessary."

Hirata nodded. "Of course. Would Mr. Hisamitsu suit your purposes? His English is acceptable, and I understand you have worked with him before."

"Thank you, sir."

"Well, if that is all I will return to my desk. Hold on for a few moments and I will send Mr. Hisamitsu in so you can bring him up to date. Thank you for your time, gentlemen, madame."

Japan (Tokyo)

Susumu Sakaguchi dug a toothpick into a piece of *yokan*, popped it into his mouth, and chewed noisily. He looked across at Ryoichi Narita, kneeling formally on the other side of the low table, and waved the toothpick in his direction. "Speak!" he commanded.

Narita kept his eyes on the delicate tea cup. "It appears, *oyabun*, that some of our overseas activities have attracted the attention of a certain organization in Geneva. An investigation has been launched."

Sakaguchi halted the movement of his mouth and a

look of rage flashed across his features. "Geneva? That fool Tokoro! How did this happen?"

"A connection was made with Japan by a diligent worker."

"Damn!" A red flush began to work itself over Sakaguchi's face. He hated incompetence and suffered fools lightly. "Get that idiot Tokoro over here, now!"

"I have already sent a car for him, *oyabun*. He should be here soon." Narita was no fan of Osamu Tokoro, but he felt sorry for him now.

"What is the name of this organization and what sort of investigation are they carrying out?"

"They are known as the International Organization for Computer Crime and are financed by the United Nations. I was informed that they have no jurisdiction over Japan and must work through our Electronic Crime Bureau and that the investigation is very low-level. A detective has been assigned to liaise with them, but he is very young and inexperienced and not considered to be a threat."

Sakaguchi grunted. Maybe it was not the end of the world after all. He hadn't deluded himself by thinking the "jobs"—as he liked to think of them—could go undetected indefinitely, and now that they knew the extent of the damage it would be easy enough to slip into recovery mode. "What is the name of this young detective?"

"Takeshi Hisamitsu, *oyabun*."

"Well, keep a firm eye on Mr. Hisamitsu. Do you hear me, Narita? Make sure that he does not find anything of interest. I will not accept failure on this and will hold you responsible." Sakaguchi curled a lip in an attempted smile. He liked to watch his minions squirm, and he knew that they equated his "nice" moods with the calm before a storm. Narita bowed his head close to the table to indicate that he understood.

Narita's servility pleased Sakaguchi. Being the leader of a small and obscure crime syndicate in Japan was not as easy as it looked. It was necessary to strike just the right amount of fear into one's enemies and subordinates in order to maintain the status quo. Words had to be closely followed by action in order to keep people in line. Sakaguchi knew servility well. His existence was tolerated by the Hirakawa-gumi—the lords of the Tokyo manor—only because of his servility and monthly stipend to them. This he accepted without bitterness. There had to be a chain of command in every aspect of life, and the natural hierarchy of business in Tokyo deemed that his organization was to be a medium-sized fish in an aquarium of sharks. So be it. He had survived this long by understanding his position, and he expected the same kind of understanding from Narita. Anybody failing to grasp this simple fact of life deserved to be bait.

The sliding door at the back of the room moved silently open and a black-suited man announced the arrival of Osamu Tokoro. Sakaguchi gestured for Narita to leave and sat back until Tokoro was kneeling on the cushion directly before the table.

"Excuse my inopportune entry, *oyabun*. I was given to understand that you wished to see me."

At thirty-four years old, Osamu Tokoro was young to be the president of a computer software company in a country where importance was placed on seniority, not ability, but the entire nation had more or less come to the tacit agreement that computers were the field of youth. It was therefore not unusual for someone of his tender years to be in charge of multimillion-yen projects, a concept that would have sent shivers through most of the population just a few years earlier. Tokoro enjoyed the status with which his position provided him and went to extremes to visibly prove himself as a member of the young elite—Valentino suits, handmade silk shirts, Versace neckties, Gucci shoes, a Rolex watch, the ever-present cellular phone, and the Louis Vuitton briefcase.

Sakaguchi leaned over the table conspiratorially and indicated that he expected Tokoro to do the same. As Tokoro leaned forward, Sakaguchi's arm whipped around in an arc and slapped him soundly across the face with the flat of his hand. Open-handed slaps, his experience had taught him, were more useful in inflicting humiliation than the more masculine punch. Taken by surprise, Tokoro was knocked slightly off balance and had to grab the edge of the table with one hand to prevent himself from toppling over. His other hand gently massaged the side of his face and he felt the back of his eyes tingle with tears of outrage. Nobody had ever attempted to raise a hand to him since junior high school, and he was struck by an almost childish feeling of injustice.

"*Oyabun* . . . why?"

Sakaguchi leaned over the table again. "Your stupid, amateurish attempts have been detected and we are now under investigation," he said softly. "What have you to say for yourself?"

"But, *oyabun*, that is impossible. We have taken every precaution."

"Every precaution? Every precaution?" Sakaguchi's

voice began to increase in volume. "How can you tell me that you have taken every precaution when your activities are now out in the open?" Sakaguchi knew that he was being overly harsh. There had been no doubts at the beginning of the project that their *modus operandi* would be clear for all to see, but they had calculated that it would be possible to erase all trails back to them, and so far this had been the case. Had he been honest with himself, he would have recognized the fact that his ire had been aroused by the investigation being initiated abroad and not in Japan, where it would be more easily controllable.

Tokoro's head drooped onto his chest. Not being in possession of the facts made it impossible for him to defend himself, and he knew that any attempts at doing so would simply anger Sakaguchi further.

"Go! Get out of here and do the job I pay you for properly. Speak to Narita before you leave and work out your next step."

Tokoro moved off the cushion and backed over to the door. Then he kneeled down again and bowed his forehead to the floor before silently exiting the room. Sakaguchi watched the door slide shut and permitted himself a slight grin. The importance of ruling with a firm hand was paramount in his business, and he congratulated himself on handling the situation well. It would be a long time before either Narita or Tokoro got careless again.

Chapter Three

Japan (Tokyo)

Ryoichi Narita took his place beside Nishina without acknowledging him formally and studiously concentrated on Uehara pitching the bottom of the fourth inning against the Tigers. Hideaki Nishina looked up in surprise and was hearty in his greetings.

"Narita-san, this is a pleasure. I had no idea you were a Giants fan. Let me get you a drink." He waved to a nearby beer-boy and paid the outrageous one thousand six hundred yen for two cardboard cups of beer. "*Kanpai*," he said, placing his unfinished cup beneath his seat and raising the new one.

Narita raised his cup in a solemn toast and turned his attention back to the game. He had still not said a single word. It suddenly occurred to Nishina that this was not a coincidence. Narita's silence was extremely rude, to say the least, and he was at a loss to understand it. Had they not conspired to complete some very successful business not a few weeks past? They were almost business partners, and he felt uncomfortable at his companion's failure to note this. He watched Uehara strike out the last batter and turned to Narita. "You wished to speak to me?" he asked.

Narita took a draft of beer and turned his eyes onto Nishina. "I think it is time we discussed our service fee," he said, managing to convey both menace and a disregard for the man's position within a single sentence.

"What?" asked Nishina, although he knew instinctively that he had become involved with a problem beyond his experience. Narita's insolence alone indicated that he was probably dealing with a member of the Japanese mob—a part of Japanese life that even a hapless motorist could become mixed up in without due care—and the fact that he had used the phrase "service fee" practically confirmed it. His heart began to beat rapidly as he searched his memory for anything that could distance himself from such people, but he realized that he was backed into a very tight corner. He glanced back to the field and Shimizu's single-baser failed to register any form of emotion within him. Nioka stepped up to the batter's box. The home crowd in the right-hand stand began to chant in support as Nioka took a few practice swings while waiting for the pitcher to prepare himself. "What are you talking about? I requested no service," said Nishina. "Our deal was clear-cut and I have paid your fee."

Narita remained silent, as if he had not heard, and concentrated on the game. As usual, he noted, the "Big Egg" was filled to capacity and the noise of the trumpets and drums from the supporters was nearly deafening. The Tigers, an Osaka-based team, had once again managed a good turnout, and in another two innings—the seventh—they would release their balloons and have the ground officials running around like simpletons in an attempt to clear the field. The balloons were the Tigers' trademark and elicited curses wherever they went—except, of course, from the manufacturers and vendors.

"What do you want?" asked Nishina. He had accepted his predicament.

"Three point five million yen per month," replied Narita.

"But why? That is a ridiculous sum! I couldn't possibly manage it."

Narita finished off his beer, dropped the cup, and turned to Nishina. "Come, come. Where are your manners? Were it not for myself and my colleagues, your company would no longer be in existence. Surely your newfound wealth will stretch to such a miserable sum. Of course, maybe you would prefer not to pay and have your competitor learn about your involvement in his sudden bankruptcy. . . ." He turned back to the game to give his words time to sink in. Nioka had struck out and Takahashi was now facing the pitcher. "Anyway, think about it. I'll have someone contact you next week."

Narita stood up and made his way to the exit. He looked back as the crowd roared and saw Akahoshi backpedaling to align himself with Takahashi's fly. The roar increased in volume as the ball hit the fence of the center stand above Akahoshi's head and bounced back into play. Of the Dome's fifty-five thousand spectators, only one man failed to be moved by this spectacle.

Hideaki Nishina was bent over with his face hidden in his hands and had not even noticed.

Switzerland (Geneva)

"Here's another one, I think," said Sylvie Keppler. Her desk was piled high with stacks of paper and files of assorted colors. A fat printout was balanced precariously on top of this mess, and she tapped it with her pen.

"Code?" asked Marceillac. He faced the computer screen on his desk and typed in the number as Keppler read it off. The digest of an Interpol file appeared on screen, and he began to read through it. "Mm, could be," he said. "The date matches up pretty well and the Japanese connection is firm. I'll post a marker on it."

Marceillac and Keppler had been working sixteen-hour days for nearly a week, and the strain was beginning to tell in their lack of enthusiasm. The discovery of a similar item just a few days earlier would have had both of them crowded around the monitor as they speculated on how the details of the crime could be matched in with the data they had already managed to gather. The task before them seemed never-ending, and their analytical skills were becoming blunt through excessive use. The translations of the Japanese cases had arrived on the same day as the data from Interpol, and they had split the work between them: Marceillac working on the Japanese files and Keppler on the Interpol files.

Of the sixty-six files received from Japan, they had determined that sixty-three warranted further investigation and had passed this list across to Hisamitsu in Tokyo. Marceillac had then read and reread every file several times to try and come up with a common factor, but so far anything of substance had evaded him. Keppler was also having trouble equating the Interpol files with the case in hand. Although she had only a mere seventeen files to work through, each file was voluminous and contained a vast range of reference data. She would read through several hundred pages of boring background only to discover that the link with Japan was nothing more than the person in question being the owner of a Toyota. Four days of work had turned up several possibilities, but even these were long shots.

"Want to give it a rest?" asked Marceillac. Sylvie nodded gratefully. "How about dinner? I'll treat you to the saumon fume at La Perle Du Lac. We can share a bottle of wine, relax and then . . . Well, who knows," he continued with a suggestive wink.

"We'll discuss the 'who knows' after I am plump with your fish," laughed Keppler. The bantering was harmless, but she had begun to feel a deep sense of respect for Armin over the past few days and could imagine her mother telling her that she should follow her instincts. The thought surprised her. Having worked with Marceillac for several years, this was the first time she had actually experienced a romantic thought about him. Their relationship was practically asexual. He regaled her with stories of his weekend conquests, and she discussed with him her rather explicit views on the size of the genitals owned by the celebrities she had crushes on. Armin's suggestive innuendos were a typical part of his physical makeup, and she knew that his lower jaw would hit the ground if she called his bluff and took him up on any of them.

Still, the possibilities were worth considering.

"Just give me a few moments to send a message to

Takeshi and I'll be right with you, mademoiselle." Marceillac swiftly punched out a message to Hisamitsu in Tokyo and hit the Send button. Two minutes later, he was sitting at his desk awaiting the arrival of Sylvie, who had gone to repair her makeup.

Japan (Tokyo)

Takeshi Hisamitsu hung up the receiver and penciled a few notes in the margin of a sheet of paper laid out on top of his desk. He was feeling pretty pleased with himself. Admittedly, everything he had so far was circumstantial, but, he kept reminding himself, he had to start somewhere, and at least he was not twiddling his fingers and scratching his head. He was also enjoying himself immensely. He was a graduate of the National Police Academy, but this was the first time he had actually been allowed a free hand on an investigation, and the fact that he was using the English that he had been so fond of since first introduced to it in junior high school was icing on the cake. It made him feel important, and at twenty-seven years of age, a feeling of importance was what he craved more than anything.

He glanced at the clock on the wall and decided that he ought to brief the director general on his findings for the day. He had been ordered to keep the director general himself abreast of all occurrences, and his daily visits to his office had occasioned a great deal of leg-pulling from his colleagues. Not that he minded, of course. It was nice to be the center of attention for a change. He collected his file together, straightened his tie, and headed toward Hirata's office.

Tsutomu Hirata's office was sparse and unattractive.

Although his position as director general was as lofty as it sounded, the Electronic Crime Bureau, being a small and relatively unimportant arm of the National Police Agency, was low on the food chain, and it would be unthinkable for its director general to have an office as comfortable as those of his contemporaries' in more substantial departments. The office, by choice, contained a gray metal desk with a glass plate laid over green felt for a worktop and was only slightly larger than the desks used by his staff. The same gray metal was used for a bank of three filing cabinets lined up along one of the walls. A black leather couch and two chairs occupied the area directly in front of Hirata's desk, and it was to this couch that Hirata waved Hisamitsu as he stood to attention by the door.

Hirata left Hisamitsu sitting on the edge of the couch for ten minutes before screwing the top on his Mont Blanc fountain pen and coming around to join him. They faced each other across a cheap and badly varnished coffee table.

"Well?" urged Hirata.

Hisamitsu cleared his throat. "Well, sir, I ran the simulation on location, but it did not help." The previous day, Hirata had ordered Hisamitsu to plot the locations of all crime victims on a map to see if any similarities arose. "The locations were liberally spread throughout Honshu, Kyushu, Hokkaido, and Shikoku. However, I did manage to get an excellent lead that I feel is worth following up."

"Go on."

"It occurred to me that some of the false data and programs loaded into the computers of the companies concerned might have been introduced through legitimate sources. So far I have only managed to contact twenty-eight of the sixty-three companies involved, but I got them to send me copies of all payments made to computer software companies over the past three months, and the only name that appears more than once is a Tokyo-based software developer called Inter-systems Incorporated. Strangely enough, this name cropped up a total of four times."

Hirata leaned over to grab a notepad from his desk and wrote the name down in neat *katakana*. He stared at the name for a moment before looking up. "Have you checked them out?" he asked.

"I ran a brief check on them, and it seems that they were operating in the red up until the end of last year, when they suddenly increased their capital base from five million yen to thirty million yen and moved to a much larger premises in Kamata. Their fiscal year runs from January through December, so there are no figures available yet for this year. I thought I would go around and check them out tonight."

"Idiot!" snapped Hirata incredulously. "It would only need an inquisitive detective asking questions to put them on their guard and destroy the whole investigation. You'll need much more evidence than this."

Hisamitsu was stung by the force of Hirata's words. How could the director general think he would be foolish enough to go knocking on their door? Surely he placed more faith in him and his training than that. "I only intended to observe them from a distance, sir."

"Forget it! A good officer is the sum of his patience. Find out more about them and build up the case before wasting your time running around town playing cops and robbers. Do I have to remind you that the best police work is carried out at one's desk?"

"No, sir." Hisamitsu bowed his head and studied his shoes.

"Anything else?"

"No, sir."

"Right, let's get back to work." Hirata slapped his knees and levered himself to his feet. Hisamitsu hurriedly excused himself and returned to his desk.

He couldn't understand it. When he had been transferred across to the ECB from the Metropolitan Police Department eleven months earlier, the first speech that Hirata had ever given him had included a ten-minute soliloquy on just how he expected his detectives to get out in the field and not spend all day putting their feet up on their desks. They had staff to work computers and fill out pieces of paper, he had said, and more was expected of his experienced officers. Hisamitsu gloomily noted the e-mail indicator on his monitor flashing. He opened the file and printed out a message from the IOCC in Geneva. Armin—they were on first-name terms already—had found two more links within the Interpol files and wanted him to check out a few names. He was rereading the message when the sound of squeaking wheels made him look up. The director general pulled up an empty chair and sat down beside him. Hisamitsu was conscious of the eyes of most of the office on him.

"I think I owe you an apology, Hisamitsu," said Hirata, once again the epitome of geniality. "I was out of line just now and have had time to reflect on my words."

"Think nothing of it, sir," stammered Hisamitsu. He

was not used to his superiors apologizing to him, and he was not sure he cared for the new experience. "You were perfectly correct, sir. I could have easily jeopardized the case."

Hisamitsu smiled and gently shook his head. "No, I was wrong. You must remember that sitting at a desk all day can sometimes deaden our sense of adventure and lead us to think that what we are doing is more important than anything else. Get your things together and go check out this company. Report to me first thing in the morning."

Hisamitsu was still sitting in a daze as Hirata phoned down to the car pool and ordered an unmarked car to be ready in ten minutes, but burst into a flurry of activity when Hirata caught his eye. He began to thrust papers into his briefcase and moved over to the lockers at the back of the room to get his jacket. Hirata picked up the cell phone from Hisamitsu's desk and weighed it in his hand. He removed the battery pack from the rear of the telephone and curiously inspected the underside, where many young people like to paste photographs of their loved ones. Finding none, he slid the battery back into position.

"Any problems and you know my number. Okay?" Hirata waved the mobile phone in Hisamitsu's direction before dropping it into the open briefcase on the desk.

"Yes, sir!"

Hirata watched Hisamitsu hurry out of the office and then returned to his own office. Had Hisamitsu taken the trouble to check, he would have discovered that a thin sheet of Perspex had been inserted between the terminals of the battery and the main unit, rendering the instrument useless.

Seated at his desk, Hirata sighed and reluctantly picked up the telephone receiver. He was not completely sure that he was doing the right thing, but he could think of no alternatives. He flipped open his address book and ran his finger down until he found an entry under "Sakaguchi." Sighing deeply once more, he punched out the number and waited for an answer.

Japan (Tokyo)

The Golden Ginza was just the place for him to drown his sorrows. The background music was low enough to soothe, the clientele spoke in gentle whispers, and the barman was well versed in his trade without being pushy. Michio Maeda sat at the counter and nursed his single shot of Glenfiddich reflectively. God, how he hated Ozaki. In fact, he hated all producers. But especially Ozaki. Twenty-two years of work destroyed because of Ozaki's blatant toadying. Damn, it hurt.

Maeda drank the remains of his whisky and signaled the barman. A measured shot of Glenfiddich was silently poured into a new glass and placed in front of him. The barman had been pouring the same drink for Maeda every night for two weeks now, and instinct told him that he was not expected to provide conversation.

Maeda had not even told his wife that he had been fired. The humiliation would provide her with enough ammunition to make his life a misery forever. He had to admit it; he would never work as a producer again. What would his wife do with that piece of information? he wondered. Could she cope with shopping in anything but the Mercedes? Could she stand life without wearing diamond earrings to her stupid tennis lessons?

Could she learn to live without two glasses of champagne with her dinner? Well, she'd have to. You don't get sacked by NHK and then have other TV companies beating a path to your door.

"May I?" The voice shook him out of his revelry. He looked up and saw a well-dressed man standing beside him with an outstretched palm indicating the adjacent stool. He nodded assent with a puzzled look. The bar was still relatively empty, and there were at least ten empty stools farther along the counter.

"Mr. Maeda?" the man asked politely.

"Yes?"

"My name is Matsumoto. Masashi Matsumoto." He handed over a name card and ordered two whiskies while Maeda studied it. "First of all, I would like to say how sorry I am to hear of your job loss."

"Who are you?" asked Maeda suspiciously. Matsumoto's company rang no bells for him, and he was startled to discover that a complete stranger knew of his predicament.

"Come, come. I am a friend, Mr. Maeda. Our destinies are intertwined." Matsumoto raised his glass in a salute. "To your reinstatement," he said.

Warily, Maeda picked up his glass, clinked it against that of his companion, and took a sip.

"It is difficult to know where to start," began Matsumoto, "but let us just say that I am fully aware of your current situation and wish nothing more than to see you back in your old position. I represent a small consortium whose interests dictate that Ichiro Ozaki does not produce the next series of Sidewinder. You, I understand, have been in charge of production ever since the beginning of the series three years ago. Is that correct?"

"Yes," answered Maeda, still slightly warily. Matsumoto was pressing the right buttons, but "luck" was not a word that featured readily in Maeda's life. "What of it?"

"We are—how shall I say?—more than satisfied with your performance so far and would like to effect your reinstatement. Would you be interested in returning?"

"Well, yes. Of course. But . . . I don't quite see."

Matsumoto finished his drink and ordered two more. He waited until the small shot glasses of golden liquid had been placed in front of them before continuing.

"Look, I am nothing more than a businessman, but I am currently in possession of some information that could coerce the director of programming to see the folly of his ways and reemploy you. It is that simple."

"But what would I have to do?"

"Absolutely nothing. Just wait at home for a phone call from the director himself and return to work to laugh over the misunderstanding with your colleagues." Matsumoto could practically see the gears clicking into place within Maeda's head. He was hooked, he was sure of it. "Of course," he continued, "there is the question of our running costs."

Maeda jerked his eyes up to the level of Matsumoto's. "How much?"

"Shall we say two million yen?" It was a reasonable sum, considering the amount Maeda stood to lose by refusing. Matsumoto watched in interest as Maeda attempted—and failed—to conceal the look of rapturous glee on his face.

"Are you sure this is possible?"

"Absolutely. In fact, you won't have to pay a penny until you are safely installed back at your old position. I fail to see how much fairer I could possibly be."

A pinprick of light appeared at the end of Maeda's dark and dismal tunnel. Could it be true? Could he really step back into the job of producing Sidewinder and flip Ozaki the bird? The temptation was simply too much for him. He understood that the means toward the end included some form of illegal wangling, possibly extortion, but what of it? He, himself, would not have to get his hands dirty and he could easily deny all knowledge if it ever came to light. He would have to leave NHK as soon as possible—he realized that—but it would be so much easier approaching the other stations when in full and productive employment than with the word "Dismissed" stamped across his files for all to see. The two million yen did not bother him in the least. His wife spent more than that on beauty treatment every year, for Christ's sake. A mere pittance when his entire career was at stake. He wondered what the consortium his companion professed to represent had against Ozaki, but decided he didn't really want to know. It was much simpler that way.

Maeda picked up his glass and touched it lightly against Matsumoto's. "You have a deal," he said, draining the liquid and signaling the waiter for two more.

Outside, Matsumoto walked down the Ginza toward Yurakucho Station. He took a cell phone from his pocket just as he reached Le Printemps department store and selected a number from the memory.

"*Oyabun*? Narita. He fell for it," he said when the connection had been made. "I spoke to Tokoro earlier and the data is ready for implanting. We will begin to turn the screw tomorrow."

Narita/Matsumoto disconnected the line and waved down a taxi. Having stated his destination and sat back, he allowed himself a small grin. Maeda would get his job back, all right. There was no doubt about that. It would cost him an arm and a leg, but he would certainly get it back.

Japan (Tokyo)

Hisamitsu sketched an image of the small building in his notebook out of boredom, not necessity. He had been watching the building for forty-five minutes from his position twenty meters away, and so far had noticed nothing but a few staff members leaving at the end of the day. The building was one of the recently popular "intelligent" buildings and, like them all, had a spotlessly gray facade finished off in mock brickwork. Only three stories in height, its very newness seemed to mark it as an outsider among the old and decrepit buildings of the backstreet leading down to Kamata Station.

The rainy season was particularly persistent this year, and a fine drizzle coated his windshield. The streetlamps reflected in the beads of collected water obscured his view to a certain extent, but there wasn't really a great deal to see. The sheen also prevented others from seeing him, he reasoned—although that was not so much of a problem. It was not unusual in Japan to come across people sitting for hours in parked cars with the air-conditioning at full blast. Most companies had rigid rules that stipulated that salesmen were not allowed in the office during working hours—for their jobs were to be out selling—and many killed time by napping in their cars. The less fortunate salesmen who were without wheels tended to spend this time in coffee bars, pachinko parlors, and cinemas.

Hisamitsu glanced at the dashboard clock and decided to give it another thirty minutes. It was seven o'clock, dark, and the number of people on the street had dwindled away to the odd businessman hurrying toward the station. His mission had not been as fruitful as he had expected, but at least he had a feel for the location now. Surely that was worth the time.

The tap on the window took him by surprise. He looked out and saw a man cowering under an umbrella and poking a finger at something on a small piece of paper. He had lost his way to the station probably, Hisamitsu thought. He pressed the button on the door console and the window hissed open, allowing the damp and humid air to waft inside. The man leaned on the open window and placed his right hand in his pocket.

"Could you tell me where to find this address?" he asked, turning the piece of paper awkwardly toward Hisamitsu as he tried to hold it and the umbrella with one hand.

Hisamitsu reached above him to turn on the light and examined the piece of paper. He looked up with a frown as he realized it was blank, and found himself staring down a dark hole that seemed to stretch into eternity. The gun looked dull and incapable of the violence it could inflict. It seemed to absorb all of the meager light that struck it like a sinister black hole. Hisamitsu had never had a weapon pointed at him before, and he felt his bowels turn over in a mixture of fear and rage.

"Open the door," the man commanded, gesturing to the passenger side of the car with the muzzle of the gun. Fearful of taking his eyes off the weapon, Hisamitsu fumbled for the button on the console that would unlock all of the doors. The door immediately swung open and a man slid in beside Hisamitsu. Another man climbed into the back.

"What do you want?" asked Hisamitsu, angry at the quaver in his voice.

"Shut up! Into the back. Quick!"

The door was opened and Hisamitsu climbed out into the rain and was hustled into the backseat. His companion in the back, he noted, was also equipped with a pistol that pointed unwaveringly in his direction. The man who had by now moved into the driver's seat switched on the engine, placed the car in gear, and moved off slowly. The lights of another car illuminated the interior as it simultaneously pulled out behind and began to follow. The man sitting beside Hisamitsu leaned over and began to pat a hand over his body. He reached inside each pocket and removed all contents: a small notepad, his wallet, his police identification folder, a coin purse, two pens, a handkerchief, a small pack of tissues, a pack of Mild Seven cigarettes, and a disposable lighter. He found the shoulder holster empty and reported this briefly to the men in front. The service revolver was located in the glove compartment, and the men seemed to relax for the first time.

"I hope you realize what you are doing . . ." said Hisamitsu lamely. He was ashamed at the fear that was slowly building up within him and couldn't think of anything clse to say. "I am a policc officcr and duly arrest you for possession of firearms and the hindrance of an officer of the law in his—" He didn't finish the sentence. The barrel of the gun whipped up smartly and hit him on the chin. There was not much power behind the movement, but the pain was considerable. Hisamitsu's head jerked back and he felt the tears of pain build up in his eyes. He moved a hand up to his face to check for blood. There was none.

None of the men spoke. This was probably the most unnerving factor. The man in the passenger seat was carefully checking through Hisamitsu's bag, but if he found anything of interest he failed to share his discovery with his colleagues. Then Hisamitsu noticed with shock that all three men were wearing surgical gloves. They were obviously going to pains to avoid fingerprints. Things did not bode well. The pain of the blow was throbbing gently, reminding him of the cost of uninvited speech, but Hisamitsu decided to try once more.

"Where are you taking me?" he asked. The man seated beside him raised the gun threateningly, and Hisamitsu subsided into silence. He looked out of the window and realized they were heading for Yokohama. The bridge over the Tama River loomed up before them and they crossed over into Kawasaki. Hisamitsu revised his guess when they turned right once in Kawasaki and began to follow the side of the river. They drove along in silence with the lights from the car behind occasionally illuminating the back of the heads of the two men in front. The tight curls of the "punch perm" hairstyle of the man in the passenger seat lent proof to Hisamitsu's supposition that he had been abducted by the Yakuza—the Japanese mob, who had no qualms about advertising their allegiance to organized crime by proudly sporting their tattoos, "punch perms," dark glasses, and flashy American cars—badges of their trade. But why had he attracted their attention? He was sure it had nothing to do with his present investigation, for he had done absolutely nothing to ruffle their feathers and had got nowhere near far enough with the case to justify being held up at gunpoint. He racked his memory for any past cases that might have forced them to come to the conclusion that he justified such treatment, but he could think of nothing. Maybe he had inadvertently parked his car in the midst of an unrelated crime and they had decided to physically remove him. But surely they would have registered surprise when they discovered he was a policeman. It was almost as if they knew his occupation, for they had made a point of searching for his service revolver.

They drove in silence for an hour. The lights of the city began to fade behind them as they reached the more isolated areas of the Tama River. The car finally pulled off the main road and turned onto an unsurfaced track leading down to the side of the river. The far side was barely visible sixty meters distant, even with the powerful illumination provided by the headlights. Hisamitsu noted that the car behind had parked at the top of the track and guessed they had reached their destination. His heart began to beat faster. He was not sure what was in store for him, but he knew it would not be pleasant. At the very least, he was in for a beating. Had they simply wanted him out of the way they would not have taken this much trouble to drive him so far, for despite the distance he was still within twenty minutes' walk of the nearest residence. He was not scared for his life. The Yakuza sometimes polished each other off during gang wars, but their activities rarely resulted in the death of nonrelated people.

The car finally came to a stop concealed from the road by a clump of bushes and assorted foliage. The driver turned on the interior light before killing the engine, extinguishing the headlights, and climbing out of the car. The man in the back covered him while his colleague in the passenger seat got out, still clutching Hisamitsu's bag, before backing out of the car himself. The driver opened the door of the backseat and pointed the gun at Hisamitsu's head. Something in the driver's eyes—a slight squint, as if waiting for a balloon to pop—warned Hisamitsu that he was witnessing his own execution. Why? The word rattled around inside his head as pressure was increased on the trigger. He heard the loud report and felt himself jerked back onto the seat, as if tugged from behind by a rope. He slumped down onto the seat and saw the rain-soaked grass outside of the door. Why was there no pain? He must have been hit, but there was no pain. Only a slight dimming of the senses, like having a dentist's injection in the brain. A slight wind blew a gust of mistlike rain onto his face. It was ironic, really. He had always expected his own death to occur on a warm and sunny day. He tried to move his arm so he could touch the wet ground for a last time. For some reason, it suddenly became the most important thing in the world to touch the ground, to link himself with Mother Nature. He didn't want to die in something man-made. Steel, plastic, and synthetic fibers were not his idea of a fitting deathbed. He knew he had to hurry. The ground was losing its focus and beginning to swirl. Slowly his fingers began to walk their way across the rough carpeting to the edge of the door, but he knew instinctively that they would never make it. The edge of his vision was shimmering black and swiftly closing in on him.

His fingers were still twenty centimeters from the edge of the door when they stopped moving forever.

The assassin grunted in approval. He quickly checked

for a pulse and then leaned into the front of the car and took the cellular telephone from its position on top of the dashboard. Sliding the battery from its bed, he tipped a small sheet of Perspex onto his open palm, then clicked the battery back into place. He made a final check of the interior before switching off the light and nodding to the other two men. They walked back along the track to the car parked above them, leaving all four of the car doors open.

Chapter Four

Japan (Takao)

Hirata sat cross-legged on the *tatami* and felt the rage boil within him. Sakaguchi faced him across the open hearth and chewed a piece of *ayu*—or sweet-fish—off its wooden skewer. Hirata had never felt the urge to trample on somebody's face until it turned into red pulp before, but he was close to it now. The fact that Sakaguchi displayed absolutely no remorse at all was the most galling factor. He wanted to grab one of the hot coals from the fire and ram it down his throat until his screams echoed up and down Mt. Takao.

Sakaguchi grinned, and the muscles on Hirata's jaw bunched up as he restrained himself. "Your fish is burning. Such a waste."

"How dare you speak to me of waste! You murdered him in cold blood, you bastard!"

Sakaguchi laughed. "You don't approve of my methods of tying up loose ends, eh? Now, isn't that a shame. Although I must admit myself to a touch of astonishment at your own pious naïveté." The smile disappeared from Sakaguchi's face, and he leaned forward slightly. "If you remember rightly, it was you who contacted me. What did you expect us to do, slap his wrists and tell him to be a good boy in future? You seem to forget that he had discovered a link with Intersystems. Fool!"

The two guards standing at the door noticed Hirata clenching and unclenching his fists and slipped the safety catches off their revolvers. Hirata wouldn't get within two feet of their boss, that was for sure.

"I won't let you get away with this, Sakaguchi. You think you can involve me in murder and then laugh it off? Do you think I am totally without honor? You have gone too far this time and will live to regret it."

Sakaguchi laughed again. He tore a piece of meat off the fish and threw it out of the screen doors into the pond outside. The carp thrashed the water into a frenzy in their efforts to grab the morsel. Sakaguchi watched in fascination. Cannibalism in any form interested him.

"So, we speak of honor, do we?" he said as the final ripples on the surface of the water faded. "And in your mind, I suppose, honor is defined by taking your own life and leaving a letter explaining all for the authorities. Correct?"

"Don't push me, Sakaguchi. Better men than me have taken the honorable way out."

"Ah, but what of your poor daughter? How old is she now? Twenty-seven and still unmarried? Disfigurement would reduce her chances of marriage, wouldn't you say?"

"You bastard!" The barrels of two pistols pointing directly at Hirata prevented him from hurling himself at Sakaguchi in fury. "Don't you ever even think of laying a finger on my daughter. She has nothing to do with this!"

"Ah, so the honorable Hirata has an Achilles' heel." Sakaguchi calmly refilled his *sake* cup and sipped the warm liquid appreciatively. "You should try some, Hirata. It is good. It may also calm you enough to realize that the fate of your daughter is totally in your hands. I can promise you that no harm will befall her just as long as our business relationship continues in the same manner of equanimity that it has enjoyed until now. I am sure you are intelligent enough to see the sense in this."

Accepting defeat, Hirata's shoulders slumped and he tried to stop his hands from shaking with pent-up rage and frustration. Would he never be free of this monster's grip? Had he not paid his price already? Had he known the cost of his present position as general director of a governmental agency, he would have happily overlooked all prospects of promotion for the rest of his career and wallowed in his obscurity contentedly. He felt like a fish on a hook. He was allowed to swim freely for the most part, but every now and then a few sharp tugs on the line would bring him within gaffing distance. His soft underbelly was exposed at the moment, and the gaff hovered close to not only him but his daughter, as well. He hated himself with a passion born of self-humiliation. How could he possibly have become mixed up in this terrible affair? What man deserves the title of father who exposes his only daughter to a danger so great? What would Machiko say if she could see him now, cowering before a man whose life had less worth than the carp swimming not two meters away? Cringing like a beaten dog.

Sakaguchi took another sip of *sake*. "And now that we have dealt with your grievance, maybe we could get onto the subject for which you were invited to this quaint and, I might add, expensive restaurant. How is Hisamitsu's death being handled?"

Hirata tried to bring his mind back into focus. "It, er . . . A full investigation has been launched by the Metropolitan Police Department," he mumbled. "It is out of my hands. There is no way I can influence the outcome."

"Of course you can't. But then, we didn't expect you to. My men left no traces, so there is nothing to worry about. All we expect of you is to ensure that no evidence remains in his computer or his desk and keep us informed of any developments. However, this will no doubt attract more attention to our computer activities, and I want to know how you intend to handle this."

"I have asked for the IOCC in Geneva to send me a consultant. I am under pressure from the NPA to sort the problem out once and for all and managed to obtain their approval for this." Hirata kept his eyes on the glowing coals and skewered fish lined up around them like soldiers. He was afraid that he would do something he would regret if he looked Sakaguchi in the eye. Sakaguchi took this as acquiescence and seemed to have completely forgotten the previous unpleasantness.

"Is that wise?" asked Sakaguchi.

"I felt that it was the only course open to us. A foreign consultant would stand out in Japan and would be denied the subtleties of the spoken and written word. It was either this or assigning several of our own detectives to the case. With a consultant, I can get away with allocating a single detective."

"Hm, well done, Hirata. You obviously have more brains than I credited you with. Do you have this consultant's name yet?"

"No. I am expecting Geneva to contact me when a suitable person has been selected."

"And the Japanese detective?"

"Another one of my young detectives. A man named Akio Murata."

"Good, good. Let's hope Mr. Murata lives through to old age." Hirata jerked his head up to stare at Sakaguchi, who was left in no doubt as to the hatred Hirata felt for him. This was acceptable. Hatred was as good a catalyst as fear for keeping people under control. "Just remember that you control Mr. Murata's destiny. Keep him away from Intersystems and his life will be long and fruitful, I am sure."

"Have you finished?" asked Hirata, his face contorted into a mask of pure contempt.

Sakaguchi looked at Hirata in mock surprise and waved his arms expansively over the uneaten food, now heavily charred by its close proximity to the hot coals. "But you have not yet tasted your food or *sake*. Where are your manners, Hirata?"

Hirata stood and walked over to the entrance without acknowledging the question. He slipped on his shoes and walked out onto the wooden walkway suspended over the pond by stilts, silently congratulating himself for having avoided the temptation to break bread with the monster. He truly hoped the insult had bitten deep, although he knew it had not as he heard Sakaguchi's laughter mocking his exit.

Switzerland (Geneva)

Armin Marceillac and Sylvie Keppler sat in shocked silence after Hewes had explained the circumstances surrounding Hisamitsu's untimely death. Rain was falling steadily outside of Hewes's office, and the director general watched it streaming down the window as he allowed them enough time to deal with the news in their own way. Keppler was the first to break the silence.

"But why?" she asked plaintively. "Was it related to the case?"

"Hirata says probably not, but I think we ought to consider the fact that it was." The lines on Jasper Hewes's brow were deeper than either Marceillac or Keppler could remember, but this could probably be put down to the fact that they had never seen him looking so despondent. The murder had certainly affected him, of that there was no doubt. "I think Hirata just does not want to admit that Japan is as potentially dangerous as the rest of the world. Huh!" Hewes laughed dryly. "That sounds good, considering the rate at which serious crime is increasing over there."

"It couldn't have been connected to this case. We haven't gotten anywhere with it yet, for God's sake." Frustration was building up within Marceillac. He and Keppler had squeezed every last drop of juice out of the files they had, but there were still no concrete leads. "Surely nobody would go to the risk of murder just because we were carrying out a few checks."

"Maybe he found something," said Sylvie softly. The words hung in the air as they all considered the implications of the case they were working on being large enough to warrant the loss of a man's life.

Hewes leaned forward and picked up his coffee cup from the table. "Are you sure there was nothing in his messages to indicate he was onto something, Armin?"

"Absolutely nothing, sir."

"Then we shall just have to leave it up to the Japanese police force. Speculation will help nobody, least of all Mr. Hisamitsu. I have arranged for flowers to be sent to his family from all of us, and I have asked Hirata to send a message of condolence in Japanese. At the moment, I'm afraid, that is all we can do."

"So where do we go from now?" asked Marceillac.

"Strangely enough, Hirata has requested that we recommend a consultant to send over to Japan to help the new man assigned to the case. He said he didn't want to take the chance of Hisamitsu's murder being connected to the current investigation and needed someone experienced in this line to provide a pointer or two. And it is no good jumping up and down in your seat like that, Armin, you are too valuable here."

The disappointment was clear on Marceillac's face. "But, Mr. Hewes, I have been involved since the beginning and know every aspect of the case. I'm the perfect choice."

"You are no such thing. We still need a coordinator here. Besides, you have had no experience of fieldwork. There is no way I am going to send you out into the unknown and have you coming back weltering in your own blood."

"Sir?" Hewes's choice of words had confused Marceillac.

"What I mean is, a man has been murdered, Armin. Do you understand what I am saying? Murdered! Do you really think I would send you in his footsteps?"

"Mr. Hewes is right, Armin." Marceillac turned incredulously on Sylvie. She was the last person he had expected to turn against him.

"Why do you say this? What danger could there be for a mere consultant?"

"I'll tell you why she says this, Armin." An impish grin had replaced the lines on Hewes's face. "She says this because she doesn't want to lose her future husband."

"Wha . . . ?"

"You can't fool me, you know. I have watched you both over the past week, and I can see the signs. Now let's have no more of it. In fact," continued Hewes, raising his right hand to block Marceillac's interruption, "I have already made my choice. I have given the subject much thought and have decided to send two people across to Japan."

Hewes stood up and collected two files from his desk. Dropping the files on the coffee table in front of Marceillac and Keppler, he said, "Frank Stockton. An Englishman who worked for me when I was in the National Criminal Intelligence Service in London. He attended school and university in Japan, speaks fluent Japanese, and knows computers like he knows his own front room. He still works for the NCIS and, as you can see, has an impressive record."

Sylvie looked over Marceillac's shoulder as he scanned the file. The flush of embarrassment occasioned by Hewes's referral to her marital status still adorned her cheeks, and she reminded herself never to underestimate the old dog again. Stockton's file was only a few pages thick and simply outlined his background—not unlike a curriculum vitae that Stockton might have sent out himself in order to gain employment. A copy of a black-and-white photograph was located on the top left-hand corner of the first page and displayed a determined-looking man whose occupation might have been in stockbrokering or advertising. A high-powered yuppie who thrived on stress and tight situations.

"Donald Mitchell," continued Hewes. Marceillac hastily closed the first file and flipped open the second. "American. A doctor of juristic science who has dedicated his life to criminology. Worked as both a research officer and field officer for the FBI for twelve years before being transferred over to the Office of International Criminal Justice. Has a reputation for being fastidious and ruthless in his efforts to put away any criminal foolish enough to cross his path."

Mitchell's photograph showed a man in his midforties with an arrogant chin and open features. Marceillac briefly noted the man's credentials and snapped the file shut.

"Okay, so I'm underqualified," he said with a grin. "I accept your choice, sir. I will sit at my desk and content myself with sending messages to these two supermen and ogling the maiden Keppler." Sylvie coyly slapped him on the arm.

"That's the spirit, Armin. I will get Stockton and Mitchell to make a stopover in Geneva on their way to Tokyo so you can brief them yourself. But," Hewes continued, a mischievous glint in his eye, "I suggest you keep a close eye on the maiden Keppler. With these men, action speaks louder than words."

United States of America (Chicago)

"You've got to be kidding me," said Don Mitchell as his boss, Bob Wretham, outlined the details of the message he had received from Geneva. "Japan? Why me?"

"How the hell should I know? Word trickled down that we have to look favorably on this. It seems like we owe the IOCC a couple." Wretham crushed out his cigarette in the ashtray. America might be ganging up on him and preventing him from smoking in every damn public area, but he'd like to meet anybody big enough and brave enough to tell him to stop smoking in his own office.

"Jeez, I really need this. Japan, for chrissake! What happens if I refuse?"

"You won't," said Wretham grimly.

"Oh, great. Thanks for the support. When am I supposed to leave?" Mitchell massaged the back of his neck with a large hand. He ran his mind over the cases he was working on at the moment and mentally began allocating them to the poor stiffs he worked with.

"You leave tomorrow for Geneva. Make your own reservations and send a message through to a guy named Marceillac to let him know when you'll be arriving. He'll meet you at the airport and take you to the Le Warwick hotel." Wretham pronounced the name of the hotel to rhyme with Lee Remick. "You'll meet up with some Brit in Geneva, stay a couple of days for a briefing, and the IOCC will arrange your tickets on to Tokyo after that."

"And when do I get back?"

"When you've solved the case, dummy." Wretham

threw the message across the desk, and Mitchell deftly grabbed it from the air. Muttering under his breath, Mitchell read through the message before getting to his feet and walking toward the door.

"Mitchell!"

"Huh?" Mitchell turned back to face Wretham with his hand on the doorknob.

"*Sayonara*," said Wretham sweetly, a happy grin spread over his craggy features.

United Kingdom (London)

Frank Stockton laid the novel down on the cushion beside him and picked up the receiver on its second ring. "Hello?"

"Hello, Frank. Gordon here." Gordon Grant, Stockton's immediate boss, sounded like a teenager on the phone. He sounded like a teenager in person, for that matter, despite his fifty-odd years.

"Hello, Gordon. What gives?"

"Look, Frank, I know you are having a few days off, but I want you to come into the office. I have a teleconference scheduled for six o'clock and I think you ought to be here."

"Why? What's happening?" Stockton knew that Grant would not disturb him during his well-earned rest unless it was important, and he felt a small tingle of anticipation begin to flutter in his chest.

"I'd rather not speak over the phone. Please?"

"Righty-ho, Gordon. Six o'clock it is."

Stockton hung up the phone and took a shower. He had promised himself five days of complete relaxation, and for the past four days had done little else but lie around, listen to music, watch rental videos, and read books. Although he had not completely neglected the elements of personal hygiene during this period, he decided that a shower and shave would improve his appearance by about six hundred percent.

It was a little after six when a well-groomed Stockton walked down the corridor of the National Criminal Intelligence Service and entered the communications room. Grant was already seated in one of the open-backed booths in front of a computer monitor, and he waved Stockton to the booth adjacent. A monitor was already set up, and Stockton recognized Jason Hewes's face below Grant's before he took his seat. He hit the function key to connect himself into the conference.

"Greetings, Frank. How are you?" said Hewes.

"Hello, Jasper. Good to see you again. And what have I done to deserve this honor?"

"Ever worked with Donald Mitchell, Frank?"

Stockton screwed up his eyes and tried to put a face to the name that rattled a memory somewhere. "Mitchell, Mitchell. I think I recognize the name."

"A Yank. Works for the OICJ in Chicago. Considered somewhat of an analytical genius. He is the one who nailed the culprits of the bank scam in Jamaica."

"Yes, of course. Mitchell," said Stockton. "I only know him by reputation, though. I've never worked with him."

"Well, you are going to," said Grant, "Jasper here has fixed you up with a nice little number that should have you jumping up and down strewing roses from your hat."

"Oh, God. I don't think I like the sound of this."

Grant was subject to overexaggeration and felt it his duty to dramatize all of the shit jobs he handed out in an effort to boost morale. Unbeknownst to him, he was doing little more than providing an early-warning system.

"Don't listen to Gordon, Frank," Hewes said, laughing. He was well aware of Grant's idiosyncrasies, having worked with him—and sometimes against him—for more than twenty-five years as they came up through the ranks of Scotland Yard together. "This one really is up your street. How would you like a trip to Japan? Yes, I thought that would grab your interest." Stockton's eyebrows had shot up at the offer. He had visited Japan only four times in the past ten years, and all of these trips had been paid for out of his own pocket.

"Are we talking expense accounts?" Stockton rubbed his hands together and faked a sneer of avarice.

"You bet we are talking expense accounts," said Hewes. "And first-class tickets courtesy of the Japanese government."

"When do I leave?"

Hewes and Grant laughed. Stockton had a reputation for basic comedy and refused to be intimidated by his so-called social superiors or events out of his control. He was exceptionally good at his job, because he had an uncanny ability to find the silver lining in even the blackest of clouds, and this enabled him to invariably see each individual tree among the other trees in the forest.

"But before you go and fill your hat with roses, you ought to know that you will be stepping into a dead man's shoes."

Hewes filled Stockton in on the details of the case, concluding with the untimely death of Takeshi Hisamitsu. Stockton punctuated the monologue with the occasional question and nodded silently as it became obvious that very little progress had been made so far.

"I want you to come over to Geneva before you fly to Japan. Armin Marceillac, the person in charge of the case here, will fill you in on some other details and you will get a chance to meet up with Don Mitchell."

"When is Mitchell due to arrive?"

"The day after tomorrow, Saturday. He'll be staying at the Le Warwick. I have also taken the liberty of reserving you a room from Saturday. Is that okay?"

Stockton considered. His passport was up to date. He had suitcases. He had enough clean clothes. Just a little shopping for toothpaste and other sundries, and he would be ready to leave. "Yes, that's fine," he replied. "That is," he added diplomatically, "presuming Gordon has given the go-ahead."

"Oh, yes," said Grant. "It has been authorized from above. Don't you worry about a thing. We'll get on fine without you."

"Marceillac will meet you at the airport, so let us have your flight number sometime tomorrow."

Chapter Five

Japan (Tokyo)

Masashi Yanagida scanned the *Nippon Keizai* newspaper and clicked his tongue in exasperation. Was Japan never going to get back on track? The media had been full of doom-laden news ever since the so-called bubble economy had collapsed in the early nineties, and now that the dollar had plummeted and stabilized out at around one hundred yen after dropping to eighty-four yen, the long-term view also held little hope. An American presidential campaign year didn't help things, either. Hardly a day passed without sanctions being threatened, and everybody knew that it was only a matter of time before the United States actually carried them out. Why did America have to choose Japan to be its whipping boy? The United States, in its typical crybaby style, had gripes with practically every country in the world, but the only nation it seemed to really enjoy hanging out to dry was Japan.

And now, not only had the Nikkei average dropped to the ten thousand mark, it was expected to drop even further, into the nine thousands. Not that he could blame that on America. The Japanese government was definitely to blame here. The same old wishy-washy politicians making nothing more than token gestures when decisive action was the order of the day; pissing into the wind, all of them. A lot of people had had hopes that the government's public flaying over their incompetence in the aftermath of the Great Hanshin Earthquake would produce a spark of initiative in the fat and bloated mechanisms of bureaucratic power, but these hopes had, like numerous hopes before them, fallen on barren ground. They had run around like headless chickens on January 17, 1995, and they were still running around like headless chickens. Yanagida yearned for a return to the days of Kakuei Tanaka, the former prime minister indicted in the Lockheed/Marubeni scandal. Now, there was a politician. A man with firm views and clearly laid-out policies. A true statesman with real, not imagined, power.

Yanagida turned the page of the newspaper and sighed deeply as his eye caught the headline informing him that the Ministry of Finance did not feel that the indicators were pointing to economic recovery. The article directly below it stated that the director general of the Economic Planning Agency had indicated his concern over an impending crisis that had placed the economy on the brink of deflation.

He folded up the paper and dropped it into the bottom drawer of his desk in disgust before reaching out for the steaming cup of green tea that stood beside his telephone. He wondered who had been on tea duty this morning. He had noted the cup being placed on his desk, but he hadn't bothered to look up and see who had brought it. The girls in the office had organized a duty rota, and each took it in turn to make the tea for their supervisors and managers. Quite right, too; a manager could not be seen making his own tea. He would rather go thirsty.

Intersystems, Inc., had fifty-seven women and seventy-two men working throughout its three floors, a relatively large workforce for a computer software developer in this day and age. The term "downsizing" had spread through Japan like a devouring flame once the economic bubble had burst, and he personally knew of scores of companies that had been driven to bankruptcy. Intersystems would have been one of them had it not been for the establishment of the back office. Despite the disrespect he felt for his boss, Osamu Tokoro, he had to admit that that had been a stroke of pure genius. The back office not only more than paid for the rest of the company, the staff in the rest of the company had absolutely no idea of what was going on in there. Considering that they were separated by nothing more than thin soundproofed walls, this in itself was a remarkable achievement. Of course, the rumors ran rife, but none of them had come even close to the truth. Most believed that work was being carried out on a secret government project, and some even thought that the Space Agency was the sponsor.

Yanagida sat back in his chair and surveyed his domain on the first floor from his position at the back of the large, open-plan room. Telephones were ringing and people were studiously getting on with their work. He himself had very little work to keep him busy, but that did not prevent him from working until past nine o'clock every night. After all, he was a manager. Managers were paid to be on standby to solve any of the thousands of small problems that cropped up in the running of an office, and he could not carry out this most important of duties if he constantly had a full in-tray. A long-haired dispatch rider with a crash helmet tucked under his arm entered the office and handed an A4-size package to one of the girls who stood to greet him. She signed the delivery chit and walked up the office to Yanagida's desk.

"*Kacho*, a package for you."

Yanagida grunted and accepted the package. He was expecting it and immediately left the office to take the elevator up to the second floor. Arriving at a door opposite the elevator, he removed a piece of plastic about the size of a credit card from his wallet and ran it through a sensor slot on the left-hand side of the door frame. The mechanism within the door buzzed, and a clicking noise told him that the lock had been disengaged. He walked into a small cubicle, about the size of one *tatami* mat, and rang the bell of the door that separated him from the actual office. After a moment, a face was revealed in the small glass panel and the door was unlocked from within.

"Where's Suzuki?" he asked as the man nodded a brief greeting.

"In the console room."

Yanagida walked across the office, picking his way around the people working at desks and numerous computer monitors, to a glass-paneled room at the back. He looked through the glass and saw Suzuki bent over a keyboard, practically concealed by a plethora of computer towers that reflected the names of the world's most famous hardware manufacturers. The floor of the console room was raised by thirty centimeters to accommodate the miles of wiring required to run all of the different computers, but it was still liberally scattered with black and gray snaking cables. Suzuki was working on the IBM S/36 console and was scrolling the lines of RPG source code on the screen. The S/36 and S/38 had been extremely popular in Japan in their heyday, and some old diehards had ignored the transition across to more modern systems and LAN networks and still battled away with their aging machines. To his knowledge, Intersystems was currently working on three jobs on these old dinosaurs. He knocked on the window to attract Suzuki's attention.

Noriyuki Suzuki looked up and acknowledged Yanagida. He saved the amendments he had made and returned the screen to the POP application before joining Yanagida in the outer office.

"It's arrived," said Yanagida, waving the package in the air.

"Let me get my jacket." Suzuki looked the part of computer nerd. At thirty-two years of age, he was unmarried, lived in a cluttered two-room apartment, and paid little attention to personal appearance. His glasses were invariably smeared with fingerprints and his hair needed the attentions of a comb, if not a barber.

The two men left the office and took the elevator up to the third floor. Osamu Tokoro's office was located ten meters down the corridor on the left, and Yanagida knocked on the door and swung it open.

Tokoro was sitting behind a glass desk in his shirt-sleeves. The office was ultramodern and contained much glass and many mirrors. Tokoro rarely removed his jacket unless he was expecting a visit from his staff; the air-conditioning was kept at a constant twenty-one degrees Celsius, so he didn't need to. His shirtsleeved figure was intended to create the image that he also worked hard and was able to raise a sweat—designer imaging. In reality, he spent most of the day reading and engaged in long telephone calls with his female acquaintances—most of whom were Filipinas working in the bars he regularly patronized.

Yanagida and Suzuki perched themselves on the high-backed, bright yellow chairs with triangular seats located in front of Tokoro's desk. They were exceedingly uncomfortable, but Tokoro shopped with looks in mind, not comfort.

"The profiles have arrived," said Yanagida, placing the unopened package on Tokoro's desk. Tokoro slit the top of the envelope with a paper knife and tipped the contents out on his desk.

"And what have we here?" Tokoro began to leaf through the three slim files, and he spent more time studying the color photographs that accompanied each than he did reading the profiles. "Now, there's ugly," he said, handing over the photograph of Donald Mitchell. He scanned the first page of the profile. "Wow, one hundred and ninety-two centimeters tall and eighty-eight kilograms in weight. We shouldn't have much trouble keeping an eye out for him, eh?" Yanagida and Suzuki laughed dutifully. "He'll stick out like a tree in a field of rice."

The three men studied the contents of each file and

came to the conclusion that the two *gaijin*, Mitchell and Stockton, would not pose any problems, but they would need to be on the alert for the ECB detective, Murata, who had no distinguishing features and would blend easily into any situation.

"Should we curtail any of our activities?" asked Suzuki. He had no time for this cloak-and-dagger stuff and was eager to get back to his console. He had two cutovers scheduled for this week and liked to check every line of code himself before compilation and subsequent deployment.

"No, there should be no need for that. Our sponsors seem to feel that these men will be provided with minimal authority and will not be allowed to get anywhere near us. All we need to do is keep a close eye out for them. Knowing the face of the enemy simply gives us an advantage. Memorize these faces and let me know immediately if you spot any of them."

The briefing complete, Yanagida and Suzuki left the office and Tokoro shrugged on his jacket. The fact that an investigation had been implemented against him made him slightly nervous, but he knew Sakaguchi would provide ample protection. After all, Sakaguchi had farther to fall than he did. He was proud of his decision to approach Sakaguchi for backing in the first place, but never in his wildest dreams had he expected the union to be so fruitful. His bank account now stood at nine digits—which, he mused, would make him a dollar millionaire if he took the trouble to work out the figures—and there was nothing Tokoro liked better than money. Sakaguchi was sometimes overbearing and failed to treat him with respect, but he could live with that as long as the cash kept rolling in.

Tokoro began to hum gently to himself as he looked up a number in his leather-bound diary and punched it out on the telephone. He jammed the receiver between his shoulder and chin and pushed the three files back into the envelope.

"Hello, sweetie," he said in broken and very accented English. "It's me, Osamu."

Japan (Tokyo)

Akio Murata waited by the luggage carousel and kept an eye on the stairs leading up to the immigration mezzanine. KL861 was already displayed over the carousel, but the conveyor belt had yet to start moving. Several Japanese tourists returning from Europe began to gather around him, but the passports of nationals were given only a cursory glance and many inspection desks were provided for them. On the other hand, only two or three desks were allocated to aliens, and the queues could sometimes be staggeringly long. The conveyor belt hummed into action and the first suitcases began to appear from the depths of the terminal.

Murata checked his watch and noted that the plane from Geneva via Amsterdam had been on the ground for nearly forty minutes. He had never had the opportunity of meeting anybody at Narita International Airport before, and the buzz he had got from flashing his ID to get him behind the customs area and into the arrival hall was still with him. A few foreigners began to collect around him, and he knew his colleagues would not be much longer. He was looking forward to meeting both Mitchell and Stockton. He had read their files several times and was deeply impressed by how early in their careers both had managed to acquire enviable reputations. Murata himself was nearing thirty and knew that his file would never impress anybody, no matter how long his career in the police force lasted. Individuals simply did not excel in Japan. If lucky, the section he was working for might receive a group commendation, but the only way his record would reflect a personal accolade would be if he was killed in the line of duty.

Like Hisamitsu.

Murata looked up and caught sight of Stockton leaning over the railings of the mezzanine, surveying the hundreds of people busily hunting out their luggage. He looked younger than his photograph, he decided. Stockton would not recognize Murata's face, but he chanced a small wave as he looked his way and was rewarded with a bow of the head and a brief grin. Both Stockton and Mitchell were aware that he would be at the airport to meet them.

Stockton was joined by a tall man a few moments later, and they moved down the stairs in his direction. Mitchell stood about twelve centimeters taller than Stockton and looked twenty years older, although, in fact, there were only ten years between them. Mitchell's face seemed slightly careworn—cynical perhaps—and lived in, whereas Stockton exuded bright confidence and open curiosity.

Murata walked across the hall and met them at the bottom of the stairs. "Welcome to Japan. My name is Akio Murata. Please call me Akio." His words ran together without any discernible punctuation, and Stockton decided that he had probably been practicing this sentence continuously for at least several hours.

"Murata-san," said Stockton heartily, taking Murata's outstretched hand. "*Toi tokoro, gokuro sama deshita.*"

"Oh, Jesus!" Mitchell raised his eyes to the ceiling. "How about us speaking English around here?"

"Of course, Mr. Mitchell. My English is not so good, but I hope you can understand me." Murata held his hand out to Mitchell and the two shook hands.

Once the introductions had been made, the three men, loaded down with luggage, left the airport and found Murata's car in the parking lot. The sun poked its head out from behind the clouds for the first time in a week as they traveled through the Chiba countryside exchanging desultory small talk. Jet lag was beginning to catch up with Mitchell and Stockton, and they had neither the energy nor the inclination to get straight down to business. There were no direct flights available from Geneva on a Monday, which meant that they had been forced to change flights with a ninety-minute stopover at Amsterdam. KLM's first-class service had been most enjoyable—neither had ever flown first class before—but fourteen hours and twenty minutes of flight time had taken its toll.

Murata's Mitsubishi Pajero—his pride and joy— handled the run into downtown Tokyo with ease. Progress slowed as they hit the midmorning traffic, but they still arrived at the Akasaka Tokyu Hotel two hours before check-in time, and even Murata's ID could not persuade the receptionist to allow them into their rooms early. They consequently adjourned to the bar and settled down with a beer each.

"So, what do you have?" asked Mitchell once they were seated in overstuffed chairs and had blown the foam off their beers.

"I think nothing that you don't already know." Murata was not used to drinking alcohol during daylight hours and wondered what his boss would say if he could see him now. "I have checked all of Mr. Hisamitsu's files, but I cannot find anything that could have provided him with any proof of foul play."

"Did he have his own computer or was he using a mainframe?" asked Stockton.

"The mainframe. Everybody in the office is allocated their own library within the main computer, and all of his files would have been stored in there."

"Any floppy disks or CD-ROMs in his desk? Scraps of paper in his locker?"

"No, I have searched everywhere."

"What about a PC in his home?"

"He had one, but it seems he only used it for personal reasons and games. It contained nothing relating to his work."

Mitchell stifled a yawn. "You know, I am beginning to wonder if Hisamitsu's death has anything to do with this at all."

"Oh, no, Mr. Mitchell . . ."

"Call me Don."

"You are wrong, Don. He was not working on anything else."

"Oh, come on. Cops make enemies. It could have been retribution for someone he nailed years ago.

"I think you're wrong, Don." Stockton drained his glass and waved to the barman for three more. "This isn't the States, you know. This style of professional execution requires a better reason than mere retribution."

"Jesus, there you go again." Mitchell shook his head in exasperation. "You're gonna have to forget your love affair with Japan, Frank." Mitchell had got the impression on the flight over that Stockton would have nothing derogatory said against Japan. Every comment he had made had been countered with a long explanation, the gist of which had stated that Japan was different and couldn't be weighed on the same set of scales. "We are talking crime, here. The basis of crime is greed, and greed is not governed by national borders. Hisamitsu obviously knew nothing about this case, so he must have made a serious enemy in the past. Pissing off people is reason enough to earn a bullet in North America, Europe, Asia—shit, the whole damn world."

Stockton grinned sardonically. "A fair comment, Don. Very impressive. But I am not disputing the basis of the crime. Sure, greed is the motivating factor, but the method will be different here. Cops just don't get croaked. Ninety-nine percent of Japanese cops have never even removed their guns from their holsters in anger, let alone necessity. The only way we are going to get anywhere in this case is if we face each item from the point of view of the culture and society."

"Bullshit!"

"Look, a few years ago the National Police Agency decided to crack down on organized crime and strengthened the law to enable them to close down any organizations that were suspected of illegal activities. Okay? Now, what would have happened in the States?"

Mitchell shrugged his shoulders. "Who knows? Increased bribe activity. Attacks on the lawmakers."

"Well, let me tell you what happened over here. The gangsters organized themselves into a peaceful demonstration and walked down the Ginza waving banners and placards protesting the crackdown. Some of the placards stated that the law was unfair for singling them out, and others reminded the public that they had children to feed as well as everybody else. A huge great rally manned by grim-looking mobsters in black suits and sunglasses who were appealing to the general public to allow them to continue committing crimes."

"Oh, come on. Give me a break."

"I'm telling you. It's true! Japan handles problems differently. You simply cannot equate it with the rest of the world."

"Okay, point taken. So who killed Hisamitsu? Somebody obviously hasn't been reading the same book of rules. Maybe things are handled differently over here, but the fact remains that Hisamitsu was given a deep-sixer. You gonna tell me that we imagined that?"

"No. What I am saying is that he must have stumbled onto something that took him as close to the core of the case as is possible. Retribution for pissing somebody off is just not on the board. The fact that he was murdered proves that we are involved in an investigation where drastic measures are the name of the game. We are going to have to proceed with great care, because the Yakuza does just not go around bumping off cops unless they are really desperate."

"May I say something, please?" Murata had watched the conversation between Mitchell and Stockton with interest. He found it refreshing that both men could speak their minds without concern for the age difference between them. Placed in the same position, he would have had to take a wide detour to persuade somebody ten years his senior of his opinions, as it would have been alien and discomforting to him to offer an open contradiction directly.

"Sure, Akio. Fire away."

"I have checked up on Mr. Hisamitsu's past activities, and he has never been in charge of a case before. He has also never been involved in an investigation into organized crime. We have a special bureau for dealing with mob crimes called the Organized Crime Control Department, and he has never worked for or been involved with this office. However, as the nature of his death points to the Yakuza, I am forced to agree with Frank. He must have discovered something concerning this case that angered them enough to arrange for his demise."

Mitchell held up his hands in defeat. "Okay, okay, you guys win. So we go ahead under the assumption that we are dealing with the mob. What's our first step?"

"I suggest we spend tomorrow going through all of Hisamitsu's files and make our decision then," said Stockton. "Maybe they will provide a hint as to where to start."

"Accepted." Mitchell placed his hands behind his head, lay back in the armchair, and closed his eyes. "Now, I need a shower and a long sleep. Any chance of checking in yet, Akio?"

"I will check with the desk," said Murata, standing up, "but there is no time for sleeping. Mr. Hirata is expecting you to report to the office this afternoon."

Mitchell smiled beatifically. "Well, tell Mr. Hirata that I appreciate his eagerness to meet me, but he will find me much more palatable after a full night's sleep. Let him know that we'll see him at nine o'clock tomorrow morning."

Japan (Tokyo)

Stockton and Mitchell arrived at the office of the Electronic Crime Bureau at nine the next morning and were introduced to the rest of the staff during the *chorei*—the morning meeting. Having been shown around the office, they finally adjourned to Hirata's office for a briefing.

"First of all, gentlemen," said Hirata after they were seated on the couch and had been served coffee, "I would like to say how much I appreciate your assistance. There have been no cases in the past where foreign nationals have been called in to act as consultants on crimes that are mostly domestic in nature, and I am sure we all have much to learn from these unprecedented circumstances.

"We have prepared a workstation and all items of stationery that you might conceivably need in one of our meeting rooms, but if you require anything else, please do not hesitate to ask Mr. Murata." Murata nodded in their direction to indicate that he was ready to accept this responsibility. "You might find our style of working somewhat prohibitive in comparison to what you are used to, but I hope you will be able to adapt to this and enjoy your stay with us. My first request of you is to provide me with an explanation of the day's progress every evening when you finish work, but this report can be made via Mr. Murata and should not inconvenience you in the least."

Both men nodded in agreement. Stockton was used to Japanese work practices and had warned Mitchell of what to expect, so neither was unduly put out by what seemed to be a perfectly reasonable request.

"There is one other point that I feel obliged to point out, gentlemen," continued Hirata. "And that is the fact that you are here as consultants and are not expected to exceed this capacity. Your duties lie within these four walls and not out on the street. If, for any reason, you feel it is necessary to leave the office in order to check out some details, I shall require a written declaration of your movements and intentions and you will not be allowed to leave until I have approved it. Is that clear?"

Mitchell shifted uncomfortably in his seat. He was not used to having his freedom of movement restricted, and he felt a jab of indignation arise from deep within him. "Now, wait a minute, there, Mr. Hirata. We are big boys and know how to take care of ourselves."

"Of course you are, Mr. Mitchell," Hirata smiled, "but while you are working for the Japanese government, I am afraid that you will have to conform to our rules. This will not cover your personal movements, naturally. Only your official activities. You must remember that a murder has been committed, and my government would be most distressed if I allowed the same fate to befall your own illustrious beings. Also, your time will be better spent here. We have people who can run your small errands and visit places on your behalf, so you can dedicate all of your time to the job in hand. Are we in agreement?"

"Well, I guess so," said Mitchell, casting his eyes between Stockton and Murata for backup. "What about you guys?"

"Seems fair to me," said Stockton.

Murata nodded.

"Good, then that is settled. So—"

"There is one other thing, Mr. Hirata," interrupted

Mitchell, grasping his chance before Hirata could end the meeting.

"Yes?"

"When will we be issued firearms?"

A look of confusion spread across Hirata's features. "Firearms, Mr. Mitchell? I don't think I understand."

"Well, I presume we will be issued side arms. We weren't able to bring our own."

"I'm afraid not, Mr. Mitchell," said Hirata firmly, shaking his head. "As I have already mentioned, you are in Japan as consultants, not detectives. There are very few police agencies in the world that would issue side arms to consultants."

"But—"

"No buts, Mr. Mitchell. The conversation is closed. Now, if that is all, Mr. Murata will show you to your working areas." Hirata stood up to indicate that the meeting was over. "Once again, I thank you for your assistance and hope you are successful in your attempts to locate the perpetrators of these despicable crimes. Gentlemen." Hirata shook hands with Stockton and Mitchell and watched Murata lead them out of his office.

Having arrived in their "office"—a small meeting room with four chairs around a table that supported a workstation and a pile of stationery—Mitchell turned on Stockton.

"Why the hell didn't you back me up in there? Do you want to fill in a lousy form every time you need to pee?"

"Come on, Don. You're overreacting, man. He only wants to know if we intend to go out on the streets and get involved in anything dangerous to body and limb. Did you really expect them to give you a free hand so you could solve the entire case single-handedly? Wyatt Earp strikes again, eh? Leave it out, Don."

"That's not the point, and you know it. I expect them to trust my judgment. I haven't survived this long by acting out of hand, and if someone decides that I deserve a bullet, then the only way I am going to be able to prevent that is not with a letter from teacher, but with freedom of movement and a gun. Jeez, this whole thing is doing serious damage to my pride."

"I'm sorry, Don, but you are going to have to take your pride and stick it where the sun don't shine for the duration. As much as I hate repeating myself, this is Japan, you know."

"You fight so much," said Murata, looking between the two men in feigned surprise. "Is this a situation where I can use the phrase 'Beam me up, Scotty'? My book tells me I can use this when I am in a situation I wish to escape. Correct?"

A grin broke out on Mitchell's face, and he slapped Murata on the back good-naturedly. "Sure, you can use it, Akio. Although I think I ought to tell you, you're using the wrong study books."

"Shall we work?" Murata waved his hands over the table and the three sat down to inspect the stationery available.

The rest of the morning was consumed by setting up a working environment in which they would all be comfortable. It was decided that a printer would have to be installed within the office, as running out to the computer room for every page printed was time-consuming as well as bothersome. Mitchell also ordered a portable coffee machine brought in and was on his second cup of Blue Mountain when they sat down to learn how to use the workstation. Efficient in the reading of the Japanese language, Stockton had no trouble learning the operations of the computer, but Mitchell was stumped from moment one and gave it up in exasperation before they had got past the log-on screen.

Actual work did not start until after lunch. They began their efforts by reviewing all of Hisamitsu's files. Hisamitsu had sent a total of fourteen messages to Geneva and received nineteen in return. They read through the messages several times before Stockton noticed a small ambiguity.

"Here, take a look at this," he said. "This message mentions 'my message of June 21,' but from what I can make out, he didn't send a message on June 21."

Mitchell frowned as he read through the message. Murata slipped into the seat in front of the workstation and began to run a search by date.

"Well, it doesn't mention what the June 21 message contained," observed Mitchell. "Do you think he just got his dates confused?"

Stockton turned his attention to Murata, who was studying the screen of the monitor. "Anything there, Akio?"

Murata shook his head. "A total of twenty-three messages were sent on-line from this office on June 21, but none by Hisamitsu. I can check the backup tapes if you want."

"No, don't bother. He must have mixed his dates up. Just in case, e-mail Marceillac and ask him to send us copies of all communications. And while you're there, is there any way that you can run a search on the domestic files to get a list of the companies and people that potentially stood to gain from other people's misfortune?

If we could come up with a short list, it would give us a place to start."

Murata thought for a moment. "Yes, I probably can if I use the English translations. I could run a spell-check on each file and then visually check the Japanese names that it does not recognize. It will take me a couple of hours, though, and some may slip through the net."

"I suggest we give it a try anyway," said Stockton. "If it works out, we can always go through the files by hand to catch the ones you missed."

"Yeah, that's not a bad idea," endorsed Mitchell. "Run it up the flagpole, Akio, my man, and let's see who salutes." Murata's questioning look forced him to add, "Go for it, Akio. Do it!"

It took twenty minutes for Murata to come up with the first file that contained information on an individual who stood to profit from a computer crime. In early April, a false order had been set in the computer of a nationwide bookstore chain requesting a publishing company to supply all of its stores with between six hundred and twenty-five hundred copies of a nonfiction book titled *Pyramid Power*, written by a relatively unknown author named Hiroshi Nagai. At the same time, a message was sent to all stores from one of the directors in the head office—who later denied all knowledge of the event—stating that the company wanted to pressure-sell the book and to set up displays in prominent locations. The publishing company went all out to meet demand and delivered close to half a million books to the two hundred and sixty outlets. Competitors, noting the trend, also began to order the books in volume, with the result that *Pyramid Power* entered the best-sellers list toward the end of April and stayed there for six weeks. The fact that the scam was a total success and that even the victim had profited detracted somewhat from the import of the crime, but the bookstore chain had reported the incident to the police out of a sense of anxiety over the fact that the security of its computer had been violated.

Murata printed out the file and passed it across to Stockton, who wrote "Hiroshi Nagai" on a pad of A4 paper.

An hour later, Murata came up with a second name. On May 5, the last day of a series of national holidays known as the Golden Week, somebody had broken into a medium-sized pharmaceutical company and linked a modem to an isolated host computer in which most of the company's internal communications were carried out. The back had been removed from the computer and the modem actually hidden within it. A truly professional job. Nothing had been suspected for a month, until one of the managers, who had been out drinking and missed his last train home, had been in the office at two o'clock in the morning and decided to get on with some work. He found it strange that he was unable to access the document he had wanted to work on because it was already in use. He checked the ID of the person who was in the computer and discovered it came from a remote source. Realizing the implications of the intrusion, he forcibly disconnected the user, effectively alerting him to the discovery, and reported the incident to his boss the next day. The ECB was contacted and an incoming trace on the line established, but the intruder never returned. Although no damage was inflicted on the data within the computer, it was discovered that the president of a rival company was now having great success in reading the trends of the market and had also made a great deal of money in dealing in the stocks of his competitor in a manner that smacked of insider trading. Lack of evidence prevented prosecution, but a close eye was being kept on his future transactions.

Stockton scanned the printout and added the name Ryuji Kagawa/Kagawa Pharmaceuticals Inc. to his list.

It was nearly five o'clock before Murata had searched all of the domestic files. Then he quickly passed the spell-checking software through the six crimes that had initially tipped off Marceillac in the IOCC and found one more name for the list—the name of the only other company in the Zaire dam construction bid.

Stockton passed his hands through his hair and slapped his face to ward off the jet lag that was creeping up on him again. He had commandeered the services of one of the office girls while Murata was busy on the computer to help him establish addresses and telephone numbers of the people on his list. "Well, I suppose three starting points is better than nothing for an afternoon's work. The names we have are Hiroshi Nagai, an author who lives in Sendai; Ryuji Kagawa, the president of Kagawa Pharmaceuticals, located in Kawasaki; and Tetsuya Ishibashi, the president of Daido Incorporated, a construction company whose head office is in Nihonbashi."

"How are you gonna approach these guys?" asked Mitchell. "The head teacher is not about to let us go interviewing people."

"We can start off with phone calls. Akio can phone each one tomorrow and either arrange a meeting or scare the shit out of them on the phone. What do you reckon, Akio? Do you think you can judge guilt on the end of a phone?"

"I think it would be better to meet with these people, but maybe I can shock them into silence by telling them we know they are guilty. Silence in Japan speaks as loudly as words."

"Good, that gives us a plan for tomorrow. Now, what do you say we all go and eat? My body clock has yet to catch up with the time difference, and I am starving." Stockton tapped his stomach to add emphasis to his words.

"First I must report to Mr. Hirata," said Murata.

"Well, go to it, Akio. We're waiting for you." Mitchell stood up to stretch his legs and poured the last of the coffee. "Did you send that message to Geneva yet?"

"No, I will do it now."

"Go and brief your boss. I'm sure Frank wouldn't mind sending it off for you. Right, Frank?"

Stockton agreed to send the message, and Murata left the room to report to Hirata. Mitchell picked up the e-mail message from Hisamitsu that referred to June 21 and read it again, a deep frown on his face.

Chapter Six

Japan (Tokyo)

"So our pet monkeys are quite bright, it would seem," said Sakaguchi as he flicked through the translated transcript of the conversations in the ECB office. "Who would have thought they would find a lead in their first few hours?"

Narita knelt on a cushion across the low table from Sakaguchi and kept his eyes on the decorative ashtray placed between them. He had already read the transcript and was feeling a little anxious at how easily the ECB were tracing leads. Two weeks ago, he would have staked his soul on the improbability of any evidence pointing in their direction, but then Hisamitsu had found a thread that had led directly to Intersystems, and now the two *gaijin* had discovered another that could finally lead back to the Sakaguchi-gumi and Sakaguchi himself. He mentally prepared himself for his boss's explosion. Sakaguchi did not tolerate mistakes, and it was obvious that mistakes had been made. For the first time in his relationship with Sakaguchi—a relationship that had lasted for more than twenty years—Narita began to fear for his life. Sakaguchi was not above making examples of failure, and he had already informed Narita that he was to be held responsible for the success of the project. When the time came, he hoped he would accept his fate with dignity. He had seen several people whom he had considered strong men dissolve into weak and simpering wretches in their final moments, pleading and groveling like ill-mannered women.

"You seem to have something on your mind, Narita? Are you bothered by something?"

Narita, startled out of his revelry, jumped slightly at the words and stammered out a reply. "For . . . forgive me, *oyabun*. I was simply reflecting upon my miserable attempts at carrying out your orders."

"Hah! You amuse me, Narita." Sakaguchi extinguished his cigarette with a delicacy that belied the stubbiness of his fingers. "You don't think that everything is going according to plan?"

"No, *oyabun*. I have provided information to the ECB that should have been concealed."

"Ah, that is where you are wrong. It is impossible to hide all evidence of a crime, but these bumbling amateurs are helping us cover our trail. Can't you see it, Narita? The idiot Hisamitsu pointed out a breach in our armor. That breach is now sealed. Not only is Hisamitsu dead, but the invoices in the companies concerned have been amended. Now the two *gaijin* and their Japanese lackey have been considerate enough to point out another breach. So how do we mend this breach . . . ?"

Narita sensed that Sakaguchi was awaiting an answer. "We remove the three people on this list from circulation, *oyabun*."

"That is correct, Narita. You are learning. Now, I suggest that you spend more time covering up these minor errors and less time reflecting upon their cause. It is my fervent wish that none of these three men will be available for the telephone calls they are destined to receive in the morning. Have I made myself clear, Narita?"

"Yes, *oyabun*. I will see to it immediately."

Narita stood up and moved across to the sliding door. Before opening it he turned back to Sakaguchi, who had lighted another cigarette and was leaning back, relishing the smoke. "*Oyabun*. Do you wish for the removal of these men to be permanent?"

"I will leave that up to your discretion, Narita. Make your own choice."

Japan (Tokyo)

The three men sat in a noisy and crowded restaurant in Shinbashi and discussed the case. Each was pleased with the progress they had made on their first day, but Stockton and Mitchell harbored a few doubts as to the next step if this gambit failed to produce results. Evidence was notably thin on the ground. The perpetrators had obviously gone to great lengths to cover their trail.

"Do you really think we are dealing with the Yakuza, Akio?" asked Stockton. The level of subtlety involved in the case so far seemed to point away from the mob. The Japanese Yakuza were notoriously clumsy in their crimes and seemed to enjoy letting the public know that they were involved, almost as if it satisfied their collective ego. They occasionally even allowed anonymous interviews with television journalists to boast of their involvement in drug dealing and gunrunning. The Yakuza constantly stated that a certain percentage of Japan's illegal drugs and firearms entered the country through the Shimonoseki ferry route in Kyushu—a major port that connected Japan's sea routes with the rest of Asia—but for some reason the customs still made only cursory checks on this entry point. The authorities, it seemed, were reluctant to believe testimony that originated from the mouths of their archenemy, so Shimonoseki remained relatively unpoliced.

Murata lifted a mouthful of buttered mushrooms with his chopsticks and chewed while pondering the question. "Yes," he said finally, "I would say that Hisamitsu's death has confirmed that. The murder in Madrid also indicates Yakuza involvement. There is a large contingent of the Japanese mob in Spain, and it would be extremely difficult for an organization or individual without such connections to arrange for a death across the other side of the world without leaving a wider trail."

Mitchell, who had decided to play safe and had ordered a pizza, which he delicately ate with the knife and fork provided, said, "Tell me more about the Yakuza. I read up on the statistics before coming over, but they just seemed like a Japanese version of the American mafia to me."

"In many ways they are similar. They just have different roots." Stockton placed his chopsticks on the edge of his plate and took a draft of beer before continuing. "From what I can gather, they go way back to the time when Japan was totally closed off from the rest of the world and, with the exception of fish, totally vegetarian. Society was arranged in a very strict hierarchy of classes. Anybody above the rank of Samurai was able to carry swords and lord it up, but the classes below this, the masterless Samurai, the merchants, farmers, fishermen, et cetera, were considered to be only on the outer boundaries of humanity. And, at the very bottom of the scale, came a group of people known as the *Eta*. These were the people who dealt in animal carcasses, like leather tanners, and they were not considered human at all. They were segregated into tiny slums on the outskirts of the towns and were not allowed to mix with the 'humans'—a situation not unlike the untouchables of India. Well, to cut a long story short, these people were, apparently, the origins of the Yakuza. They involved themselves in the black market and hired out their dubious services to rich and poor alike. Given the turbulence of the times, it appears that they had no shortage of clients.

"The typical modern-day Yakuza group is relatively small—although most maintain connections with the larger groups—runs a legal front office to cover itself, and involves itself in loan-sharking, extortion, blackmail, drug dealing, and gunrunning."

"Bless them," said Mitchell, who had discovered a liking for Japanese beer and was already on his fourth medium-sized "jockey."

"You know about my country very well," said Murata. Most Japanese people would feel reluctant to converse openly about the Yakuza in a public location, and he was impressed, although slightly disconcerted, at Stockton's knowledge of the dark side of Japan. The Japanese mentality, in general, exhibited great embarrassment when non-Japanese people were aware of the secrets they would rather keep quiet. The first reaction to the spate of serious crimes that were prevalent in Japan had been "Oh, my. What will the rest of the world think of us?"

"I was brought up over here, Akio. My father was transferred to Japan when I was twelve years old, and I stayed here until I was twenty-five."

"You must have had a very interesting life."

"Depends on what you think is interesting. I went to an International School in Yokohama, then on to Sofia University in Tokyo, worked as a translator for one of the major Japanese electronics manufacturers, and then worked two years for the British Tourist Authority."

"How did you manage to worm your way into the NCIS?" Mitchell asked.

"The director of the Tourist Authority had lots of contacts, and when I expressed a desire to return to England, he phoned a few people on my behalf. This was back when computers were just beginning to feature heavily in serious crime, and he managed to get a job for me in Scotland Yard as a civilian intelligence comptroller in the computer division. I got on well with my supervisor, and he suggested that I enroll for a two-year course at the British Police Staff College to make me into a real cop, which I did. I returned to the computer division of Scotland Yard, was later promoted to inspector of computer crime, and was then transferred across to the National Criminal Intelligence Service. The rest is history."

"My girlfriend, Hiroko, also attended an American school," said Murata brightly.

"Not an American school, Akio." Stockton waved an admonishing finger at Murata. "An international school. I went to the Yokohama International School in Yamate, and we were strongly aware of our superiority over the American schools."

Mitchell looked up in surprise. "And what's wrong with an American school, you stuck-up Brit? American schools teach men to be men."

"Yeah, and women to be men," scoffed Stockton.

"You see what he's saying about your girlfriend there, Akio? I wouldn't stand for that. Here, let me hold your coat while you kick the shit out of him."

Murata recognized that the two men were joking and laughed himself. "You two are crazy," he said, "but I think you are good friends."

"No way, pal!" said Stockton with a grin. "I choose my friends carefully, and all have to be at least a three on the beauty scale of ten. Don here checks in at just under zero point five."

"So tell us about your girlfriend, Akio," invited Mitchell.

Murata launched into a lengthy explanation of his girlfriend, Hiroko Ito. Although there was no trace of foreign blood in her family, her father had decided to send her to the American school in Japan from elementary school upward to give her a better chance in life. Her father ran his own distribution company and did not want his beloved daughter serving tea to ungrateful men until she was fired upon marriage, as was the case for most of Japan's female workforce in the past. She graduated from the ASIJ and went on to the International Christian University in Tokyo, where she excelled at International Business. She became a freelance translator upon graduation and set up office in a condominium—or "mansion," as they were known in Japan—in Gotanda, in which she also lived. Murata had met her eighteen months previously through a mutual friend, and they had dated ever since.

Mitchell and Stockton listened patiently until Murata had finished. "Let's get her over here," said Mitchell. "What do you say, Frank? I think a touch of female beauty would brighten the place up."

"I'll certainly agree with that. Go on, Akio. Phone her and get her over here."

Murata was finally persuaded to phone Hiroko, and she agreed to come. Gotanda, being separated from Shinbashi by a mere six stations on the Yamanote line, was only a thirty-minute door-to-door journey away for Hiroko, and it was not long before a pretty girl with long black hair pushed her way through the other customers in the restaurant and settled down at the three men's table.

"Hiroko, meet Don and Frank," said Murata proudly. Hiroko was looking flawless in a lemon one-piece dress, which gave her an air of casual sophistication. She looked stunning, thought Murata in awe.

"Woof!" said Mitchell appreciatively.

"Pleased to meet you, Hiroko. I'm Frank," said Stockton, kicking Mitchell in the ankle under the table.

The introductions complete, they ordered a bottle of whisky and a cocktail for Hiroko.

"Akio told me that you were coming across, but I didn't expect to get the chance to meet you," said Hiroko in perfect English. "I suppose it is you that I have to thank for the invitation, and not Akio. Akio was absent from school on the day they taught social graces."

Stockton mumbled something self-consciously, and Murata looked suitably embarrassed.

"Do you have any sisters?" asked Mitchell.

Stockton threw a rolled-up napkin at him. "Ignore him, Hiroko. He was absent on the same day as Akio. He is about as subtle as a backed-up toilet. Apparently, you have to be like that in order to be accepted into the FBI. They don't like anybody with a social conscience."

"The FBI? How exciting!" She turned a full grin on Mitchell, who wilted with a groan.

"So how did you get into the FBI, anyway, Don?" asked Stockton. Mitchell had removed his jacket and rolled up his sleeves. The whisky made a pleasant change from the beer they had consumed, and Mitchell's insistence at drinking it neat—as opposed to the watered-down Japanese version—had occasioned coos of admiration from Murata, who was already slightly drunk.

"Well, I left college with a well-earned degree and moved to New York, where I worked as a research clerk in a lawyer's office. I met my wife during this, and—"

"You're married, you old dark horse you!" exclaimed Stockton.

"Not anymore. I was recruited into the FBI by a friend and worked for a couple of years as a research officer, but when I had the chance to become a field agent I jumped at it. Things began to go downhill after that, until we were finally divorced."

"Did you have any children, Don?" asked Hiroko. The way her lips puckered around the straw of her cocktail, decided Mitchell, was probably the cutest thing he had ever seen.

"Yeah. A boy named Richard. He's fourteen years old now."

"Do you ever get to see him?"

"Sure. They still live in New York, but he comes over to Chicago every now and then to stay with me. He's a good kid."

"I want Hiroko to have my baby," announced Murata.

"Way to go, Akio!" Mitchell laughed. "But remember, kids bring heartbreak as well as joy. The day Richard had to have his first vaccination, I was a bag of nerves. I would have given anything in the world to take the pain on his behalf. I left for work that morning with the knowledge that an adult and probably very ugly man was going to be sticking pins in my baby and my baby was going to hurt."

"But vaccinations are necessary, Don," said Murata. "Doctors don't want to hurt babies."

"Sure they do. That's their job. You ask a pediatrician to sum up his work in a single sentence, and nine out of ten that guy is gonna say, 'I hurt babies.' Even dogs sense that doctors are evil. We used to have a dog that chased doctors first and postmen second, for God's sake."

Stockton knocked back his Scotch and water and said, "The slight exaggeration overlooked, why don't we change the subject back to Hiroko having Akio's baby. I think I preferred that conversation."

"You're durned tooting!" Mitchell leaned both elbows on the table and looked deep into Hiroko's eyes. "And how do you feel about this, Hiroko? Are you willing to have this man's baby?"

Hiroko matched his stare and said, "I don't think he is capable. Did he ever tell you my nickname for him?"

"Hiroko!" said Murata, obviously astounded.

"I call him Ultraman," she continued impishly.

Stockton burst into laughter and nearly spilled his drink all over the table. Murata looked sheepish for a moment before breaking into laughter himself. Mitchell passed his eyes between the two men and said, "Hold on, there. What have I missed?"

Murata was incapable of answering, and Hiroko avoided his eyes. It wasn't until he had brought the palm of his hand sharply down onto the table that Stockton managed to control himself and utter a reply.

"Ultraman is one of these Japanese heroes that beat the proverbial crap out of Godzilla and all those other monsters," he began.

"So?"

"Well, Ultraman is a normal human being with the power to change into this superbeing, but he is only allowed three minutes before all his power is drained. I think Hiroko is insinuating that poor old Akio here is a three-minute egg."

Understanding dawned on Mitchell's face. He unscrewed the cap of the whisky and poured a generous amount into Murata's glass and then topped up his own. "Akio, we need to talk, man. Now, where would you like to start?"

Japan (Sendai)

Hiroshi Nagai was on his way home from his favorite bar when he noticed the car pacing him step for step. He looked around at the gray Aristo but could not make out the face of anybody inside. He was not worried. The word "mugging" had yet to reach as far north as Sendai, and he decided that it must be one of his neighbors trying to visually confirm that it was him before offering him a lift home. He reversed his direction and walked over to the car.

As he approached, the window of the passenger seat rolled down and he found himself looking into the eyes of a man he had never met. He was still not overly unsettled—a lot of unknown faces had followed him since the success of his book—but the look in the man's eyes told him that this was no autograph hunter.

"May I help you?" he asked, the first stirrings of fear beginning to flutter within his chest.

The man said nothing, but opened the door and climbed out of the car. He released the catch on the backseat door and gestured with his head for Nagai to get in.

"Who are you?" said Nagai, now seriously worried.

The man grabbed him by the arm and forced him into the backseat. At sixty-eight years of age, Hiroshi Nagai was not going to argue. He allowed himself to be guided into the car. The car started moving and before long left the city of Sendai, headed toward Matsushima. Nagai suddenly had an urgent need to go to the toilet. He was more worried than he had ever been in his life. His recent dealings with the mob had left him a nervous wreck, and he was pretty sure that that was in whose hands he now was. He farted loudly, but apart from opening the windows, the men in the front of the car made no comment.

The car continued along the country roads until a vision of the sea was revealed ahead of them, dark and foreboding in the blackness of night. Fifty minutes after being picked up, Nagai was driven up the driveway of one of the hundreds of hot-spring hotels that lined the coast of Matsushima, bustled from the car, and frog-marched through a garden and into a small self-contained cabin.

Nagai sat fearfully on the floor, aching to pour a cup of green tea from the vacuum pot that stood on the low table before him. The inside of his mouth felt as dry as sandpaper. His two companions on the drive from Sendai stood by the door with their eyes staring into the middle distance approximately one meter above his head. Ten minutes later, the door opened and the man who had had the temerity to subject him to blackmail walked confidently through the door.

"Ah, Mr. Nagai. Glad to see you have made yourself comfortable."

The man seated himself at the table and poured two cups of tea. He handed one to Nagai, who gulped it down convulsively. Then he nodded to one of the guards, who left his position at the door, collected a telephone from a small cabinet located beside the refrigerator, and placed it on the table before the two men.

"Now, Mr. Nagai," he continued, pouring another cup of tea, "I want you to look upon this as a holiday. Yes, you are to be my guest for a short period of time."

He picked up the receiver of the telephone and dialed a number from memory. "Now, please inform your wife that you have decided to take a short break and will see her in a week or two."

He held out the receiver to Nagai.

"You—you cannot do this to me," stammered Nagai. He felt himself hyperventilating and couldn't find the correct words to express the mixture of emotions he was experiencing.

"We could always kill you if you refuse." The man smiled sweetly, continuing to hold out the receiver. The ringing tone was audible to both.

Nagai licked his lips. His wife would by now have left her position in front of the television and be hobbling across to the telephone located in the hall just outside of the front room. He could imagine her reaching out to open the door just halfway. She would then lift the receiver without looking and bring it inside the room without taking her eyes off her favorite program.

The line clicked and a voice said, *"Hai, Nagai desu ga."*

Nagai grabbed the phone.

"It's me," he said gruffly. He always spoke gruffly to his wife and didn't want to alert her to anything that could threaten his life. He noticed the man watching him with an encouraging smile on his face and felt sickened. "I'm going away for a while. I have an idea for a book, and I need isolation. I'll keep in touch." Before she could reply, he slammed the receiver down in its cradle.

"Satisfied?" he asked, his voice unsteady.

"Perfectly," said the man, removing a small set of cardboard cards from his pocket. "Do you play *hanafuda*? It seems as if we have a lot of time on our hands."

Japan (Yokohama)

Motomachi, located in the glitzier area of Yokohama, was nothing like Japan at all. The hodgepodge of Western buildings seemed to suggest an architect's nightmare. Traditional Greek buildings complete with fluted columns competed against bright silver monoliths that would not look out of place on the Strip in Las Vegas, and Tudor-beamed English cottages snuggled up alongside country-music bars decorated as log cabins. Ryuji Kagawa walked along the mostly deserted street and hummed lightly to himself. He was considering buying a property in one of the backstreets of Motomachi and had come to familiarize himself with the locality. The cost of land in the area was exorbitant, but what the hell? He could afford it, couldn't he?

Kagawa was only three years away from retirement and was looking forward to the moment when he would walk out of Kagawa Pharmaceuticals for the last time. He hated the damn place. Being the eldest son, it had almost been a foregone conclusion that he would succeed to his father's throne in the company started by his grandfather in the ninth year of the Taisho era. His own eldest son was now the vice president and was being groomed to take over in three years time. Good luck to him!

A voice called him from across the street, and he stopped and squinted into the darkness. He recognized the overemphasized swagger of the man who was into his pocket for two million yen every month and straightened his back in a display of dignity. He didn't want the scum to think he had a weakness.

"What do you want?" he asked sharply, noting that

111

the man's two accomplices had fanned out to prevent him from trying to escape.

The man pulled a toothpick out of his mouth and flicked it a few meters down the street. "You!" he said simply.

Before he could stop himself, Kagawa had pulled his fist back and let it fly at the man's face. "Bastard!" he screamed. The man easily dodged the punch, but he hadn't expected Kagawa to follow up with a kick. Kagawa's foot caught him just below the knee, and he yelped in pain. The two other men had also been caught unexpectedly, but quickly shook off their surprise and launched themselves at Kagawa. Outnumbered but feeling invincible, Kagawa began to swung in all directions with his fists and was satisfied when he felt his left hand crunch into the jaw of one of his assailants—although which one he had no idea. He was stopped dead in his tracks by a powerful punch that caught him just under the rib cage. All of the breath was knocked out of him and he involuntarily crouched over, wheezing in an effort to force air back into his tortured lungs. He saw the knee coming up into his face but was powerless to stop it. It crashed into the side of his cheek, and he felt, more than heard, the crack of his cheekbone fracturing. A double-handed sledgehammer slammed into the back of his neck, and he realized with surprise a moment later that he was sprawled out on the pavement. It was his last coherent thought before he slipped into unconsciousness.

The man who had been kicked in the leg hobbled over to the supine form and spat on his back in contempt. "I'll bring the car around," he said. "Watch him!"

Two minutes later, the unconscious body of Ryuji Kagawa was unceremoniously bundled into the back of a car and driven off to a small private hospital in Isogo, a few kilometers down the road.

The doctor was reluctant to accept his new patient, but finally agreed when a price of half a million yen was mentioned. The patient was loaded onto a trolley and wheeled into a private room, where the doctor fussed about setting up the IV. His instructions were to keep the man in a coma until someone was sent to pick him up, and he was glad to follow these instructions to the letter. Considering the beating he had taken, this man would be in an extremely bad mood if allowed to wake up, and the doctor did not wish to be among those present when he did.

Japan (Tokyo)

Tetsuya Ishibashi was pouring his second can of beer when the doorbell rang. He lowered the volume of the television and went to answer it.

"Mr. Matsumoto, how nice to see you. Please come in."

Ryoichi Narita, alias Matsumoto, walked through into the front room and looked around at the clothes strewn all over the place and the empty cups and plates on the table. *What a way to treat a house that could be sold on the open market for nearly two hundred million yen*, he thought.

"I expected that I would get neater once I reached middle age," said Ishibashi sheepishly. "But I didn't. Ever since my wife died, well . . ."

"It is of no importance." Narita reached into the inside pocket of his jacket and removed a blue envelope.

He moved aside an overflowing ashtray and placed it on the table.

"Please, sit down. Can I get you a beer?"

"We don't have time. Your flight leaves in less than ninety minutes."

"My flight? I don't understand."

"It seems that the police have gotten wind of the Zaire job and are planning to take you in for questioning tomorrow." Ishibashi's eyes opened wide. "It is not serious, but it might be prudent if you were unavailable. That envelope contains an open ticket to Hokkaido. I suggest that you find a nice, quiet hotel somewhere out in the countryside and check in under a false name. Phone me to let me have your number when you are there so I can contact you when the coast is clear. But don't contact anybody else."

"I could go to Hawaii. I have a condo there."

"No. International travel leaves a paper trail. It is best to stay inside Japan."

"But just how close are they?"

Ishibashi was one of Narita's few clients who did not mind paying the monthly stipend. He probably didn't even look upon it as blackmail, thought Narita. It was not that he was stupid, it was just that the amount of money involved in a project the size of a dam construction made the sum of ten million yen per month seem like peanuts. He didn't even have to pay it out of his own pocket; it was written off as a consultation fee.

"Nowhere near, really. It will have all blown over in a few days. Now, throw some clothes in a suitcase and let's get going."

Ten minutes later, Narita and Ishibashi were driving toward Haneda Airport. When they arrived, Ishibashi phoned one of his directors from the departure lobby and told him he would be out of town for a few days. A cousin had been involved in a traffic accident near Lake Como in Italy and was at death's door in a Milan hospital, he explained. He just had to go to him. The director said that he understood perfectly and hoped everything would turn out all right.

Narita watched Ishibashi walk through to the boarding gate and lost sight of him in the crowds. He wandered across to the self-service coffee bar and sat on an uncomfortable stool drinking a cup of black coffee until the flight had departed. Satisfied, he walked out to the parking lot and drove back into central Tokyo.

Chapter Seven

Japan (Tokyo)

Don Mitchell looked across at Murata and raised an eyebrow. He himself was feeling the effects of the whisky from the night before, and the fact that Murata was bouncing around and humming cheerfully grated on his nerves—especially since Murata had been in an even worse condition when they had finally arrived at the hotel bar for a nightcap. Akio caught his glance and stopped humming.

Mitchell turned his concentration back to the file in front of him. In addition to contacting the three people they already had on their list, they had decided that Stockton and Mitchell would spend the day going through all of the domestic crime files to see if there were any more they could add. Murata was about to lift the phone to make the first call when the computer

117

beeped and the indicator telling them that e-mail was waiting began to flash.

"Probably the files from Geneva," said Mitchell.

Murata went to the computer and confirmed this. Stockton handed him the original files, and he began to check them off one by one with the data on the screen. They matched perfectly, with the exception of a new message from Marceillac stating that he wanted a teleconference at nine-thirty Geneva time that day—four-thirty P.M. in Tokyo.

It was a little after noon when Murata hung up the phone for the last time and sucked the end of his pen thoughtfully. He had not been able to contact even one of the men on his list, and nobody had been able to provide him with a forwarding number or address.

"Problem?"

Murata looked up at Stockton. "Yes," he said. "None of them are available and nobody knows where they are."

"Oh, come on. That's impossible!"

"That's what I thought. I contacted Nagai's wife, and she said her husband hadn't returned from a bar last night but had phoned to say he would be out of touch for a few days."

"Does he do that often?" asked Mitchell.

"The first time, apparently. She seemed quite worried."

"Has she contacted the police?"

"She said it was not necessary. He had phoned himself so she didn't have to worry about him being involved in an accident. She will just wait patiently until he returns."

"But that's ridiculous. He could be in trouble."

"This is the Japanese way, Don. They are an old couple and live by traditional values. The man is master in his house and can do what he wants. Old people also live in fear of causing *meiwaku*, or trouble, for other people. She thinks that it is not her place to transfer her burden over to the police. He will come home when he is ready."

"Jesus! What does she think the police are for?"

Before Murata could answer, Stockton interrupted. "What about Kagawa?"

"Kagawa has also gone missing. He didn't return home last night or turn up for work this morning. Nobody knows where he is."

"Dare I ask?" said Mitchell sardonically, his chin propped in a cupped hand.

"A missing-persons claim has not yet been filed."

"Well, surprise, surprise!"

"A person has to be missing for more than twenty-four hours before they are officially considered missing. I think the law is the same in most countries of the world."

"Never mind. Never mind. What about the other guy?"

"Ishibashi was called across to Italy yesterday, where a relation was involved in a car accident."

"That's better," said Stockton. "We can get hold of him at the hotel." He paused and looked across at Murata. "Provided we have a hotel name . . . ?"

Murata shook his head.

"Flights to Italy? Passport control?"

Murata shook his head again.

"Well, that's just great!" Mitchell slammed his pen down on his desk. "All of these dudes went missing yesterday and nobody knows where to find them. What the hell is going on?"

The odds against the three presumably unacquainted men leaving their homes on the same day were astronomical, and this, added to the fact that nobody knew where to contact them, multiplied the unlikelihood by millions. It was practically impossible to disappear without a trace unless the person in question made a concerted effort. There was always a hint to a wife or friend, an entry in a desk diary, or even an overheard telephone call. Here there seemed to be nothing.

A look of suspicion crept across Mitchell's face. "You don't think . . . ?" he said, pointing a finger at the ceiling and miming a man holding a microphone.

"No, that's ridiculous," said Stockton. "This is a government building, for God's sake."

"Well, I think it is obvious that our conversations have been monitored," said Murata. "The coincidence is just too much. I think we should trace over our steps of yesterday and try to remember exactly where we spoke these men's names outside of this office."

Stockton shook his head. "Hang on, there, Akio. Maybe it seems a coincidence from where we are sitting, but there could have been a lot of other people whose names we don't yet have who also went missing yesterday. Maybe the only coincidence is the day. It could have been planned from the beginning."

"What do you suggest?"

"Well, it won't do any harm going over our movements of yesterday, but I think we should concentrate on these files and see if we can squeeze another name out of them first. All we need is one more name and we can confirm whether we are in fact being monitored or simply chasing phantoms."

"I agree," said Murata.

"Don?"

"Me too. Let's get to work."

They worked ploddingly through the files. The going was slow, for each file was comprehensively written and hastily—possibly even badly—translated. They would find a link that made it seem probable that only a taxi company could possibly have benefited from a certain crime, only to discover that there were twenty small taxi companies in the locality of the victim. It was also impossible to tell if the culprit in question was a company or an individual. They asked one of the office girls to bring them in some sandwiches from the local convenience store and worked right through lunch, without success, up until the time of the teleconference with Geneva.

Stockton was elected as the spokesman. They could have all joined the conference, but it would have meant splitting up into different rooms, and this was not considered necessary. Murata set the equipment up and raised the direction of the camera slightly to get Stockton's full face on screen.

At exactly four-thirty, the screen flickered and Marceillac's face appeared. A moment later, it was reduced in size as Sylvie Keppler joined the conference.

"Good afternoon, Frank," said Marceillac. "The necktie suits you."

Stockton laughed and looked down at his dove-gray tie. "Well, you know how it is. When in Rome . . ."

They chatted about general things, such as the flight

121

over and the hotel accommodation, for several minutes before getting down to business.

"We have one or two leads," said Stockton in answer to Marceillac's inquiry on progress. "But strange things have been happening. We had three people to speak to today, but they all mysteriously disappeared overnight. We are now trying to find out if this was a coincidence."

"What do you mean, disappeared?" asked Sylvie.

Stockton filled them in on events so far and was cautioned to take extreme care. "These men seem to be desperate, Frank. Maybe this is not such a good idea, after all. If anything happened to you or Don, the Japanese government would be placed on the hot spot."

"Oh, don't be such a wuss, Armin. We're just beginning to have fun. Anyway, we have to get close before we put ourselves in danger, and from the looks of things we are more likely to die of old age before we gain any footage. Anyway, why did you call the conference?"

Although Stockton was not aware of it, Keppler's terminal was located beside Marceillac's and they were holding hands under the table. She could sense the worry in Armin and realized the pressure this whole thing was placing him under. A few short weeks ago he was a simple office clerk, and now he was placed in a position where he felt responsible for the lives of other men. It was simply too much for a man not trained in such fields. It had been he who had initiated the investigation, and so far one man had already lost his life. He had taken Hisamitsu's death very personally. The shock had not settled in until they were dining together in a restaurant the same night that Hewes had informed them of his murder. He was fine until the wine bottle had been reduced to only one-quarter full, and then the shaking had started, the realization of what he had done clear on his face. They had left the restaurant hurriedly and taken a taxi back to his apartment, where she had cradled his head until the tears had run dry and the hacking sobs subsided. She had cradled him like that all night, both fully clothed on the sofa. He had cracked the usual chauvinistic jokes the following day about it being the only time he had spent a night with a woman and she had kept her clothes on, but the gratitude in his eyes was obvious. She knew that he was now worried about Stockton, Mitchell, and Murata. She dreaded to think how another death would affect him. In fact, she wouldn't think about it. She pushed the thought aside and concentrated on what Marceillac was saying.

"I wanted to know what you thought about the Interpol file I sent you. The connection is very faint, but I thought it might be worth checking out."

Stockton raised an eyebrow to Murata, who shook his head. "I'm sorry, Armin, but we haven't received it yet. When did you send it?"

"About thirty minutes ago. Are you sure it hasn't arrived?"

"Hold on, I'll check."

Stockton grabbed the mouse and double-clicked one of the buttons displayed at the top of the screen. A white screen laid itself over the faces on the terminal. He clicked the file menu and called up the "Messages Waiting" file. A single line of Japanese script appeared, stating that no messages addressed to this terminal were waiting. He closed the application and the faces of Marceillac and Keppler were revealed once more.

"No, nothing has come in," he said. "Are you sure you sent it properly?"

Marceillac checked his terminal and came back a few moments later. "Yes, it has definitely gone. The address is correct, too."

"Strange. Listen, chase it through on your end and see if you have any line trouble. Send it again just to be sure, and we'll have another teleconference at the same time tomorrow. Okay?"

Marceillac agreed and terminated the connection.

"That's weird," said Mitchell, walking over to the coffee machine for a refill.

"No, not really. Probably a spot of line trouble somewhere. It's not uncommon." Stockton looked back at the pile of unfinished files in the middle of the table and sighed. He was about to sit down when the workstation beeped. Craning his head around the side of the monitor, he noted that the e-mail indicator was flashing. "Ah, here it is. It looks like Armin has located the problem after all."

Murata sat in front of the computer and hit the Print button. The printer began to spool out twenty-one pages. Mitchell, coffee in hand, wandered across to the printer and scanned the contents as they were being printed. His eyes flickered up to the top of the first page and he halted the progress of the coffee cup to his mouth. He glanced at his watch and then at the wall clock to confirm that it was correct.

He looked across to Murata. "Akio. Let me have a printout of those files we received from Geneva this morning, will you?"

"They are the same. I checked."

"It don't matter. Just print them out, please."

Murata placed the job on the queue and three minutes later it began to list out immediately in the wake of the Interpol file. Mitchell only had to glance at the top of the first page to know his assumption was right. He walked back to his seat, scribbled a message on a pad of paper, and handed it to Stockton.

Stockton took the pad and read it slowly, a look of incredulity spreading across his features. Having read it, he looked up at Mitchell, who matched his gaze before passing it wordlessly across to Murata.

Murata read the message three times before looking up in shock. Mitchell nodded to him and he went into action. His act was slightly exaggerated but served its purpose. He yawned loudly and suggested that they leave the office a little earlier tonight. Last night's whisky, he said, had caught up with him and he just could not face another file. Stockton and Mitchell, their performances slightly more convincing, agreed and began to tidy up the files.

Twenty-five minutes later, Stockton and Mitchell sat at the back of a coffee bar in front of Toranomon Station, where they had a view of the entire shop. As the working day for most companies had yet to finish, they were the only customers. They sipped their coffees while they awaited the arrival of Murata, who was briefing Hirata on the day's progress.

"Are you sure about this, Don?" asked Stockton. He pulled the crumpled sheet out of his pocket and laid it on the table. It said:

DON'T READ THIS OUT LOUD
I think we are being monitored from within this office.
End the day smoothly and adjourn to the coffee bar we went to after lunch yesterday.

Akio, brief Hirata truthfully on everything that happened up until ten minutes ago.
ACT NATURALLY!

"Yeah, certain. Our messages are being censored. But wait till Akio gets here. I don't want to have to repeat myself."

Stockton pondered on this and sipped his coffee. If it was true, then things were really out of hand. The Yakuza regularly donated to political parties, but there was no precedent for their infiltrating a government agency. At least, no known precedent. Unstable under normal circumstances, the Japanese government would not simply topple if the press ever got hold of this, it would be smashed to smithereens. With the introduction into Japan of Western morals, things that were overlooked in the past were no longer acceptable. Scandal after scandal had rocked the Liberal Democratic Party until it had finally been replaced by a weak coalition of the Socialist Party and several other puny break-off factions. Most of the scandals had included bribe-taking, which, until a few years earlier, had been nothing out of the usual. Japanese culture was based upon accepting money from acquaintances. Kids were given cash on New Year's Day, newly married couples were given cash at their weddings, attendance at a funeral meant that cash had to be presented; cash was a way of life. The telling phrase was "*Okozukai.*" *Okozukai*, loosely translated, means "pocket money," but relatives were expected to provide *Okozukai* to anyone going on holiday, regardless of their age, and *Okozukai* was presented to people in payment for favors. Politicians also received *Okozukai* in great abundance until the public of Japan began to translate the word into the more popular Western nuance—bribe money. Politicians consequently no longer received *Okozukai*, they received *Wairo*, or bribes. The mass media had been quick to jump onto this ambiguity and immediately began to hound any politician or company employee who was brash enough to stretch out a hand anywhere near unsolicited cash. Politicians had begun to batten down the hatches by checking out the source of all political donations, and this, presumably, had placed the Yakuza in a corner. They could no longer guarantee the planning permission for golf courses and governmental construction jobs that they had received via the *"Ten-no-koe"* in the past. The *Ten-no-koe*—the voice from heaven—was the local slang for a high-ranking official giving his approval to the tender of a company in return for monetary favors. This avenue now barred, the Yakuza appeared to be extending their horizons by infiltrating the government agencies that they had previously controlled from without.

They were on their second cup of coffee when Murata arrived and ordered an iced tea.

"Explain," said Stockton, looking across at Mitchell.

Mitchell took a deep breath and marshaled his thoughts. "All of our mail is being monitored. The time stamp on the Interpol file from Geneva indicated that it had arrived in ECB exactly twenty-eight minutes before it was passed across to our terminal. I then checked the time stamp on the Hisamitsu files and saw they had arrived just before midnight last night. We, however, didn't get them until nearly eleven o'clock this morning. Somebody is checking everything addressed to our terminal and only letting through what they want."

Murata and Stockton digested this news in silence. Murata was the first to speak.

"That is impossible, Don. In order for this to happen, the programs must have been tampered with. Our system is checked for rogue programs and viruses every single morning. There is no way the code could be modified without detection."

"How does the virus checker work?" asked Stockton.

Murata quickly explained how the ECB host system worked. All programs were assigned a starting number that could be anything between one and one hundred thousand, and each line of code in the programs was allocated a series of numbers that ran upward in sequence from this assigned starting number. The virus-checking software ran through all programs in the computer and checked that these serial numbers ran in sequence. Any program to which a line of code had been added or deleted would instantly trigger an alarm. The serial numbers were also encoded to prevent anybody without access to the encoding software, which was not stored within the computer, from amending the numbers to fit the original sequence. Alarms would also be triggered if a program not recognized by the software was resident within the computer.

"That doesn't mean it is impossible, Akio," said Mitchell. "It means that modifications were sanctioned. Is there any way we can check the programs tomorrow?"

"No, internal security places all program members out of reach. The only way we could check it would be to get hold of the master source programs that are stored on tape for backup purposes."

"Can you get hold of the master tapes, Akio?" asked Stockton.

"Well, I don't know. I know where they are kept, but if I am found stealing them I would be in great trouble. Even if I do get them, I do not have access to a computer that is capable of reading them. It would be impossible to use the ECB computer."

"I might have an idea." Stockton removed a small address book from his inside pocket and flipped it open. "I have a friend who runs a computer company in Yokohama. If I could get the tapes to him, I'm sure he'll check them out for me."

"Is your friend likely to have an on-line account with an Internet server?" asked Mitchell.

"Sure. Why?"

"Maybe we could get Geneva to send over Hisamitsu's files again and we could check to see if a June 21 message exists."

"I'll give him a ring. There's a telephone outside."

Stockton returned three minutes later and made a circle with his thumb and forefinger. "It's all set. He invited us round for dinner. Let's grab a taxi."

Japan (Yokohama)

Narita drove past the taxi, turned the next corner, and parked. He got out of the car and walked back to the corner just in time to see the three men enter one of the large, detached houses of Yamate, an expensive residential area of Yokohama that housed many of the city's foreign residents. He waited until the door had closed and then walked casually along the road, his route taking him past the front gate of the house, where he memorized the name and number on the postbox.

He walked all the way around the block to avoid having to pass the house again, and, upon reaching his car, punched out a number on his mobile phone.

"*Oyabun*. They left the office and are now in Yokohama. I followed them to a house owned by a *gaijin* named Crawford."

He pressed the button to disconnect the line and started the engine of the car. He drove down to the end, where he made a U-turn before returning to the street on which Crawford's house was located. Selecting a parking place where he could keep an eye on the house, he switched the engine off and settled back to await their departure.

Japan (Yokohama)

Mitchell popped the can of Kirin lager, took a swig, and looked around him. "A nice house you have here. I thought Japanese houses were supposed to be small and cramped."

"A lot are, but if you stay away from the city centers, most places are not too bad." Timothy Crawford sat back on the white leather sofa and raised his can to Mitchell and Murata. Crawford's wife was showing Stockton to the study, where he could phone Geneva. "So how are you enjoying Japan, Don?"

"It's okay, I guess. A bit confusing, but I think I could grow to like it. Frank tells me you've lived here since you were a kid. Any plans to go back to England?"

"Not at the moment. I run my own computer company and couldn't just throw it away after all the work

I've put into it. It takes several years to build up confidence in clients, and it is only in the past couple of years that I have started to make a reasonable profit. Things are not always easy for a foreigner doing business in Japan, but I think I have finally earned my credibility."

"How many staff do you have?" asked Murata.

"At the moment only eight. Anything we can't handle ourselves we subcontract out to other companies."

The door of the front room opened and Stockton entered, followed by Crawford's wife, Yoko.

"What are you doing?" exclaimed Yoko in horror. She ran to a cabinet and returned with glasses and coasters. "You cannot expect guests to drink out of cans, Tim."

Crawford grinned and raised his eyes to the ceiling. "They're only *gaijins*, Yoko. Not real guests."

"What about Mr. Murata here? He must have a glass." Murata allowed Yoko to take his can of beer and pour it into the glass, a look of abject embarrassment on his face.

"Did you speak to Marceillac, Frank?" asked Mitchell.

"Yes. He said he would send them straight through to Tim's e-mail address. Maybe we should give it thirty minutes before we check."

In fact, it was an hour before they all went into Crawford's study. Stockton and Crawford had both attended the Yokohama International School—the same school that Crawford's two children were currently attending—and had then gone on to Sofia University together. The stories they had of the faculty of Comparative Culture kept everybody amused, and time was overlooked until Yoko announced that dinner was ready. Crawford pleaded for an extra thirty minutes and they all trooped into his study, where he fired up a personal desktop computer and connected through to his server. He then started up the mail software and was rewarded with an indicator informing him that he had thirty-six messages waiting.

It didn't take long for the messages to be downloaded, and soon afterward his printer began to spew out the contents.

"Well, lookee here," said Mitchell, holding up the printout, "a message from Hisamitsu sent on June 21! It seems as if I was right."

Stockton and Murata leaned over his shoulder as he read through the message. They suspected that it must contain something of import, but whatever it was, it was not conspicuous. It was simply a general message thanking Marceillac for his previous message and outlining a few questions.

"Do you think the P.S. has anything to do with it?" asked Murata, leaning over and pointing out a single line at the bottom of the message. "It says he will be checking out some invoices the next day."

"Who knows. I think we need to see if there were any other messages that we never received. If my math is reliable, I think there are three messages that we have never seen. We only received thirty-three this morning, but there are thirty-six waiting now. We can check them out back at the hotel tonight."

"I think we ought to go in to dinner before Yoko throws a wobbler," said Crawford, getting to his feet. "We can leave the printer on while we eat. What's going on, anyway?"

Stockton grabbed his friend's arm and led him out the door, followed by Mitchell and Murata. "Nothing, really, Tim. We are just a little curious about something, that's all. I also have something else to ask you. Could you check out some source programs for me? I'll send you a tape in the next couple of days."

"Sure, no problem. What do you want me to check for?"

"I want you to look at the communication software and see if you can spot any recent amendments. Something like all incoming and outgoing mail being passed across to a holding file for approval before being delivered."

"Okay. Is this official business or a favor?"

"A favor, I'm afraid, mate. But it's worth a case of Scotch. How's that?"

"Done! Now let's get some dinner."

Japan (Yokohama/Tokyo)

Narita stayed four cars behind the taxi that contained Mitchell, Stockton, and Murata as it joined the highway into Tokyo from the Yokohama Interchange. He reached down for his cell phone and pressed the redial button. The telephone was answered on the third ring.

"*Oyabun.* They have left Yokohama and are heading back to Tokyo. I imagine they are heading for the hotel, but will contact you again if they have a different destination. The Crawford *gaijin* is not with them."

He hung up the connection and concentrated on driving.

Japan (Yokohama/Tokyo)

Stockton looked out of the taxi window at the grim scenery that surrounded Kawasaki, the industrial area located between Tokyo and Yokohama. The filthy factories lined back-to-back made Kawasaki one of the ugliest places in the whole of Japan. *The very sphincter of the Kanto region*, Stockton thought. It provided the industrial muscle that Tokyo needed, but was still nothing more than a shithole.

Stockton returned his gaze to the front as Murata shifted his position beside the driver to give him a view into the backseat. "I don't think I can do it, Don. My whole career would be destroyed."

Mitchell smiled sadly at the agony of decision that Murata was going through. "I wouldn't suggest it if I didn't think it was necessary, Akio. You would be in great danger if you stayed. I think it is now clear that the disappearance of the three men we wanted to question is not a coincidence. Not only are our messages being monitored, but our conversation, too. Don't forget what happened to Hisamitsu."

"Don's right, Akio." Stockton had a greater understanding of Murata's plight than Mitchell. The lifetime employment system was prevalent in Japan, and the chances of a disgraced detective getting another job were slim. He pitied Murata for the decision he would have to make. "Your career can only stay on track if we find out who is responsible. The NPA might not smile on your methods, but they couldn't ignore the motives once we get this out in the open. Anyway, what sort of salary are you picking up now? About two hundred thousand a month?"

"My status is class five, rank three. My basic salary is exactly two hundred four thousand and seven hundred yen per month."

"Well, there you go. I'll make you a promise. If you

are not accepted back into the ranks when all this is over, I'll persuade Tim Crawford to give you a job at double that. Or even more."

"But I could go to prison for going against orders." The plaintive note in Murata's voice was heartrending. To stay might cost him his life, but to follow Mitchell's plan and leave might cost him his job. In Japan, the two choices represented a devil's alternative. To live with no job led to disgrace. To die with a job led to . . . death.

"Akio, listen to me." Mitchell placed his face closer to Murata's, and the concern visible there surprised even Murata himself. "A man has been killed, and at this moment there are people plotting to kill you. Do you understand what I am saying?" Murata nodded. "I cannot let you throw your life away for appearances alone. We have to do this, but we have to do it together. If Frank and I suddenly disappeared, we would be writing your death warrant. I'm pleading with you, Akio."

Murata turned back to the front. He knew that what Mitchell was saying made sense, but an ingrained inability to disobey authority was a tough obstacle to overcome. He turned around to the back again.

"Just let me speak to Mr. Hirata about it. If I could get his authorization, there would be no problem."

Stockton answered, "Where would you speak to him about it? What if his office is bugged, too? What if Hirata himself is the leak? Akio, you are just going to have to take the plunge here. I realize how difficult this must be for you, but you have got to understand the situation we are in. We cannot trust anybody!"

Murata tried to distance himself from the problem and view himself from other people's eyes. What advice would Hiroko give him? He knew without thinking.

She would tell him to follow his heart, and his heart had already made up its mind. The problem was his brain. He was thinking too hard about consequences. He had read somewhere once that Japanese people worried too much about tomorrow, had too many regrets about yesterday, and in the process totally forgot to live for today. Was this awful stereotype applicable to himself, too? Yes, it probably was. What would his father say? He would tell him that his duty was more important than anything else and running away would solve no problems. Yes, that was his father. But wait! What if his father knew that his duty might ultimately end in his death? He had to provide his father with all possible permutations in order to be fair.

His father would tell him to run. . . .

He sighed and swiveled around in his seat. "You are right," he said. "Tell me what I must do."

Neither Mitchell nor Stockton smiled. Both realized the battle that had gone on inside Murata, and neither sensed a victory. Conversely, they both felt empty and sad.

Chapter Eight

Japan (Tokyo)

Stockton opened the door of his hotel room and glanced along the corridor. There was nobody in sight, but he reasoned that any person wishing to keep a covert eye on him would hardly camp out on his doorstep. He wouldn't have to worry until he walked into the reception area. They still had no evidence of anybody following them, but he didn't want to take any chances. Mitchell and Murata, who had stayed the night in the hotel with them, had left for the office some thirty minutes earlier with a story about Stockton having caught a touch of gastroenteritis, forcing him to take the day off and rest up. It was a weak story, but sometimes weak stories were the most plausible.

Stockton walked down to the elevator hall and pressed the button. The silver door of the elevator provided a reflection, and he decided his disguise was good enough to fool most Japanese people as long as they didn't get too close. The black hair dye Murata had purchased from the hotel's pharmacy had not turned his blond hair completely black, but it had darkened it enough, and the unfamiliar parting contributing to this had changed his image considerably. His eyebrows had taken the dye a lot easier and were a slightly darker color than his hair, but they did not look overly out of place. The mustache was the trickiest part and could be his potential downfall. They had pondered on how to fabricate a false mustache on such short notice for several hours, and in the end had trimmed a chunk of hair from Murata's head and painstakingly stuck it to Stockton's upper lip with spirit gum. It would never pass a close inspection, but it would suffice from a distance of a few meters. The rolled-up tissues in his cheeks had totally altered the shape of his face, and he was sure he could walk past his mother without her recognizing him.

The doors of the elevator opened to reveal three people standing inside. Stockton held his hand up to his mouth as if to stifle a yawn, entered the elevator, and quickly turned his face to the front. So far so good. Two more people got on a few floors down, but nobody took any notice of him.

The doors opened onto the reception area and Stockton was relieved to see an equal number of both Japanese and foreigners milling about. Not wanting to seem in too much of a rush, he wandered slowly across the reception as naturally as possible until he reached the main entrance. The doorman asked him if he wanted a taxi, and shaking his head in refusal, he stepped outside and began to walk down the road in the direction of Akasaka-Mitsuke Station.

He purchased a copy of the *Japan Times* from the kiosk in the station and stood beside the wickets to the Marunouchi line as if waiting for somebody. Using the newspaper to cover the lower half of his face, he scanned the area for anybody who was acting as if they did not belong there. After ten minutes he decided he was safe, purchased a ticket from the ticket machine, and passed through the wickets down onto the platform of the Marunouchi line, where he caught a train to Ike-bukuro. At Ikebukuro Station, he left the subway and went aboveground to catch the Yamanote line. He had an eleven-o'clock appointment with Hiroko at Tamachi Station, and a glance at his watch informed him that he still had plenty of time in hand. He decided to waste some of this time on the platform and missed three trains while he surreptitiously removed the sodden tissues from his mouth and slowly drank a can of iced coffee from the vending machine. Ikebukuro Station was located on the opposite side to Tamachi on the circular Yamanote line, so he could have got a train in either direction. He decided, however, to go via Ueno, as fewer people used this route and anybody following him would be more obvious.

Thirty minutes later, he walked through the wickets at Tamachi Station and turned right out toward the Tokyo Bay exit. Hiroko was already waiting for him, parked in Murata's metallic-red Pajero, and she leaned across and pushed the passenger door open as he walked over.

"Frank-san, *ohayo gozaimasu.*"

Stockton returned the greeting and climbed up into the big four-wheel-drive vehicle. He looked into the back of the car and noticed his luggage sitting next to Mitchell's. "No trouble getting the bags?"

"No, none at all. I just walked in, grabbed them, and walked out. Nobody even looked at me twice. What about you? Were you followed?"

"No. I have been riding the trains around Tokyo all morning and not a sniff of a tail. Either the disguise worked well or the bugged office is considered sufficient to keep an eye on us. What do you think, anyway?" Stockton used the forefinger and thumb of both hands to make a frame around his face.

"You look silly," said Hiroko with a giggle. "Especially that mustache. Don't you think you should take it off? Our appointment is in thirty minutes."

"How far from here?"

"Just two minutes around the corner. I'll drive around while you remove it."

Removing the mustache was a painful experience and one that kept Hiroko in fits of laughter. The last vestiges of spirit gum were removed with nail-polish remover, and Stockton was just combing his parting back into its original position when Hiroko parked the car in front of a white apartment building.

"Bay Heights," she announced with a grin. "Fully furnished condominiums rented out on a weekly basis. Our appointment is with a Mr. Uchida."

They walked into the building and looked around. Stockton counted the mailboxes lined along a wall and noted that names were attached to only twelve of the sixteen available. Good, that meant vacancies. A small window opened out onto the hall, and Hiroko went over and asked for Mr. Uchida. They were invited into the room and provided with green tea while they awaited Uchida's arrival.

Uchida arrived a few moments later, and Hiroko exchanged business cards with him. Then she introduced Stockton as a business client from overseas, and Stockton apologized in flawless Japanese for not having his cards with him, eliciting Uchida's admiration.

"So how many weeks will you be staying?" Uchida asked, a registration form open on his desk.

"Initially three weeks, but if business goes well we might extend that."

"Our rates are sixty-five thousand yen per week plus one month's deposit. Payable in advance. Rates include gas and electricity, but the telephone bill must be paid separately. I also need to see the passports of non-Japanese residents."

Stockton pulled out his wallet and peeled off the required sum. He was running short on cash, but Mitchell still had plenty and both had credit cards. He placed the cash and his passport on the table in front of Uchida. "I will bring my colleague's passport in this evening when he arrives. I hope that is not a problem."

"No problem at all. And I shall also need a guarantor."

"I am Mr. Stockton's guarantor, Mr. Uchida."

Uchida took down Stockton's, Mitchell's, and Murata's names, filled out the necessary parts of the form, and then led them up to the third floor, on which their apartment was located.

"Not bad at all," said Stockton as he looked around. The apartment contained two bedrooms—each with two beds—a living room, and a small kitchen. The furniture was cheap but serviceable, and the air conditioner worked. A nineteen-inch television set also stood on a cabinet in the corner. "I shall need a desk to work on," he said to Uchida. "Can you provide one?"

"I will have one brought up this afternoon. Where would you like it situated?"

Stockton indicated a location just in front of the window, and Uchida made a note on his notepad. Stockton then moved over to the telephone and checked for a dial tone. It worked.

"The number is written on the base." Uchida walked over to him, picked up the telephone, and turned it over, revealing a number written on a piece of white tape. "Dial three for an outside line, one for reception." Stockton memorized the number.

The negotiations complete, Uchida handed over three keys and returned to his office while Stockton and Hiroko brought the luggage up from the car. It was decided that Stockton and Mitchell would share one room and Murata would take the other with the spare bed, just in case Hiroko ever needed to stay over. They agreed that neither could be bothered to find a restaurant for lunch and ordered *Tendon* delivered from a local restaurant, the number of which was on a vinyl-covered card providing useful numbers located in the drawer of the telephone table.

"You will take care of Akio, won't you?" said Hiroko over lunch. "He is not exactly what Europe or America would consider a hard-boiled cop, but he is a very good man."

Stockton smiled and laid down his chopsticks. "I promise you that he is in good hands. I understand just how much courage it must have taken to agree to take a runner, but he really will be much safer away from that office. I wonder how some of my so-called brave colleagues back in London would have handled this situation given the same cultural background." He reached over and took Hiroko's hand in his. "Akio is one of the best, Hiroko, and he will come out of this without a stain on him. I promise!"

"You know, he has so much respect for you and Don that it is almost pitiful. When we left you the other night, the only thing he spoke about all the way home was his new friends. He was boasting about you, as if being connected to you somehow made him a better man." She withdrew her hand and ate a small portion of rice. "I don't wish to be disrespectful, Frank, but your company won't make him a better man. He is already good enough."

"I know that, Hiroko," said Stockton softly. "And he has made the right decision. We will nail these people, find out who the mole is, and Akio will be back in his desk before you know it."

"You really don't understand, do you?" Fire flashed in Hiroko's eyes and she tapped her *Tendon* bowl with the chopsticks in frustration. "I would have thought that your experience of Japan would give you a clearer picture! A governmental employee over here cannot simply take the law into his own hands and become a vigilante. There are procedures to follow. Akio is not just agreeing to find the culprit, he is agreeing to destroy his whole life. When this is all over, he will be crucified for not taking the problem to his boss, Hirata."

"But Hirata could be the mole!"

"If he has sufficient suspicions to feel that, then his duty is to approach somebody in the National Police Agency, or even the Metropolitan Police Department! Under no circumstances will he ever be forgiven for going it alone. The only heroes that Japan can produce are ballplayers who make it into the majors! A low-level policeman who discovers the identity of Jack the Ripper would be fired if it could be proved that he did so out of office hours. Can't you understand that?"

Stockton rubbed his face with his hands. He suddenly felt very tired. "God, you're right. I must have been away for too long." He looked up and watched Hiroko storm out to the kitchen and noisily pour a glass of *Oolong-cha*, slamming the plastic bottle down on the worktop when the glass was full. "Maybe we could persuade him to contact the NPA. It's not too late."

Hiroko leaned against the jamb of the kitchen door and sipped her tea. "No, it is already too late. He is probably stealing those damn tapes at this very moment." She walked back to the table and sat down heavily, her rage burnt out as quickly as it had been ignited. "My point is, Akio is trying his best to emulate these two big, tough cops from the West, but the truth of the matter is, his sacrifice is one thousandfold that of yours. When everything is over, you and Don will be hailed as heroes for having come up against and beaten Japanese bureaucracy, and Akio will be lucky if he can get a job serving noodles. I just want you to remember that."

"Point taken, Hiroko. I think we need to discuss this some more when Akio and Don get here."

"No. He has made up his mind, and now nothing will change it. But make his sacrifice worthwhile. Find the people who have committed these crimes and make them pay. Not only for Akio, but for Hisamitsu."

Stockton nodded and pushed his bowl away from him. The sauce on top of the deep-fried prawns had congealed and he no longer felt hungry. If anything, he felt sick.

"And now," said Hiroko, functioning once again as a friend and conspirator, "I think we should get moving. We have much to do before nightfall."

Hiroko washed out the bowls and placed them outside the door for pickup before they left in the Pajero for Akihabara, Tokyo's mecca for electronic equipment. They found a backstreet to park the car and walked the few hundred meters to La-Ox, a large store on the main street renowned for its bargains. Once inside, they purchased a personal laptop computer with a built-in landline modem and assorted software, an inkjet printer, three cellular telephones, and a facsimile machine. They haggled over the price and managed to get an additional ten percent discount on top of the already discounted prices, and Stockton paid the full sum with one of his credit cards. Hiroko brought the car around to the side of the store, where three eager salesmen loaded the gear into the back.

"A successful shopping spree, wouldn't you say?" Stockton lay back in his seat and let Hiroko worry about the midafternoon traffic. He had found that his foot was constantly pressing an imaginary brake as she wound in and out of the traffic, and decided it would be better not to look.

"We're not finished yet," she answered, skillfully avoiding an impatient taxi. "You are going to need food and drink."

She stopped at a convenience store in Tamachi, and the two of them entered. Stockton looked around for the booze counter and, not finding one, left Hiroko on her own and walked down the street in search of a liquor store. He found one a block down and purchased a case of twenty-four beers, two bottles of Scotch, and a

145

few bottles of ready-mixed cocktails. Staggering under his load, he still managed to reach the car before Hiroko left the convenience store, weighed down under the burden of several carrier bags. He peeked into one and saw fresh orange juice, milk, coffee, bread, margarine, cornflakes, instant noodles, and several other items required to keep three grown men sustained for the foreseeable future.

Hiroko fumbled for the car keys and noticed what Stockton was carrying. "Huh!" she said. "Typical man!"

Stockton peeked into another bag and saw the ice cream, candy, and magazines contained within. "Huh!" he said. "Typical woman!"

Japan (Tokyo)

Murata's heart thumped within his chest despite the fact that he had full authority to be in the computer room. He felt suspicious and was sure that it was visible at a glance. Only three people remained in the office on lunchtime duty, and the fact that he had an excellent chance of smuggling the master tapes out of the computer room provided no solace for his racing mind.

The master tapes were kept in a small gray cabinet with sliding doors beneath an air conditioner. Murata crouched down in front of the cabinet, slipped the key into the lock, and opened the door. Inside were thirty-one magnetic tapes. Twenty-five had red seals and represented the data backup tapes—five for each day of the week—and the remaining six had blue seals indicating the system backup tapes. Murata slid the cardboard box he had brought with him along the floor and began to place the tapes with the blue seals into it. When all of the tapes were safely inside, he took six new tapes down from a rack against the opposite wall and put them in their place. They would not fool anybody who was searching for the system tapes, but they would quell the curiosity of the person on data backup duty.

He locked the cabinet and left the room with the box under his arm. Walking over to the reception desk, he took a *Takkyu-bin* label from a drawer and wrote Tim Crawford's business address on it from memory. He used brown adhesive tape to secure the box and stuck the address label on its upper surface before placing it with the three other packages awaiting pickup. The representative of the *Takkyu-bin* company would collect the box at two o'clock and it would be delivered to Crawford's address by ten o'clock the following morning.

Murata returned the key of the tape cabinet to the manager's desk and heaved a sigh of relief. He could not totally relax until the box had actually left the office, but at least the hardest part was over. He mopped his brow with his handkerchief and returned to the meeting room, where Mitchell was eating his sandwiches and listening to music on a Walkman.

Japan (Tokyo)

Mitchell and Murata did not leave the office until nearly seven o'clock that evening. It would be the last time they stepped inside the building, and they wanted to gather as much information as possible before all lines of communication were severed. Mitchell was also hoping that they could whittle the identity of the potential mole down to the number of people who were left in the office at that time of night, but when they shouted their good-nights and left the office, everybody else was still working hard at their desks. Mitchell shook his head in puzzlement as they took the elevator down to the first floor.

The rush hour was still at its peak as they entered Kasumigaseki Station and split up. They were to meet Stockton at a coffee bar inside Shinagawa Station at eight-thirty, and would spend the next ninety minutes shaking their tails by using different routes. If, of course, they were being tailed.

Stockton arrived at the self-service coffee bar located at the top of the steps to the Keihin Tohoku line and Yamanote line thirty minutes early, purchased a cup of coffee, and selected a seat that provided a perfect view of the entrance and most of the seats. His hair was once again parted in a different position and the rolled-up tissues were back in his mouth. The only difference was that he no longer sported a mustache; he now wore a white face mask designed to prevent flu germs from being passed on, not dissimilar to the mask a surgeon would wear during an operation. The mask hindered his attempts to drink the coffee, but he was not really thirsty anyway.

Murata arrived first and took a seat several tables down without acknowledging Stockton. Ten minutes later Mitchell arrived, purchased a beer at the counter, and sat down at the large, rectangular table located in the center. They stayed there for forty more minutes, until Stockton was sure that everybody who had entered within several minutes of Murata and Mitchell had finished their coffee and left. Stockton then stood up and moved toward the door. He turned left and went down the steps to the platform of the Yamanote line and walked to the end of the platform. Having made sure that Mitchell and Murata had followed him down onto the platform, he got on the next train and began to walk through the carriages until he met up with Mitchell. He winked, and the two walked through a little farther until they came across Murata.

They got off at the next stop, Tamachi, and walked out of the station and along the road to Bay Heights.

The smell of cooking greeted them as they pushed open the door to the apartment and climbed over an assortment of empty cartons into the living room. Hiroko greeted them with a can of cold beer each. They popped the cans and Stockton held his up in a toast.

"Ladies and gentlemen. May I have order, please? We are now well and truly on our own and must live off our wits. All except Don, of course, who doesn't have any. . . ."

"Asshole!" muttered Mitchell.

"Good luck, everybody!" Stockton clinked his can against the side of each person's in turn and drained it in one gulp. He then crumpled the can with his hand and threw it against the wall. They all laughed and followed suit, except Hiroko, who couldn't finish the beer in time.

Hiroko dished up steaks and french-fried potatoes with a large bowl of tossed salad, and they sat down to eat. Hiroko darted worried eyes across to Murata every now and again, but if he was regretting his decision it did not show in his demeanor. He was joining in the merriment as if he had just finished a normal working day.

Mitchell sat back, pushed his empty plate away from him, and took another swig of beer. "I hope you are not expecting me to clear this mess up tonight." He looked around at the cardboard cartons, Styrofoam packaging, and plastic bags that littered the place.

Stockton glanced at his watch. "I suppose it will wait until tomorrow. It's nearly ten o'clock already. I have to phone Tim to let him know the tapes are on their way, but after that maybe we could crack open a bottle of Scotch and work out a schedule."

"Sounds pretty good to me. What about you, Hiroko? Can you stay around any longer? It's getting late."

"I think I will stay the night and help you clear the place up tomorrow." She looked across at Murata, who was struggling to remove the cap from the first bottle of whisky. "That is, of course, if I am invited."

"Akio, the lady's talking to you."

"Hmm?" Murata looked up and saw all three of them staring at him. He self-consciously placed the bottle of Scotch on the table and sat on his hands.

Stockton cupped a hand over his mouth and muffled his voice in an imitation of a B-movie narration. "We have a damsel in distress here who is calling on Ultraman. Will our intrepid crusader arrive in time to save her from a fate worse than death?"

Hiroko giggled, and Murata raised his eyes to the ceiling.

"Beam me up, Scotty!" he said.

Japan (Mobara)

"You useless, stupid . . . Damn!" Sakaguchi slammed his notebook down on the table, his eyes wide open with rage. "How could this happen?"

Narita noticed that several of the residents and staff gathered in the reception of the High Range Country

Golf Club and Hotel were looking in their direction and tried to calm Sakaguchi down. "*Oyabun*, people are looking."

"What do I care if people look?" Sakaguchi screamed. He jumped to his feet and directed his anger at everybody unfortunate enough to be close at hand. "Get on with your own damn business, bastards!" An embarrassed silence followed during which the people present turned their backs on Sakaguchi and pretended he was not there. "Idiots!" He kicked the leg of the table, knocking the two drinks to the floor and upsetting a delicate vase holding a single rose.

"*Oyabun*, I beg you. They will call the police if you don't stop."

Sakaguchi kicked out again and one of the glasses slid gracefully across the deep pile of the carpet and came to rest just two meters before the reception desk. Narita could see the female receptionist reaching for the telephone.

"*Oyabun*, you must calm down. This will get us nowhere. If they call the police, we will be arrested for causing a public nuisance. Please, just sit down and I will sort it out."

"Damn!" shouted Sakaguchi, slumping down in the leather upholstery, his rage spent for the moment.

Narita walked over to the reception, slapped his hands purposefully on the counter, and called loudly to the receptionist. "I want the manager, this instant!" he said.

Before she could answer, the leather-padded door behind the counter opened and a man in a black bow-tie appeared. The receptionist had obviously called him and not the police, as Narita had suspected.

"Are you the manager?" he asked briskly. The man nodded and walked over, his eyes sweeping the reception area for the troublemaker. "Well, how do you explain mouse shit in a glass of gin and tonic? My client has a lot of stress at the moment, and such filth in a hotel of this class has upset him considerably."

The manager was immediately on the defensive. He was well capable of handling a drunk in the reception—in fact, he had done so on several occasions—but the knowledge that a tantrum had been brought on by an error for which the hotel could be blamed took the wind out of his sails. Narita saw the change and relaxed a little. At least they would no longer have to worry about the police. Maybe they could even profit out of it.

"I'm sorry, sir. I do not understand."

"If you don't know what mouse shit is, then you ought not to be in charge of a hotel like this." Narita purposely raised his voice a little to ensure that the other people in the reception could hear. The manager took the bait and leaned across the counter.

"Excuse me, sir, but maybe we could discuss this in my office." He held a hand out in an invitation for Narita to come behind the counter.

"Why? The problem is simple. I have probably lost a client through your stupidity, and you want me to pay you a visit! How dare you insult me in this manner."

The manager wilted. He realized that he had to placate this man as quickly as possible before other people began to gather. It had the classic signs of an all-out confrontation, and part of his job was to prevent such scenes. He stood to attention, slapped his open palms to his thighs, and bowed deeply.

"Please accept the humble apologies of the hotel, sir.

You will of course be our guest for the duration of your stay, and I can assure you that nothing else untoward will occur."

"I should think so, too." Narita nodded across to Sakaguchi. "We shall need two more drinks over there. Make sure you check the glasses before serving them." Narita turned his back huffily on the reception and walked back to Sakaguchi.

"Excellent, Narita." Sakaguchi had a broad grin on his face, causing Narita to marvel at his ability to change emotions as if they were mere garments. "It is good to see you in action. You must excuse my outbreak of a few moments ago, but I am sure you can understand how frustrating this is for me. I give out a few orders and nobody seems capable of carrying them out. Were it not for a strong heart, I would have been shocked into my grave a long time ago. So let us carry on. Our monkeys have escaped, you say?"

"Yes, *oyabun*. All three somehow managed to slip our men and are now missing. They have not checked out of the hotel, but their rooms contain no luggage. We have lost them."

Sakaguchi saw one of the hotel staff heading in their direction and waited until the new drinks had been placed before them. The table was swabbed and the vase removed.

"Does Hirata know of this?"

"I do not know, *oyabun*. Maybe."

"Well, let's give him a call and see."

Narita removed a mobile phone from his case, dialed Hirata's home number, and passed it across to Sakaguchi.

"Ah, good evening, Hirata."

"What the hell do you think you are doing calling me at home?" Hirata had been reading a book and sipping a whisky before bed. The television reminded him of his wife, and apart from the occasional sports program and news, he rarely watched it anymore.

"I am calling to ask where you think your two *gaijin* might be. We have mislaid them and wondered if you knew."

"You're crazy! What the hell are you talking about?"

"It seems as if the two *keto* are no longer in the hotel. Are you expecting them in for work tomorrow?"

Hirata felt his heart tighten. Could they possibly have suspected the surveillance? No, it was impossible. The only lead they had was the author and the other two men who had disappeared, and he had heard them himself discussing the fact that the coincidence was too great. They had decided to hunt for more names before considering a leak. "Well, yes I am. I was briefed on to-day's work and it matched the tapes perfectly. I can think of no reason why they should not come in to work. Maybe they are staying the night at a friend's house or something."

"Well, I shall expect your call in the morning if they do not arrive. And, if they have decided to go under-ground, I shall want them found, but not by your blundering police department. Is that clear?"

"But—but how else can I find them?"

Sakaguchi took a sip of his drink before continuing. He felt much calmer now, and the gin soothed him even further. "You do not need to even try, Hirata. I will find them myself. Just make sure that the news of their disappearance is kept quiet. Can you manage that?"

"Of course!" said Hirata indignantly. "I do not need to report to anyone on their activities."

Sakaguchi hung up and dismissed Narita with a wave of his hand. Apart from the brief fit of rage this evening, he had had a pretty good day. He had managed to get around eighteen holes in ninety-eight strokes, the first time his score had been under one hundred for more than a year, and he had free accommodation for the night. What more could a man want? Those damn *gaijin* were causing trouble, of course, but he could now deal with them in the same way he had dealt with Hisamitsu. They were no longer under the protective wing of Hirata and were subsequently fair game. He wondered if they were aware that the hunting season had just begun.

Chapter Nine

Japan (Tokyo)

It was eleven o'clock before all of the packages were unpacked and the cartons collapsed and tied up. Murata and Mitchell volunteered to take them out to the garbage area while Hiroko vacuumed the floor. The living room now resembled the study of a professional businessman, with the computer neatly positioned on the desk in front of the window and the fax machine set up beside it. They had yet to sign up with an Internet server, but that would be tackled that afternoon.

Stockton sat at the desk and sipped a can of sports drink. He waited until the noise of the vacuum cleaner had died out before flipping open his address book and punching out an international number.

It rang seven times before the sleepy voice of Armin Marceillac answered.

"Allo?"

"Armin, it's Frank. Good morning."

A heavy sigh floated across the line. "Frank, it is four o'clock in the morning. Has something happened?"

"You bet something's happened!" Stockton quickly ran through the events that had caused them to suspect their movements were being monitored and go underground.

"I don't know if this is a good idea, Frank. It may cause problems between the IOCC and the Japanese government." Marceillac was now wide awake. "Are you sure you are doing the right thing?"

"We had to, Armin. We have no idea who the mole is, and staying there could have endangered our lives."

"Well, I suppose the decision is yours, but I don't know what Hewes is going to say about it. He is in a position of responsibility and might be forced to call you back."

"That is one of the reasons I called you, Armin." Murata and Mitchell returned and, realizing who Stockton was speaking to, sat down at the table to listen. Hiroko brought them out a can of sports drink each, and Stockton had to stifle a giggle as he watched Mitchell stare in disbelief at the title—*Pocari Sweat*. "I want you to keep cooperating with the ECB as if nothing has happened. They must not find out that you know where we are. I will keep in regular contact with you, but in the meantime I want you to keep sending messages to the ECB addressed to myself, Don, or Akio. Nothing important, of course. Just simple, routine stuff."

"That is easy enough, but I must leave the final decision up to Hewes."

"I understand that, Armin, but please try and persuade him to give us a chance. We are all convinced that this is the only way we are going to solve this case. Pulling us out now would only give victory to the opponent by default."

"Okay, I will try. How can I contact you?"

Stockton gave him their new address and telephone number. "We will be signing up on an on-line server later today. I will send you a message the moment I have a mail address. I would appreciate it if you would e-mail us whenever there are any developments."

"Okay, Frank. I'll do what I can. And, Frank . . ."

"Yes, Armin?"

"Just be careful, okay?"

Japan (Tokyo)

Hirata's grip on the telephone was so tight he knew that it was only a matter of time before it cracked into a million pieces. Unless the bones in his hand gave out first, of course. Things were beginning to get out of control and the butterflies of fear were active in his stomach.

"So, I was right." Sakaguchi's loathsome voice floated from the other end of the connection. "Do you have any idea where they might be?"

"None whatsoever. I presume they have checked into another hotel somewhere in Tokyo."

"In which case I shall find them. It is just a matter of time."

"There is more."

A pregnant silence followed. Hirata was about to continue when Sakaguchi said, "What do you mean, more? I hope this is not going to upset me."

"The master tapes to our computer are missing. Probably taken by the *gaijin* and Murata."

"So?"

"I had the system modified by Intersystems to allow me to read all incoming and outgoing mail. This enabled me to edit out all incriminating facts."

"And now the *gaijin* have them. . . ."

"Actually, no. A package was sent from this office yesterday to another *gaijin* in Yokohama. I have asked around and nobody in my office sent it. It must have been them."

"Would the name of this other *gaijin* be Crawford, by any chance?"

"Yes," answered Hirata in surprise. How could Sakaguchi have possibly known that?

"Then you have nothing to fear. Leave Mr. Crawford to me. I will have your precious tapes returned by tomorrow. And may I suggest that you have Intersystems remove any modifications they have made? I am also surprised that you stored them in an accessible location where anyone could get their hands on them. Maybe you don't realize the implications of such carelessness."

"I do. It was just an oversight."

"Well, make sure that no other incriminating evidence is left lying around."

"I . . ." began Hirata, but the line clicked and went dead.

Japan (Tokyo)

Murata studied the introduction pack to the Global-Serve host, provided by the electrical store in Akihabara, while Stockton set up the on-line software. They had selected GlobalServe out of the many on-line servers available in Japan because all services were provided in both Japanese-language and English-language menus, which could be switched at the click of a button. When the software was up and running, Murata sat in front of the computer and dialed into the local access port. Once the connection had been made, he entered SGN to allow on-line sign-up, then tapped in the serial number and agreement number that were listed in the introduction pack.

He followed the onscreen instructions and registered Hiroko's name, address, and credit-card number in addition to all of the other questions the machine prompted him to answer. He was finally presented with a user ID and a temporary password. They now had Internet access and an e-mail address.

He disconnected the line and immediately redialed it. This time he entered "SVC" as the connection ID and then the user ID and temporary password. GlobalServe's top menu scrolled out on screen. He selected PASSWORD and amended the temporary password to AKIO3min3$SCOTTY before severing the connection once more.

Murata stood and held his hands out palms up to Stockton, who slapped them as if accepting the tag. Stockton then slipped into the seat and finished off the fine details, such as setting the parameters for the e-mail software in accordance with the instructions provided by GlobalServe, and making sure that the icons for the software they would most commonly use were situated on the screen's desktop. It took twenty minutes for this to be completed, and then he fired up the e-mail software to check that it was working properly. It was.

"Your turn, Don."

Stockton tagged Mitchell, who then spent five min-

utes typing out an e-mail message to Marceillac, basically outlining what Stockton had already told him on
the telephone that morning. The tag was then passed
back to Murata, who sent the message.

"What do you think of that, Hiroko?" said Murata.
"Real teamwork, huh?"

Hiroko walked over to him and placed a small kiss on
his cheek. "I don't even want to comment. I am going
back home now to leave you boys with your games."

"Oh, no . . . " all three men chorused in unison.

Hiroko slipped her arm through Murata's and guided
him to the door. "Come and say good-bye to me properly. Out of view of your playmates."

"Bye, Hiroko," said Stockton. "Thanks for all your
help. And don't take Akio too far. We can't spare him
for long."

"Yeah, not even three minutes," added Mitchell.

When Murata returned, they sat down at the table
with a full jug of freshly made coffee and began to work
out their plans. They decided that the rest of the afternoon would be spent on printing out the files that had
been sent from Geneva to Tim Crawford's computer—
copies of which Crawford had loaded onto a floppy
disk—and then going through them for any further
leads. While they were printing out, Murata would try
to contact the three people on their original list to see if
any further news was available.

"We'll also need guns," said Mitchell. "Can you get
some, Akio?"

Murata slowly replaced his coffee cup on the saucer.
"That is impossible, Don. I cannot allow it."

"Oh, Jesus! Don't go all prudish on me. There are
people out there who want us dead, man. Don't you

think we have the right to protect ourselves? Tell him, Frank."

Stockton rubbed a hand over his chin. "Much as I am loath to admit it, I think he has a point, Akio. We already know that our adversaries are armed, and a little backup is not going to hurt."

"But guns are dangerous. Innocent people could be killed."

Mitchell sighed. "Look, Akio. I have carried a gun around with me everywhere for the past twelve years, and I have yet to shoot an innocent bystander. Remember that Frank and I are cops. We know what we are doing."

Murata looked down at the table and pondered on the request. If it was ever found out that he had armed foreign nationals on Japanese soil, he would never see the light of day again. His actions already had more or less guaranteed his dismissal from the police force, but with the exception of stealing the tapes, he had done nothing that would put him in line for a prison term. It just wasn't fair. Two big decisions in two consecutive days. He had agreed to go underground because of the danger to his life. For some reason, the more he had thought about it the idea of being out of a job had dimmed into insignificance when placed alongside the possibility of his death. Now he was being asked to risk his freedom by committing a crime that carried a long prison sentence. The most tormenting factor was that the request was quite reasonable in itself. Who wouldn't want a gun to protect himself if he knew somebody had a similar weapon pointed at him?

Murata looked up and took a sip of coffee. "I will do it," he said.

"Attaboy, Akio!" Mitchell slapped him on the back.

"But there is one problem."

"What's that?"

"I have no idea where to get guns."

"Oh, come on. You must have. You're a cop, aren't you?"

The logic of this argument was totally lost on Murata, but he bent his mind to the problem anyway. He knew *theoretically* where to get guns, he just didn't know how to contact the people who dealt in them. He finally decided to phone an old friend from his National Police Academy days and see if he had any idea. Mitchell and Stockton watched him as he made three phone calls from the desk. Twenty minutes later, he stood up and beamed his delight.

"I have ordered two pistols and will pick them up tomorrow afternoon, together with twenty rounds of ammunition." The deal had given him a strange feeling of elation. It had never occurred to him just how easy it was to obtain firearms in Japan, and the fact that he had completed the negotiations in less than thirty minutes made him feel like an actor in an action movie.

"Way to go, Akio!"

The rest of the afternoon was spent printing out the files. Stockton visited the local convenience store and came back with a pile of notebooks, pens, and a stapler. As each file was printed out, they placed a cover sheet of blank paper at the front on which comments could be written, and stapled it into a single booklet. The files were then placed in chronological order.

The telephone rang just before six o'clock, and they all looked at each other. It was the first time that the phone had rung since their arrival. Stockton walked over to it and picked it up.

"*Moshi, moshi*," he said.

"Don't you moshi-moshi me, you bastard. What the hell is going on?"

"Tim, what's the problem, mate?" Stockton looked across to the other two and shrugged his shoulders.

"I'll tell you what the problem is! Three blokes walked into my office not twenty minutes ago and trashed my computer. They walked off with those tapes you sent me."

"Oh, Jesus, you're kidding!"

"No, I'm not bloody kidding! What's going on, Frank?"

"Look, Tim. Stay calm about this. We are in a spot of trouble, but it's nothing to worry about. I am really sorry about your computer, but we'll pay for all damages. Did you have a backup?"

"Of course I have a backup. But that is not the point! I want to know what's going on!"

Murata and Mitchell could hear Crawford's fury leaking out of the earpiece. Although each word was indistinct, they could guess what had happened from Stockton's side of the conversation.

"I'm sorry, Tim, but I really can't tell you yet. As soon as we have sorted this out, I promise you'll be the first to get the full story. Trust me, mate."

"Jesus, man! That's asking a lot. Can't you even give me a hint?"

"Sorry, Tim. Did you get a chance to look at the tapes?"

"I got a glance at them. I was going to work on them this evening."

"Did you notice anything out of place?"

"Nothing actually out of place. I looked at the program that processes incoming mail and found a few amendments to store the messages in a holding file, but this was not a hack job, Frank. The programmer even signed his work."

Stockton held his breath. Could this be the lead they needed? "Go on."

"Each amended line of code was signed INTSYS/N.SUZUKI."

Japan (Yokohama)

Crawford hung up the phone and leaned back in his executive chair with his hands behind his head. Somehow Stockton had managed to take the boil off his rage, but he was not quite sure how he had managed it. Maybe he himself had sensed that his friend was in trouble. Bigger trouble than a trashed computer.

He sighed and picked up the phone again. He had sent all of his staff home already. He didn't want to have to pay overtime so people could stare at blank screens. He hoped the machine itself wasn't damaged. He had arranged for an engineer to visit the following morning, and if everything was well they could restore the backup and be up to full operations by late afternoon. But what if the computer was irreparable? He would have to phone the police tonight in order to get the insurance company to pay up. But what would he tell them? Stockton had probably stolen the tapes in the first place, and he didn't want to add to his friend's trouble. Well, at least he had offered to pay for the damages.

If the insurance company didn't pay up, then let him!

He brought the receiver up to his ear, pressed the quick-dial button for his home, and told his wife that he was coming home early. She asked him to pick their daughter up from the YCAC, where she was swimming with her friends.

He got a taxi up to the Yokohama Country and Athletic Club and waved to a few friends he spotted. He quickly located his daughter and told her it was time to go home. They lived only a five-minute walk from the club, so Erika simply wrapped a towel around herself, stuffed her clothes into her bag, and said good-bye to her friends. She followed her father out onto the street, leaving a wet trail behind her.

Erika was ten years old and, like her brother, Jason, had been born in Yokohama. They both spoke fluent English and Japanese, and Timothy Crawford was dreading the time when they reached the twelfth grade and had to decide on a university. The teachers at the YIS were contemptuous of Japanese universities and tried their utmost to persuade their charges to attend prestigious colleges in America or Europe. He didn't want to be separated from his children by several thousand kilometers when they were only eighteen years old. He fervently prayed that they would decide to attend Sofia University in Tokyo, as he had.

"Did you have a good day, love?" asked Crawford as they left the club. The sun had already gone down, but the air was still hot and humid. He felt a trickle of sweat run down his back.

"Janie said that Jason's cool," said Erika. She was at the age when boys were either "cool" or "gross," and her conversation invariably ran along similar lines.

"Well, maybe he is. You never know."

She looked a bit dubious about this but let the matter ride. "Oh, yes. Angie's dad gave me a letter for you." She hunkered down on the street and began scrabbling inside her bag, finally producing a damp and crumpled envelope. Crawford stuck the envelope into his back pocket.

When they reached home, Erika rushed off to take a shower before dinner and Crawford walked into the bedroom to change out of his business suit. He placed the envelope on the dresser while he changed, and picked it up on his way to his study to check if any faxes had arrived. He grabbed a paper knife from the top of his desk and perched himself on the edge of the windowsill while he opened it. Removing a single sheet of white paper, he felt a chill of fear run through his whole body as he read it. A ridge of sweat broke out on his upper lip. He read the message five times before rushing over to his desk and searching frantically for the small gray telephone directory of all students at the YIS.

He found Angie Hannegan's name and dragged the telephone across the desk toward him. With trembling fingers, he punched out the number and waited for an answer.

"Hello?"

"Ah, Mrs. Hannegan? My name is Crawford. I believe my daughter, Erika, is in the same class as Angie."

"Well, hello, Mr. Crawford. Angie tells me so much about Erika. What can I do for you?"

"Is your husband there?"

"I'm afraid not. Is there anything I can do?"

Crawford closed his eyes and rested his head in a cupped hand. "Actually, I need to speak to your husband. If you would be so kind as to let me have his business number . . ."

"Well, of course, if you wish. But my husband is out of the country at the moment. He is in the States on business, but he should be back by next Tuesday."

"Oh, really?" Crawford tried to keep his voice level. "Well, it doesn't matter, then. I'll speak to him when he gets back."

He broke the connection and walked over to the door. Opening it, he hurried down the hall to the bathroom and shouted through the door. "Erika? Is Angie's dad Japanese or American?"

The door opened and Erika's face popped around the edge.

"There's no need to shout, Dad. I can hear you."

Crawford crouched down until his eyes were level with his daughter's and repeated the question. "Is Angie's dad Japanese or American?"

"Japanese."

"Okay, thanks, love." Crawford walked back to his study and sat down in the chair. The YIS telephone directory stated that both of Angie's parents were of American nationality. His daughter was so used to seeing people of mixed nationality every day of her life that it just never occurred to her to wonder why a blond-haired, blue-eyed little girl would have a Japanese father.

He reached out for the telephone and keyed in Stockton's number.

Japan (Tokyo)

Stockton, Mitchell, and Murata had just finished sharing a huge pizza when the telephone rang. Stockton wiped his lips on a paper napkin and sat down at the desk.

"Frank, it's Tim. My family has been threatened. I think you ought to give me some more details."

Stockton shivered involuntarily. Crawford's voice had lost the tone of anger that had been apparent during their previous conversation. It was now flat and resigned.

"Tell me what happened."

"Somebody pretending to be the father of one of my daughter's friends handed her a letter addressed to me. It says, roughly translated, 'Don't get involved. You see how easy it is to lose a daughter?' "

"Oh, my God." Stockton rubbed his eyes with his free hand, his mind racing. "Listen, Tim. I don't think we should continue this conversation over the telephone. Do you remember the URL of that 'over the top' CB we used to use?"

"The hacker's site? Yes, of course."

"Do you remember the password?"

"Yes, I think so," replied Crawford after a short pause. "Over the top, screw you buddy, right?"

"That's the one. Okay. E-three. I'm Sophia, you're YIS. Are you with me?"

"Yes, I've got you. I'll be there in a few minutes."

Stockton hung up the phone and switched the computer on.

"What was all that about?" asked Mitchell.

"Tim's daughter was threatened with abduction. They are trying to warn him off. I'll have to let him know what is happening. The poor guy sounds distraught." He clicked on the icon to start up the Internet browser. "I have just arranged to meet him on a chat room we used to use back in college. Channel E, board three. I don't want to take the chance of his phone being tapped."

"What about the 'screw you buddy' stuff?"

"Hackers never write down passwords. They are always memorized, and treating part of the password as an acronym helps you remember it. 'Over the top' and 'screw you buddy' represent part of the password for the chat room."

"So you guys were hackers?"

"In a very loose sense of the word. We thought hackers were cool, and used to hang about in the chat rooms and use the hackers' vocabulary. We wrote a few simple programs together and really thought we were gurus. All pretty low-level stuff, really, although Tim was a lot better than me."

Once connected to the Internet, Stockton tapped out an HTTP address from memory and accessed a website. When the front page was displayed, he moved the mouse pointer down to the bottom and began to move it systematically across the entire width of the screen, from left to right and back again, until a hidden link suddenly showed up in the status bar. He clicked on it, and a dialog box with a single entry field was displayed. He keyed in q$j%98ott[ru[j5]sybzz%.

A new window displaying an entry field and a list of channels and board numbers was overlaid on the screen. He typed "SOPHIA" as his handle, then selected channel E, board three. All text on the screen disappeared, and all that was left was a black surface on which a prompt blinked at the top left-hand corner. He punched in "/USERS" to show if anybody else was on the board. The list displayed his handle only.

The CB board was basically a visual telephone service, although the one Stockton was on was a closely guarded secret used predominantly by hackers who loved nothing better than to spend the majority of their time boasting of their conquests and sharing information on how to seize root of the world's most (supposedly) impenetrable computers. Anybody sharing the board could read every word that other people logged onto the same board had typed out on their computers, and vice versa. The hackers mainly congregated on the boards linked to channels A and B, and left the other channels free for private conservations.

Stockton called out the list of users at five-second intervals until the handle YIS was displayed under SOPHIA. He punched in a greeting and pressed the return key. His line of characters was immediately displayed on the board, preceded by his handle.

(3,SOPHIA)   Hi! Glad you understood me.

(3,YIS)   Hi! My hands are trembling. Expect typing errors.

(3,SOPHIA)   What can I say, man? I really am sorry.

(3,YIS)   Just tell me what is going on.

Murata and Mitchell pulled their chairs closer to the desk and watched the conversation evolve on screen.

(3,SOPHIA)   The part about us acting as consultants for the Japanese government is true. What I didn't mention is that we suspect the Yakuza of being involved. Our office in the ECB was bugged so we had to clear out. We are now undercover.

(3,YIS)	What about the tapes?
(3,SOPHIA)	ECB host system.
(3,YIS)	Did you steal them?
(3,SOPHIA)	Yes.

Stockton typed in "/USERS" again to ensure nobody was monitoring the conversation. Nobody was.

(3,YIS)	So those clowns who visited me were from the mob?
(3,SOPHIA)	Probably.
(3,YIS)	Excuse me while I reach for the toilet paper.

"At least his sense of humor is still intact," said Mitchell with a short bark of laughter. "You Brits are crazy!"

(3,SOPHIA)	But this complicates matters a bit.
(3,YIS)	Tell me about it . . .
(3,SOPHIA)	Fortunately you were only threatened. Maybe you should avoid all further contact with us. I'll get in touch with you when it is all over. You should be safe.
(3,YIS)	Fortunately . . . ? Maybe . . . ? Should be . . . ? Are you serious, man? Let me have your address. I will be around tomorrow evening after I have sent my wife and kids off to her parents.

"Oh, Jesus," muttered Stockton. "This is all we need."

173

(3,SOPHIA)	Negative! Stay put and you'll be fine.
(3,YIS)	No way, pal. I am already involved. I can't sit back and "hope" that my kids won't be hurt.
(3,SOPHIA)	We are talking danger, here. If you feel insecure, just send your wife and kids off and let it stand at that.
(3,YIS)	Maybe I can help. I can get you into any database you want. I can get information from places you didn't even know places existed.
(3,SOPHIA)	No.
(3,YIS)	Is Don there?
(3,SOPHIA)	Yes.
(3,YIS)	Ask him.

Stockton swiveled around in his seat. "What do you think?"

"I think he should go off to the country with his wife and kids. We have obviously placed him in danger, and anybody who is desperate enough might try to use him as leverage if we do get close enough. Whatever happens, we can't leave him exposed."

Stockton turned back to the screen.

(3,SOPHIA)	Don says you're an insufferable prick.
(3,YIS)	Tell him I love him, too.
(3,SOPHIA)	We think there might be danger if you stay where you are. Can you go off to the country with your family?
(3,YIS)	Blow it out your ass!

"Don?"

"Well, I guess we'll have to drag him in. Make sure he gets rid of his family, though."

(3,SOPHIA)   Okay, you win. Get a train to Tamachi Station after you have packed off the wife and kids and then give us a ring. I'll come and pick you up.

(3,YIS)   You've got it. See you tomorrow.

(3,SOPHIA)   Don't forget to bring a toothbrush.

(3,YIS)   Bye . . .

Stockton called out the list of users and noted that he was alone. Crawford had already signed off. He exited the CB and ended the connection.

"So," he said when the computer had been switched off, "our numbers increase. You'll have to share your bedroom from tomorrow, Akio."

"No problem."

Mitchell noticed the frown on Murata's face. "What's the problem, Akio? What are you thinking about?"

Murata looked up and the lines were wiped from his face. "Oh, nothing," he said brightly. "I was just wondering what 'screw you, buddy' means."

Chapter Ten

Switzerland (Geneva)

Hewes stood with his back to the office and stared out of the window, his hands clasped tightly behind him. The idea of an informer in a governmental office sickened him. He had dedicated the whole of his life to the ideal of eradicating crime, and the thought that somebody in a position of trust was doing just the opposite set a tangible lump of hot anger in his gut.

"They have no idea who it is?"

"No, sir. But it must be somebody relatively high up to have arranged it. From my calculations, it could be any one of six people, excluding Mr. Hirata."

"Are they absolutely sure? I mean, they couldn't have made a mistake, could they?"

Marceillac looked at Keppler and shrugged.

Keppler answered. "It is possible, sir, but we have to

trust their judgment. I am sure they would not take such drastic steps unless they felt it necessary."

Hewes grunted in reply. Marceillac and Keppler watched him as he returned to the couch.

"How much information do we have on these six people?"

"Very little, sir. Just their names and jobs, really."

Hewes slipped into a thoughtful silence. It was obvious that they would have to continue supplying Tokyo with information as if nothing had happened. That was not a problem. He was worried about appearances when it was finally discovered that he had withheld information from a member nation. The United Nations needed all the friends it could get nowadays, and he did not want to be the cause of even further scorn being poured on a UN agency.

But his first priority was to protect his men. If anything happened to Stockton and Mitchell, his agency would be in for a double whammy; not only would they be hung out to dry for withholding information, they would also be raked across the coals for allowing agents to operate illegally on foreign soil. The loss of two good men notwithstanding, this scenario was totally unacceptable. But he had to protect his men at all costs. If they brought home the bacon, they would be hailed as persecuted heroes. If they didn't . . . Well, that didn't even stand thinking about.

"I agree," he said finally.

Marceillac looked up in surprise. He had been expecting his boss to make a meal out of this, and was not prepared for such swift acquiescence. "Then we can continue to send them information, sir?"

"Yes. But make sure you are careful in what you send.

Keep back anything that you think might be useful to them."

"Yes, sir," said Marceillac dryly. So far they had come across absolutely nothing that could be of use to anybody.

"And I want to know of every small development."

"Yes, sir."

Marceillac and Sylvie, understanding that the meeting was over, gathered their belongings together and left the office. Hewes continued to sit on the couch with his hands steepled before him. He wondered why Hirata had not informed him of Stockton and Mitchell's disappearance the day before, but presumed he was giving them the benefit of the doubt. A single day away from the office hardly constituted a basis for screaming foul, after all. He felt sorry for Hirata. When the truth finally came out, he would be in deep trouble for not detecting the mole earlier. People of his position were paid to take the responsibility for such things. Maybe he should tip him off. A few moments on the phone would not only save the IOCC from any later ridicule, it would also give Hirata a chance to clean house before the curtain came down. Maybe he could save two careers with one stone. The more he thought about it, the better he liked the idea. Hirata was no fool and would simply keep an eye out until whoever it was made a wrong step and incriminated himself—or herself. He could give him Stockton's phone number and allow the two three, counting Mitchell—to solve the problem together.

He leaned forward and plucked the sheet of paper given to him by Marceillac from the coffee table. He stared at Stockton's address and telephone number.

Slapping the arm of the couch decisively, he got to his feet and walked across to his desk. His watch told him it was nearly two-thirty in the afternoon. Nine-thirty at night was a little early in Japan perhaps, but there was a good chance that he would catch Hirata at home. He wanted to avoid Hirata's office telephone for obvious reasons. He tapped a few keys on his laptop computer and used the scroll key to locate Hirata's private number. He reached across for the telephone and began to punch in the number.

Japan (Tokyo)

The end of the rainy season had been officially announced, and a breath of fresh morning air wafted through the open door, fluttering the tablecloth into movement. The warm sun shone down brightly, but the humidity was low enough to curtail the use of the air-conditioning. Hirata watched Sakaguchi butter another slice of toast and crunch on it. He chewed noisily and washed the mouthful down with a slurp of coffee. Hirata's breakfast lay untouched on the table before him.

"I am very proud of you, Hirata," said Sakaguchi patronizingly. "Now that our pet monkeys have been found, we can turn our attention to more pressing matters. How did you manage to locate them?"

"That is none of your business. But I assure you, nobody from the NPA was involved."

Sakaguchi raised a hand and an aide rushed over to refill his coffee cup. "It is of no importance. As long as we know where they are."

"What do you intend to do?"

"If I may borrow your own phrase, that is none of your business. Don't worry yourself about it."

"The international pressure that will result from their removal might give you more trouble than you bargain for."

"We will cross that bridge when we come to it. In the meantime, go back to your office and keep in close contact."

Hirata stood and left the restaurant, a beaten man. He knew that Sakaguchi planned to kill Stockton, Mitchell, and Murata that day, but he was powerless to do anything about it. If any of the three men were left alive, he himself would be in danger, and he was aware of a strange emotion that actually wished for their deaths. If only he had the courage to call Sakaguchi's bluff and take his own life. But what if Sakaguchi was not bluffing? He couldn't possibly place his own daughter in danger.

Machiko, his only child, could do no wrong in his eyes. Although she was now twenty-seven years old, he still thought of her as his little girl. Even more so since the death of his wife. His dearest memories were of Machiko as a small girl: when she would come running in from her bath, pink and warm in her tiny pajamas, and jump onto his lap with squeals of laughter; when she would curl up in the crook of his arm and doze while he lay on the *tatami* amid the summer heat and watched the high-school baseball tournament on television; when she would creep into his bed and nuzzle up against him on Sunday mornings.

How would she react when she discovered his betrayal of everything he had ever stood for?

He felt a prickle of heat behind his eyes and had to

blink to clear them. Crying would solve nothing. He despised himself deeply for the self-pity he was feeling.

But one thing was for sure. If he could ever find an opportunity to make Sakaguchi pay for his atrocities, he would grab it with both hands.

Japan (Odawara)

The Pacific Ocean was no longer visible, but the smell of salt and seaweed drying in the warm sunshine reminded them all of its proximity. Erika and Jason were in high spirits and bounced about excitedly in the backseat. Yoko was pale and drawn, but tried to hide her anxiety from the children.

Crawford had decided not to tell her everything—just enough to worry her into agreeing to the trip. If he admitted to receiving an actual kidnap threat, Yoko would become hysterical and burn up the lines to the police station. Maybe he should have contacted the police himself. But no. That would have served no purpose at all. The police would have questioned him for an hour, sent somebody around to the school to ask a few questions, and then stamped the file "Perpetrator Unknown" before sticking it in a filing cabinet forever. In the meantime, his daughter and son would still have to go to school armed with nothing more than the knowledge that they should not speak to strangers.

No, there were no doubts in his mind. He was doing the right thing.

They drove past Odawara Castle and up into the hills beyond it. The vegetation became denser as they left the city behind, and the sunlight flickered through the trees annoyingly. Crawford was glad he had his sunglasses with him. The road was narrower now, and he hoped that he did not meet a car coming in the other direction. Another kilometer and he turned into a narrow dirt path and drove along it at fifteen kilometers per hour. The rainy season had washed much of the topsoil away and the surface was pitted and very bumpy, so he had to drive slowly to protect his suspension. Erika and Jason laughed in delight behind him. They always enjoyed visiting their grandmother and grandfather. There was so much to do in the country.

They caught sight of the house through the trees, and the kids started to jump up and down. He looked across at Yoko, and she smiled wanly at him. He winked encouragingly in return. Two minutes later he pulled into a circular driveway, the gravel bouncing up and clicking against the underside of the car. The door to the house stood wide open—as it always did—and the kids were halfway there before Yoko's mother appeared in the opening and clapped her hands in delight as she caught sight of her grandchildren. Yoko followed the children across at a more leisurely pace and kissed her mother on the cheek. Crawford got their bags out of the trunk and followed them all inside, acknowledging the wave from his mother-in-law.

Crawford placed the bags just inside the door and walked in his stockinged feet along the well-polished floorboards to the back of the house. He could hear Erika and Jason making a nuisance of themselves in the kitchen as he slid open the door to the room in which he knew he would find his father-in-law.

This room was his father-in-law's favorite place. Apart from a low table in the center and an antique cupboard up against the wall, it was totally devoid of furniture. This did not detract from its charm, however. The floor was covered with twelve *tatami* mats, and the paper sliding doors on the far side opened onto a glass-covered wooden corridor that looked out into the garden. Hidemitsu Murayama, Yoko's father, had opened the paper doors and the glass French-windows and was sitting with his feet outside in the garden. He was reading a book on *shogi* strategy. When the sun moved around to make his position uncomfortably hot, Crawford knew that he would move inside and set up his *shogi* board at the table and sit in front of it until dinner, probably making only one or two moves an hour.

"Ah, Tim-san. I thought I heard your car."

Crawford moved across and sat down beside him on the edge of the raised floorboards. "I hope my telephone call did not alarm you."

"Very little alarms me these days." Murayama placed a piece of paper in the book to mark his place and turned his gaze onto the garden. The garden contained very few flowers, mostly trees, bushes, and strategically placed rocks. It exuded an aura of peace and calmness. Crawford was beginning to understand his father-in-law's affection for this spot. He found that he could stare out at the garden in total serenity, not unlike when he was a child and could stare fascinated for hours into the flames of an open fire.

"We are in a little trouble."

"So I gathered. Do you want to tell me about it?"

Crawford took a deep breath and wondered where to start. He knew his father-in-law would not be fobbed off with only half of the story, like Yoko. Despite his laid-back demeanor, Murayama was a very shrewd man. "The Yakuza have threatened the kids."

Murayama raised an eyebrow and looked across at Crawford. He had expected financial trouble and had been wondering how much it would cost him. "You are involved with these people?"

"No, nothing like that. I have a friend who is currently working for the United Nations. He is in Japan as a guest of the Japanese government in the capacity of consultant. Unfortunately, the subject on which he is providing his services concerns the Yakuza rather heavily."

"You move in hallowed circles, Tim-san. I am impressed." Murayama looked back out at the garden, his silence encouraging Crawford to continue.

"Well, this friend asked me to check something out for him. A computer tape. I agreed and was visited by three men, who took it back forcibly. I later learned the connection with the Yakuza."

Murayama said nothing.

"And then I received a note threatening Erika. I have it here." He brought the sheet of paper out of his pocket and handed it to Murayama, who read through it several times.

"This is serious, Tim-san," Murayama said without emotion. "What do you intend to do?"

"I haven't decided yet," he lied. "But for the time being, I don't want Yoko and the children at home. It might complicate matters."

"You told me on the telephone that you needed help, Tim-san. Allowing my own daughter and grandchildren to stay at my house is not help. What else do you have in mind?"

"I want you to take them to Karuizawa." Murayama, a retired bank manager, maintained a country *besso* in Karuizawa, an expensive resort area of Japan to which the rich flooded in order to escape the summer heat of the metropolis.

"Why not stay here?"

"I don't know. I just feel nervous with the thought that they were only sixty kilometers away."

"Maybe you should take them back to England. Surely that would be far enough."

"Father, please. You know that is impossible."

"And what of you?"

"My friend has offered me protection. I will be safe." Two lies in as many minutes. Not bad going for someone who constantly told his children that lying was the greatest sin.

"Your Japanese is improving, Tim-san." Crawford knew that Murayama was playing for time while he juggled the information available in his mind. Crawford had been lucky in the fact that both of his parents-in-law had taken to him from the first and had not objected to him marrying their daughter. He had many friends—both male and female—who had gone through hell on the route to the altar. Despite this, Murayama seemed to feel it his duty to remind Tim that he was not Japanese. Crawford had lived nearly all of his life in Japan and knew that his Japanese was as good as—if not better than—Murayama's, but he was informed on every visit that his Japanese was improving.

"Do you realize just how dangerous the Yakuza can be, Tim-san?"

"Yes, I do."

"How much of this story does Yoko know?"

"Very little. I simply told her that my friend had incurred the ire of the Yakuza and he had contacted me to say that he feared their anger might be directed against me or my family."

"Has she seen this?" Murayama held up the letter.

"No. And I would appreciate it if she never did."

Murayama yawned heavily and stretched his body until his legs stuck out straight before him. "Well, I suppose we ought to be moving. It's a long drive to Karuizawa."

Japan (Tokyo)

Murata sat on the edge of his seat and sipped his iced coffee nervously. He was about to commit a crime, and that bothered him more than he had expected. He checked his inside pocket once again for the envelope. It was still there.

He was in a coffee bar on the underground level of Shinjuku Station, and from his position he could see hundreds of businessmen rushing to and from trains. He wondered where they all came from and where they were going. No matter what time of day he took a train in Tokyo, it was always crowded with men in suits and neckties. Didn't anybody stay in the office anymore? Was all that valuable real estate out there empty? He sighed and took another sip of coffee.

A glance at his watch told him that his appointment was late. Five minutes late. Damn, he hated sloppiness. People spent a fortune on clocks and watches and still couldn't be on time. He looked at the magazine he had placed on the table and wanted to read it. He felt stupid doing nothing. He inspected the other people sitting at the tables, and all of them were doing something. Some were reading books, some newspapers. Some were writing. There was even one girl repairing her makeup. The only person doing absolutely nothing was him. He had been told to purchase a copy of the *Friday* magazine and leave it faceup on the table so his contact could recognize him, but it seemed so unnatural. He wondered if it was only in Japan that a man could look so out of place simply because he was doing nothing.

"Excuse me. Is this seat taken?"

He looked up into the eyes of a young man with a punch-perm haircut. His contact had arrived at last. A *chinpira*, he thought; a young mobster with so little authority that he had to scare the public with his appearance, as a skunk would with its stench.

"Please, help yourself."

The man sat down and poured gum syrup into his iced coffee. He stirred it and took a drink from the straw before leaning back and crossing one leg over the other in an act of open arrogance. "Your name?"

"Murata."

"I think you have something for me." He sneered as if to show that he was totally in control of the situation.

Murata was not intimidated. Such scum were nothing. He placed his elbows on the table and looked the *chinpira* in the eye. "You first," he said.

The man casually hooked two fingers into the top pocket of his gaudy Hawaiian shirt and pulled out a key to a coin locker. A number was written on it, but Murata could not make it out.

"Now you."

Murata looked around him and pulled the envelope

188

from his pocket. He placed it on the table and pushed it across until it was touching the other man's glass. He reached a little farther and grabbed the key. The man took the envelope and brought it down until it was just below the level of the table. He opened the top and looked inside. Satisfied, he looked up.

"The set of lockers on this level at the exit to the Odakyu line."

Murata got silently to his feet and began to leave.

"Hoy!"

He stopped and looked back, his muscles clenching in anticipation of trouble.

"You've forgotten your magazine."

"Keep it," he said.

Japan (Tokyo)

Mitchell was taking a nap with his head resting on his folded arms when the phone rang. The sudden noise exploding not ten centimeters from his ear made him jump awake in panic.

"Shit!" he said as his hand went automatically for the receiver. "Hullo? Oh, hi, Tim. How'd it go?"

Crawford explained that he was now a bachelor and was waiting patiently at Tamachi Station.

"We'll be down in about ten minutes. Have you eaten?" Mitchell looked across at Stockton, who had just come out of the shower. The constant shampooing was slowly returning his hair to its original color, but it was still a dirty brown, like the business end of a baby's diaper, as Mitchell had noted. "Neither have we. We'll grab a bite while we're down there."

189

He hung up the phone and stretched out his long frame. "Tim's at the station now. Let's go eat."

Japan (Tokyo)

Murata located the locker without any problem and turned the key. The door prevented the hordes of people exiting the Odakyu line from seeing inside, and he carried out a quick inspection by feel. The locker contained a cheap canvas bag—the type that kids carry their gym shoes to school in—and was both bulky and heavy. He unzipped the top and felt inside. Greaseproof paper covered the unmistakable shape of two handguns. He assumed the small box beside them must contain the ammunition. Rezipping the bag, he hurriedly put it into his own small sports bag.

The entrance to the Yamanote line was on the same level as the exit to the Odakyu line, and he purchased a ticket and joined the rush hour. He was not used to Shinjuku Station and had to keep a sharp lookout for the steps that led up to the correct platform. Five minutes later, he was on the train and crushed up against several people, many of whom tried to read their newspapers despite the crowded conditions, leaving him with even less room. The crowds thinned out a little at Shibuya, but he was still perspiring heavily when he reached Tamachi.

He arrived at Bay Heights and walked over to check the postbox—not that he was expecting anything—and a shadow caught the corner of his eye. He turned around in time to see a large man rushing toward him from behind one of the two columns decorating the foyer of the building. Sensing danger, he sidestepped and swung the bag forcibly in the direction of his assailant. It glanced off his arm without doing him serious damage, but it provided Murata with enough time to make a break for the door.

"He's coming out!" the man shouted.

Dusk was in its advanced stages when Murata reached the entrance, but it was light enough for him to see two men running around the side of a car in his direction to cut off his escape. He could move neither left nor right, and he sensed the original man closing on him from behind. He had no choice but to fight. He wondered where the hell Mr. Uchida, the building manager, was. Probably up in his room watching baseball on television.

Murata backed over to one side where he could keep an eye on all three men. He hefted the small bag before him and placed one foot behind the other to give himself the best possible balance. He had studied Karate, Judo, and Kendo in his school and academy years, but probably his assailants had, too. Most people did. Three against one were bad odds, but he knew that a sense of desperation would give him a better-than-average chance. The men closed in on him warily. They had recognized his stance and knew he would be trained in unarmed combat.

Murata went for the man in the middle. He didn't want to give them the advantage by allowing them to start the attack, so he leapt forward and administered three powerful kicks in quick succession to the man's thigh before jumping back out of reach again. The man yelped and went down on one knee, his leg numb and useless. Before they could react to the attack, he swiftly moved over to the left and swung the bag heavily at the head of another of the men. The man ducked instinctively, but the solid contents of the bag caught him just above the temple and made him stagger to his right, a thin trickle of blood running from his hairline.

The momentum of the bag swung Murata off balance for a brief moment, but it was all the third man needed. He ran in at full power and crashed into Murata just below the chest. The breath rushed out of Murata, and he felt his head hit hard against the concrete wall. He shook aside the pain, grabbed the bag in both hands, and brought it down with all his strength upon the top of the man's head, who had not released his hold and was now squeezing him in a fierce bear hug. The grip relaxed, and Murata hit him with the bag again. The irony of the situation struck Murata as the man backed off with both hands held to the back of his head. Here he was with a bag containing two pistols and twenty rounds of ammunition, and all he could do was beat his assailants around the head with it.

A sharp kick to the side brought him back to his senses. The kick hurt like crazy, but he could not afford the luxury of dwelling on it. He straightened his fingers, flashed his hand out in a blur, and hit the man in the neck just below the ear, the glancing blow causing his nails to scratch out three lines of flesh. Before the man could recover, Murata put all of his weight onto one foot and lashed out with the other. The kick caught the man perfectly on the side of the head and sent him careening into the wall before falling in a pile at its base.

Sensing victory, Murata swung the bag up as hard as he could and caught the man who was still holding the top of his head under the chin. He staggered backward and went down like a ton of bricks. A line of blood flowed out of his broken jaw and dripped onto the ground.

Two down, one to go. The remaining assailant was still down on one knee, the nerves in his leg damaged by Murata's hard leather street shoes. He held up his hand with the palm facing forward to indicate that he had had enough, his faced screwed up in pain. Murata was not in a mood to take prisoners. He lashed out with his foot again and kicked the man viciously in his injured leg. The man screamed in agony and rolled over onto the ground.

Murata decided that it was time to leave. He straightened the lapels of his jacket and stepped pointedly over the man, who was moaning through his misshapen jaw, and slowly began to walk away from the carnage. Had he realized the way events were unfolding behind him, he would have taken to his heels and sprinted like a rabbit.

The man with the injured leg got painfully to his original one-kneed stance and plunged a hand beneath his jacket, bringing out a lethal-looking Smith & Wesson revolver. He held the weapon in both hands and steadied it on his good knee, drawing a bead on the head of Murata, who was now nearly three meters distant. The man had never shot anybody before and quavered before applying pressure to the trigger, but he knew that if he did not shoot now he would probably miss. The pain in his leg was intensified by his position, and this prompted him to get the thing over as quickly as possible. He pulled the trigger.

The bullet hit Murata at the top of the spinal cord, and its trajectory helped it deflect up into the brainpan, where it inflicted massive trauma. Murata was dead before his legs realized that mission control was out of action and gave way beneath him.

Japan (Tokyo)

"You eat this stuff all the time, man?" asked Mitchell. He and Stockton had met Crawford at Tamachi Station and gone for a meal of grilled eels. Mitchell had not been impressed.

"Sure. About once a month, at least," Crawford said.

Mitchell shook his head in pity. "Jeez, man, that was gross! It was like cotton wool soaked in grease. How'd you manage to get a liking for that sort of thing?"

"When you come from Britain, even greasy cotton wool tastes good," said Stockton with a laugh. "You, I take it, prefer hamburgers and grits, right?"

"Damn right I do! I thought I was going to be eating sushi all the time. I haven't seen a slice of raw fish since I've been here. Do they only sell it in Chicago?"

"Yes," said Stockton, nudging Crawford into silence. "Sushi is a joke on America that Japan devised to prove what a bunch of dickheads you all are. Think about it, Don. Do you really think that people would eat fish raw? Nah, nobody would go that far. Unless, of course, it was introduced to America with enough advertising to build it up as not only ethnic, but also healthy. I hear you lot lapped it up, mate. Whenever an American businessman visits Japan and asks for sushi now, the whole of Japan sniggers behind its hand. One up for the empire, mate."

"You're full of shit!"

"Shit, maybe, but not raw fish, old son. You know,

restaurants in Japan now actually stock the stuff to serve to Americans. None of the locals eat it, of course."

"How the hell did I get saddled with a shithead Brit? I know the chances of meeting any Englishman with an IQ of more than seventy are almost nonexistent, but why did I have to get the only one who . . . Whoa!"

Mitchell stuck out a hand to halt the progress of Stockton and Crawford. They had turned the corner into the road on which Bay Heights was located, and Mitchell had noticed a commotion farther down the street.

"What do you think is going on?" he asked.

"Looks like an accident," Crawford said, viewing the police cars and ambulances with their lights flashing.

"But it's right outside our place."

"Tim, take a wander down there and see if you can find out what is happening, will you? Don and I will stay here."

Stockton and Mitchell watched Crawford walk down the road toward Bay Heights. There were masses of people milling around the area, but they were able to see the yellow and black tape of a police cordon. A van with the words "Nippon Television" screeched around the corner and skidded to a halt ten meters away from the crowds, effectively blocking their view of the ambulance. They both had a feeling of dread in their stomachs. Could it be Akio?

Crawford was gone for only three minutes, but it seemed like three hours to Stockton and Mitchell. He finally came back down the road at a gentle jog.

"Well?"

"It's difficult to say for sure, but I think there has been a shooting."

Mitchell, a look of horror on his face, said, "You don't think . . . ?"

"Well, there's only one way to find out. You bring your cell phone?"

"No. You?"

"No. Let's find a public telephone and ask Uchida." Stockton began to stride off in the direction of the station without waiting for a reply. Mitchell and Crawford ran after him.

The nearest public telephone they knew of was located just outside Tamachi Station. Stockton flung open the door and fumbled in his pocket for some ten yen coins, which he fed into the machine with shaking hands.

"Mr. Uchida? This is Frank Stockton. I . . ." He lapsed into silence and dropped his head onto his chest as he listened. "Are you sure? There is no chance that he . . . ? No, I understand. Thank you."

He hung up the phone listlessly and turned to his two friends.

"He's dead. The bastards have killed Akio!"

Chapter Eleven

Japan (Tokyo)

Hiroko opened the door and immediately turned back inside to hide her tear-stained face. Mitchell removed his shoes and followed her into the living room.

"You heard?"

She nodded and sniffed loudly. "Akio's mother phoned me."

Mitchell looked at Hiroko and felt the strings of his heart twang. She stood defensively in the center of the room, a picture of abject misery. She seemed smaller than he remembered, and he had to make an effort to prevent himself from rushing over to comfort her in his arms. Rage was boiling unceasingly within Mitchell, and he looked around for something on which to vent his emotions. There was nothing available.

"Can I get you anything?" he asked gently.

Hiroko shook her head and flopped down onto the

couch. The room was small but well appointed. A small table stood in the center of the white carpet, surrounded on three sides by a couch and two armchairs. Mitchell looked across at her work area set up in the corner. A desk, computer, and bookcase containing many thick dictionaries and reference books. He wondered how long it would be before she found the incentive to return to work.

Mitchell sat down on the other end of the couch and placed his elbows on his knees.

"He was a good man, Hiroko. One of the best. I can't tell you how sorry I am."

"Have you done this many times in the past?"

The question caught him off balance. "Done what?"

"Comfort the friends and family of dead policemen."

"What do you mean?"

"You must be used to your colleagues dying all over the place. An occupational hazard, right? How many partners have you been through in your career? Ten? Twenty?"

Mitchell realized she was using him to exhaust her own emotions and accepted his fate stoically. In fact, he had seen three men close to him die in the past, but none in such a violent manner. He kept his eyes on his clenched fingers and remained silent.

"I suppose this type of action makes you feel at home. The streets of Chicago brought to metropolitan Tokyo. Lots of nice violence and shootings to help you get accustomed to the place." Hiroko looked across at Mitchell and saw the sadness in his face. A twinge of guilt ran through her. "Oh, I'm sorry, Don." She moved over to sit beside him. "I shouldn't be taking this out on you. It's just that, it's just that . . ." She broke into tears and buried her face in her hands.

Mitchell avoided looking at her. He felt like crying himself. He had grown incredibly fond of Akio in the brief time he had known him, and could not think of anyone who deserved death less. He was just a small man caught up in a situation out of his control. But he was such a nice guy! Why did things like this always have to happen to the nice guys?

Hiroko's shoulders heaved as the sobs racked her body. For the first time in his life, Mitchell felt totally useless. He didn't have a clue what to do. If Hiroko were American he could have put his arm around her to provide comfort, but he guessed that such actions might not go down so well in Japan, and he did not want her to think that he was trying a number on her. In the end, she solved his dilemma.

"Hold me, Don," she said between sobs. "I don't want to be alone."

Mitchell put his arms around her and pulled her head gently onto his shoulder. He suddenly realized that he wanted to protect this woman for the rest of her life. She felt small and childlike in his arms, and her shaking body hardened his resolve to make sure the people responsible for her misery would be punished. Punished hard.

"I'll get them, Hiroko. I promise you that. I'll get them and make them pay."

Hiroko raised her head and a thin smile broke through the tears like the sun through clouds. She sniffed and leaned forward to take a tissue from the box on the table. "I'm sorry for what I said, Don. I know you are not to blame for all this. I should be thanking you for trying to help Akio." She nestled back onto Mitchell's shoulder with the tissue held to her mouth. "You know, Akio was always convinced that a person's whole life is determined at the moment of conception. Even down to the actual minute of death. If this is true, there is nothing you could have done to have kept him alive, Don. He would have died even if you had never come to Japan. I want you to remember that."

"I will. Thank you."

"What do you intend to do now? You cannot return to Tamachi."

"We are moving out of town to a place called Zushi. Crawford has a weekend cottage or something there. As the situation stands, we have nowhere else to run. We'll continue the hunt from there."

Hiroko took another tissue and blew her nose. "So I might not see you again."

"I want you to come with us, Hiroko." The unbidden words poured from his mouth before he could stop them. He had not planned on saying that. Examination of the logic behind the phrase made him realize that it was the best course of action. Hiroko could be in danger if left alone in Tokyo. There was no knowing who would visit her on the off chance that Murata had confided in her. "I want to keep an eye on you. It could be dangerous for you to stay here. Will you come?"

"I can't, Don. Akio's funeral will be held just as soon as the authorities release the body. I can't miss that."

"I'm afraid you might have to. The guys who did this probably already know about you and your relationship with us. They might come looking for you, and the funeral would be the obvious place to start. If they don't already know your address, that is."

"But I can't miss the funeral. What would Akio's parents think?"

"It is already past that, Hiroko." Mitchell saw the misery in her eyes and felt his heart strings twang again. "You have to protect yourself."

"I don't know, Don. Maybe it's not such a good idea. I could be in the way."

"I insist."

Hiroko reached up and kissed him on the cheek. "You're sweet, Don. I accept your offer, but not today. I want to spend the night thinking of Akio. I have to say good-bye to him in my own way. Do you see?"

"Of course I see, Hiroko. You do what you must."

"Tomorrow I will be back to normal. Tonight I still belong to Akio and must comfort him while his spirit is confused. He needs direction to pass on to the next life."

Mitchell nodded his understanding, although he felt slightly uncomfortable at the direction the conversation was taking.

"Would you stay with me?" Hiroko continued.

"But I thought . . ."

"I will make up a bed on the couch. I would feel safer if you were here."

"Of course I'll stay, Hiroko."

Japan (Tokyo)

Narita saw the blow coming but did nothing to avoid it. The open palm smashed into the side of his face and stars exploded in his head. The backhand swipe was not as powerful, but Sakaguchi's ring caught him on the cheek and gouged a thick graze from his cheek to the edge of his jaw. He fought the pain with clenched teeth while he awaited the next blow. It never came.

Sakaguchi's shoulders heaved from exertion and anger. He had been let down again. Blood dripped from Narita's chin and a red stain blossomed on his shirt. Good! Serves the bastard right! Could he do nothing right? Hadn't he given him enough chances?

He pointed a finger threateningly at Narita, and his voice was strained with anger. "You fail me one more time and you will be feeding the fish in Tokyo Bay. Do you understand?"

"Yes, *oyabun*. I understand."

Sakaguchi walked over to the table and lit a cigarette. "So let me go over this again. You let the two *keto* escape. Right?"

"Correct, *oyabun*."

"You failed to capture Murata alive. Right?"

"Yes, *oyabun*."

"And you have lost track of the Crawford *gaijin*. Right?"

"Yes, *oyabun*." The blood dripped freely from Narita's jaw, but he made no move to wipe it away.

Sakaguchi sat down behind the table and lowered his head in thought. "Right," he said after a minute, "things are getting too hot. Get over to Intersystems and tell them to suspend all operations until further notice. I want all incriminating evidence removed from their computers and stored elsewhere. Tell Tokoro to keep an eye out for the *gaijin*, but to contact me if they are spotted. Under no circumstances is he to approach them himself. Is that clear?"

"Yes, *oyabun*. I will see to it immediately."

Japan (Zushi)

Stockton scanned the front page of the *Japan Times* looking for details of Murata's murder. He turned to the next page and finally located a small article near the bottom.

"Here, listen to this." Mitchell, Crawford, and Hiroko passed their attention over to him. " 'A spokesman for the Electronic Crime Bureau confirmed that Murata's movements over the past few weeks have been strange and hinted at a mob connection,' " Stockton quoted.

"I don't believe it!" Mitchell said. "They are trying to cover it up. Does it name the spokesman?"

Stockton read a little further. "No, it doesn't. They mention the guns, though. They insinuate that possession of the guns positively incriminates him as a runner for the Yakuza. Damn!"

Crawford leaned over Stockton's shoulders and read through the article. "You know, you'd have to be pretty high up to put out that sort of information. Anything quoted to the newspapers is the official stance. Whoever put this out is near the top of the ladder."

"You don't think it could be Hirata, do you, Don?" asked Stockton.

"Anything's possible, I guess." He turned to Hiroko. "Did Akio ever mention noticing anything strange about his boss?"

"Not that I remember," she said.

"We need more information before we can make a decision on that. Maybe we could suggest it to Geneva and see what they think. Maybe they can find something out."

Mitchell walked over to the open window and stared out at the sea. The weather was beautiful again, and the sea breeze carried away the humidity. They were in Crawford's weekend getaway. He maintained a three-bedroom apartment in Zushi, a coastal resort popular for its ninety-minute proximity to downtown Tokyo. The apartment was not registered in Crawford's name—it was officially rented by his company—so they didn't think their location would be discovered. The manner in which the apartment in Tamachi had been burned remained a mystery to them, but they presumed it was because they had used their real names—an unavoidable necessity, because they had had to show their passports. Either that or the IOCC in Geneva had also been infiltrated. Nobody wanted to think about that.

Mitchell turned back into the room and looked across at Crawford. "Have you tried that database yet, Tim?"

"Not yet. I was just about to."

Mitchell noticed Hiroko looking at him and felt his heart jump. He could understand the sense of responsibility he felt for this girl—quite natural really, considering the circumstances—but he was confused by the fact that his heart was in the throes of mistaking it for love. That was ridiculous, of course, but he couldn't get away from the fact that the center of his chest tingled whenever she looked at him and he had a constant desire to rush over and wrap his arms around her. He smiled warmly back at her. They had got up early that morning and caught the first train through to Zushi from Shina-gawa Station. Mitchell had been slightly disconcerted at the way in which Hiroko had seemingly put Murata's death behind her and returned to normal. Her eyes were hollow and she sometimes stared off into the distance, but apart from that she seemed to be at peace with herself. Hiroko, noticing his confusion, had explained that she had said her good-byes to Akio and locked his memory away in a special compartment of her heart—a compartment to which only she had the key. She said that she would unlock these memories every night for the next forty-nine nights—the accepted period of mourning—and cry then until the tears came no more.

"What database is that, Tim?" asked Stockton.

"I thought I'd try the Teikoku Databank to see if we could get a leg up on this INTSYS thing. I was talking to Don earlier, and he said he remembered the name Suzuki cropping up once before, but couldn't remember where. It could provide a lead."

"That's right. Now you come to mention it, I have read that name before, too. In Geneva, right, Don?"

Mitchell screwed his eyes up. "Maybe you're right. Yes, I think it was in Geneva. Something to do with those original six cases that Armin briefed us on."

"I've got it!" Stockton clapped his hands loudly. "The name in the virus that wiped the Korean computer clean."

Mitchell gave a noncommittal shrug. "Your guess is as good as mine."

"Well, we can check that out later when we get the files re-sent, but in the meantime I suggest you carry on, Tim."

The Teikoku Databank contained information on all companies registered on the Tokyo Stock Exchange. Apart from providing information on each company's business address and capital, et cetera, it also gave data on pre-tax and post-tax revenue, number of employees, and a credit rating. The name, address, and telephone number of the president were also thoughtfully included.

Crawford fired up the laptop computer he kept in the apartment and quickly managed to access the databank. He selected a search by name and typed in "INTSYS." The machine failed to come up with any items with this name, so he then tried again with "INT" and thirty-seven entries were retrieved. He downloaded them all and disconnected the line.

It took nearly thirty minutes to print them all out—he kept only a small printer in the apartment—and he separated the printouts into two independent piles, one larger than the other.

"Okay, folks!" he said. "Gather round and view the results."

They all moved to the kitchen table, onto which Crawford slapped the two piles of printed paper. He placed one hand on the smaller pile. "Five companies that have both 'INT' and 'SYS' in their titles." He moved his hand to the other pile. "Thirty-two companies with only 'INT' in their titles. If the INTSYS we are looking for is a *kabushiki-gaisha*, a company registered with the Tokyo Stock Exchange, then it is here." He moved his hand back to the small pile.

"Now you're talking!" said Mitchell. Going by the luck they had had so far, he was convinced it would be the larger pile.

Crawford picked up the few sheets of paper and began to read off the company names. "International System Technology; Interlogical Systems, K.K.; Intersystems, Inc.; International SysTech, Ltd.; Intrafoam Systems, K.K."

"They all sound suspicious to me," Hiroko said.

"I vote we give them all a ring and ask for a Suzuki-san," said Stockton, reading through the data. "We can prepare a sentence that only the guilty Suzuki will fall for, and try to force him or her into incriminating the company. Any suggestions?"

"What about something really dramatic, like 'We know your game. Prepare twenty million yen in used notes and deliver it to Hibiya Koen at the stroke of midnight.'" Crawford dodged the empty can of coffee that Stockton threw at him.

"No, maybe he has got something." Mitchell held up his hand and frowned as he worked out his thoughts. "From my experience, it is only vanity that will induce a man to sign his work. I doubt if the ringleaders are aware that this guy is leaving a trail behind him, and if we can convince him that we know all about the Korean scam and his involvement in these crimes, he might agree to a meeting and prove the company's involvement without blabbing to his superiors. Just to save his own neck."

Stockton nodded thoughtfully. "Okay, let's work out a guv'nor of a sentence!"

They put their heads together and ten minutes later decided upon the conversation that would be used. Hiroko was elected to make the calls, and Crawford brought the telephone over to the table and placed it in front of her. She picked up the data sheet for the first company and punched out the number.

"May I speak to Suzuki-san, please?" She was asked to wait a moment and mouthed "Okay" to the others. "Suzuki-san?" she continued as a female voice answered. "You don't know me, but I wonder if the mob knows that you have been leaving your name in the programs? I know all about the Korean job and many others. I think we should speak."

Hiroko listened for a few moments before hanging up the phone. She looked up at the expectant faces of the three men. "Not a chance," she said. "I put the poor girl into total confusion."

"But there can't be that many Suzukis around," Mitchell said. "Maybe she's bluffing."

"Our Suzuki is equal to your Smith," said Hiroko. "We might find a Suzuki in every one of these five companies. Anyway, we can always come back if there aren't."

She phoned the next company and was informed that nobody by the name of Suzuki worked there. Shrugging, she hit the number for Intersystems, Inc.

"May I speak to Suzuki-san, please?"

"Hold the line, please."

Two minutes later, a male voice came on the line.

"Suzuki-san? You don't know me, but I wonder if the mob knows that you have been leaving your name in the programs? I know all about the Korean job and many others. I think we should speak."

A pause met her revelation. "Who are you?" the voice asked after a moment. Hiroko circled her thumb and forefinger and grinned widely.

"A friend. But I must speak to you. Alone."

"How do you know these things?"

"I can tell you that when we meet. Believe me, I am on your side and want to help. Without my assistance, you could be in big trouble."

"Where?"

"Eight o'clock at the Marunouchi exit of Tokyo Station."

"I'll be there."

The line clicked and went dead.

"Gotcha, you bastard!" enthused Stockton.

For form's sake they rang the two remaining companies, but a Suzuki worked in neither.

It was decided that Stockton, Mitchell, and Hiroko would travel into Tokyo for the meeting and Crawford would stay in Zushi. Before they left, Stockton phoned Geneva and broke the news of Murata's death to Marceillac.

"Oh, my God! But how?"

"Well, that's what we don't know, Armin. It was either our apartment registration cards that let us down, or you have a leak in the IOCC. We are also slightly suspicious of Hirata, but we can't come up with any plausible reason for his knowing the address. Maybe you could look into it on your side."

"But that is terrible! Another man killed?"

"I'm afraid so, Armin. We have a lead that we will follow up tonight, but in the meantime I hope you won't mind if I don't give you our address and telephone number. We don't want to risk the chance of a mole at your end. But we do have a new e-mail address that you can use to contact us. Have you got a pen?"

Marceillac took down the details, said he understood, and the connection was broken.

209

Japan (Tokyo)

Tokoro, Yanagida, and Suzuki listened to Narita's instructions to halt Intersystems's operations with mixed feelings. It would certainly delay the schedules of several projects, but the stress of being involved in illegal activities for twenty-four hours of every day was beginning to tell on them all. A brief respite from this stress—albeit temporary—would provide a welcome break.

"How long will it take you to clean out the computers?" asked Narita.

Suzuki jotted a few notes down on a pad of paper. "Three days," he said. "There is only one problem."

"And that is?"

"We will miss the Korean Central Bank cut-over and will have to scrap the project."

"But that cut-over is not for another month," said Tokoro.

"We will still never be ready in time. We are working on it around the clock at the moment, and a delay of even one week would mean we could not meet the deadline."

The Korean Central Bank project was the largest project undertaken by Intersystems to date. The system was being developed by a Seoul-based company called Korean Postal Data and Communications Technology, Ltd., and consisted of a cash reconciliation system to check payments against remittances for member banks. The reconciliation window was opened at the end of each working day and payment requests checked for sufficient funds. If an account had insufficient funds, a digital signal was sent to the member bank in question requesting augmentation of funds. Each account was assigned a credit rating, and augmentation was automatically approved or rejected in accordance with this rating and the sum involved. A rejection simply meant that the request was returned and the check subsequently bounced, but an approval meant that the member bank accepted responsibility for the payment and covered the cost of the transaction out of its own funds, allowing, in effect, the holder of the account an overdraft.

The modifications that Intersystems were working on overrode the rejection flag if the account requesting payment was one of six already established in separate member banks spread throughout Korea. The idea was that on the first day of trading with the new system, payment requests for massive amounts would be sent from these six accounts in accordance with checks written on six other bogus accounts, each of which contained the equivalent of approximately one hundred U.S. dollars. The augmentation of insufficient funds would be approved and the sums duly transferred across to the accounts requesting payment. These sums would be withdrawn the following day and the accounts never used again.

The total profit expected exceeded twenty-six million U.S. dollars, and the termination of the project presented Narita with a difficult decision. It was a lot of money to throw away, and the chances of lining up the logistics to reinstate the project at a later date were practically nonexistent.

"Okay, go for it. But only this one project. I want all others suspended."

Chapter Twelve

Switzerland (Geneva)

Armin Marceillac sat at his desk with his head in his hands, the official report from Japan open before him. The knowledge that another man had lost his life had affected him considerably, and this added to the possibility that the leak could be within his own office had contributed to a depression such as he had never experienced in his life before. Although anybody in the office would technically have access to the details of the case so far, the only people who knew enough about the case apart from himself were Jasper Hewes and Sylvie Keppler.

But he knew it couldn't be either. Or did he?

Damn, the indecision was driving him crazy. He was powerless to do anything alone, so had to confide his fears in somebody—anybody! He was sure Sylvie was not to blame. A strange sort of relationship had built up between them over the past few weeks—a relationship that verged on the borders of love, but which both were striving to keep within the realms of simple friendship—and he knew she had been affected by events as deeply as he himself. No, it was definitely not Sylvie.

That left Hewes. The thought itself was so improbable that it bordered on the ridiculous. He knew he should not confuse improbability with impossibility, but surely the line between the two meanings in this case was so small as to be practically nonexistent.

He looked up at Sylvie, who sat across from him, and winked. She smiled gently but said nothing. Marceillac's listlessness was worrying her, but she knew he had to fight his own demons in his own way. "We need to talk to Hewes," he said. He had decided to seek advice.

Hewes was reading the report on Murata's demise from Japan when they knocked on the door. The lines of worry were back on his face, and Marceillac was convinced that he had come to the right decision. No actor could add ten years to his age this convincingly.

Before Hewes could greet them, Marceillac blurted out, "I received another call from Stockton this morning."

Hewes left his desk and moved over to the couch. When they were all seated, he gestured for Marceillac to continue.

"Stockton thinks that we may have a leak in this office." He watched Hewes's reaction closely.

"Here?" The surprise was clear on Hewes's face, and Marceillac relaxed a little. "But that's impossible. Why, only us three know the full story. Have you noticed any tampering with your files?"

Marceillac and Keppler both shook their heads.

"What makes him think that?"

"Simple process of elimination, from what I can gather. There is no doubt that their apartment was burned, and they can only think of three ways that this could have happened. The registration cards they filled out when they rented the apartment, a leak in this office, or the leak in the ECB."

"Phew, I'm glad it is only speculation. You had me worried for a moment, there."

"Stockton also mentioned that Hirata is high on their list of suspects."

"Hirata? That's ridiculous! He is the director general, for God's sake." Hewes waved away the accusation with contempt.

"Stockton agreed that the basis for suspicion is weak because there is no way the ECB could have got their address, but it would have taken somebody as high up as Hirata to manipulate the press release. Mr. Hewes . . . ?"

Hewes had gone pale and his mouth was open. Marceillac began to fear he was having a mild heart attack. "Oh, my God!" he said.

"Are you all right?" Keppler made as if to move around the table to help him, but Hewes waved her back into her seat.

"I know who our mole is," he said softly. "Damn, how stupid!" He looked up into Marceillac's eyes. "Armin, you are going to have to forgive me for what I am about to say. You must understand that I thought I was working in the best interests of everybody concerned."

A look of suspicion crept into Marceillac's eyes. "Go on, sir."

"I gave Hirata the address. I am your unwitting mole."

215

"What?" Marceillac jumped to his feet. "What are you saying?"

Sylvie Keppler grabbed hold of Marceillac's arm and pulled him down into his seat. "Armin, take it easy. Let Mr. Hewes explain." Marceillac allowed himself to be calmed down, but anger blazed in his eyes as he stared at his boss.

"After our meeting the other day, I thought it was my duty to warn Hirata that there was a serious leak in his office. My concern was that it would eventually come out that I had withheld information from a foreign government." Hewes extracted a cigar and lit it with shaking hands. "I phoned him at home in case his office was tapped. Who would have thought that . . . ?"

"But this is impossible! We agreed to withhold this information. What made you do it?"

"I am sorry, Armin, but you must remember that my position is largely political. A substantial part of my job is to prevent the IOCC from being exposed to criticism. Although in retrospect my actions were inexcusable, I still believe that I did the right thing."

Marceillac's anger was replaced with frustration. He realized that there was sense in what Hewes said, but he was unable to accept the fact that Murata's death had been the result of a political decision. He smashed his fist into the arm of the chair, wishing it were Hirata's face. "So where do we go from now? How can we get Hirata put away forever?"

Hewes pondered on the question. A certain amount of color was returning to his face, but it was still deathly white. "I'm afraid we still do not know for sure if Hirata is the culprit." He held up a hand to prevent Marceillac's interruption. "He could have unknowingly given the address to any one of the people in his office. He could have jotted it down in his diary. His phone could be tapped. We still have no concrete proof that he is responsible."

"He is right, Armin," Keppler said. "We cannot let our emotions fool us into making the situation worse than it already is. We have to view facts clinically."

Marceillac's head slumped. Was he the only person who was unable to be objective about this case? He realized how stupid he looked, jumping at every shadow and seeking vengeance like a child who has had his candy stolen. He would, as Sylvie had pointed out, have to learn to curb his emotions and begin to work professionally.

"You are right. I am being foolish. I apologize."

Hewes felt a sudden stab of pity for Marceillac. It was unfair to subject a bureaucrat to life-and-death decisions, but who could have foreseen the direction in which this case would turn? He hoped it could be resolved without further bloodshed. "We could try to trap Hirata into a false move. If he grabs the bait, we know we have our man."

Marceillac and Keppler nodded in agreement.

"I have a plan, but we will need Stockton and Crawford's assistance. Do you know where they are now?"

"No, Frank wouldn't tell me. But we can contact them through e-mail. I have a new contact address for them."

"Right. Send them this message." Hewes walked over to his desk and began to write on a pad of paper.

Japan (Tokyo)

The view through the door of the coffee bar was restricted to a certain extent, but Hiroko was able to keep an eye on the Marunouchi entrance to Tokyo Station by craning her neck a little. Stockton and Mitchell kept their backs to the door and sipped on beers.

Hiroko kept up a running commentary: "A girl has just run up to the first man, and the two are walking toward the wickets. That leaves just two men remaining. The scruffy one keeps glancing at his watch and seems very nervous. I would put my money on him. Oh, hang on. The other man has just disappeared from view and is taking something out of his inside pocket. I'd say he is going to make a phone call.

"Another man with a briefcase has stopped. No, he has spotted his date standing outside and has moved off."

Stockton glanced at his watch. It was fifteen minutes past eight o'clock. The only person who had been waiting for the entire fifteen minutes was the man they had named the Scruff. He risked turning his head and caught sight of the man as he impatiently tapped an umbrella against his leg.

"I think that's our man, Don. Take a look while he is facing in the other direction."

Mitchell turned around and examined the Scruff. The man wore a crumpled suit that had probably never seen the inside of a dry cleaner's, and was constantly pushing his glasses up onto the ridge of his nose. "Handsome sort of guy, wouldn't you say? I must say, those white socks go well with the dark gray suit."

"Hmm, very tasteful," agreed Stockton.

The man who had disappeared from view returned, but walked directly over to the ticket machines at the far side of the circular waiting area and purchased a ticket. Then he walked through the wickets and was lost from view again.

It was just after eight-thirty when the Scruff finally gave up the vigil and walked out of the station. Crawford and Stockton got to their feet and waited until he had passed out into the street before following him. They waved a brief farewell to Hiroko, who remained seated.

They maintained a twenty-meter distance between themselves and the Scruff as he crossed the road and walked up toward the Marunouchi Hotel before heading down into the Otemachi subway station. They just caught sight of him as he turned left at the bottom of the steps. The Scruff obviously had no inclination that he was being tailed, and it did not occur to him to check behind him. He purchased a ticket at the machine and passed through into the Chiyoda line. Stockton quickly bought two tickets, and they followed him through. The rush hour had finished, but there were still enough people around to provide cover.

The Scruff boarded the first train and stood in front of the sliding doors. Stockton and Mitchell boarded the next carriage and managed to gain positions beside the connecting door where they could keep an eye on their target. The Scruff got off the train two stops before the terminal, at Kita-Senju Station.

They had walked northeast for approximately ten minutes when the Scruff turned into a small apartment block and climbed the fire-escape stairs onto the first landing. The block contained six apartments—three down, three up—and was typical of low-priced housing in Tokyo. Each apartment, Stockton knew, would have two small rooms, one of six *tatami* mats and one of four and a half *tatami* mats, a small kitchen, and a bathroom. The Scruff probably paid about sixty thousand yen per month in rent for this hovel.

The Scruff walked to the last apartment on the second floor and fiddled with the letter box.

"Now, that's helpful," Stockton said. "He leaves the key inside the letter box. Probably on a piece of string."

When the Scruff had entered his apartment and shut the door, Stockton told Mitchell to stay where he was and ran over to the staircase. He looked around to make sure he was not being observed before running silently up the stairs two at a time. He walked down the landing to the end apartment and read the name on the door and then retraced his steps until he was standing beside Mitchell again.

He removed a cellular phone—a prepaid unit purchased earlier that day to replace the one left in Tamachi—from his pocket and tapped out a number. "Hello, Hiroko. We were right, his name is Suzuki. First name Noriyuki. His address is 405 Ryuta-so, 36 Senju 2-Chome. Got that?"

He broke the connection and pointed to a parking lot on the other side of the road. "I think we ought to go over there. He should be leaving soon and will be passing by here."

The two men crossed the road and melted into the shadows of the car park.

Japan (Tokyo)

Hiroko dialed one-zero-four for directory inquiries and obtained Suzuki's telephone number by providing his full name and address. She wrote the number down on her notepad and took another sip of her iced coffee before punching out the number. She was beginning to feel a bit embarrassed about staying in the same coffee bar for hours on end, but had justified her presence with three cups of coffee.

"Suzuki-san? I am sorry for missing the appointment. I arrived at about eight-forty, but you had already left." Suzuki grunted his displeasure down the phone. "But I must meet with you. You are in grave trouble, and I want to help you. Can you come back into town? I will meet you outside the main entrance to the Marunouchi Building by Otemachi Station."

"Well, I don't know. Can't you give me some more details?"

"Not over the phone. This is very important, and I don't want to put you in greater danger. Please."

"All right. What time?"

"Now. I am already in Tokyo Station, so will be there before you. Please, I beg you."

Suzuki agreed to the meeting, and Hiroko immediately telephoned Stockton to warn him of Suzuki's imminent departure.

Japan (Tokyo)

Stockton disconnected the telephone, slipped it back into his pocket, and winked at Mitchell. "Any moment now."

They sank farther back into the shadows and were rewarded a few moments later as the door to the apartment opened and Suzuki hurried out and began to walk speedily toward Kita-Senju Station.

They waited until he had turned the corner before casually walking across the road and mounting the steps to the first landing of the apartment. Mitchell leaned on the railing and surveyed the area while Stockton thrust his hand into the letter box and pulled out the key. The string was just long enough to allow the key to reach the lock, and Stockton quickly turned it and gained entrance to the apartment. They closed the door before turning on the lights.

The inside of the apartment was messy and smelled dank. An unmade futon was laid out in the center of the room and the floor around it littered with clothes, novels, and comic books. Picking their way over the rubbish, the men started a cursory search of the place. Mitchell began to look through the drawers of a cabinet, and Stockton walked over to the smaller room and fired up a personal desktop computer. The area around the computer was littered with computer magazines and software manuals, and Stockton flicked through these while the operating system was loading. He found nothing of interest.

Stockton began to search through the hard disk for anything that might be incriminating, but not knowing exactly what he was looking for made the task difficult. The directories indicated that Suzuki mostly used the computer for games and e-mailing his friends, and Stockton could find no compressed files that might conceivably contain something incriminating. The only files that seemed to be of any interest were text files, but these simply appeared to be casual letters that he was exchanging with an on-line pen pal. Nevertheless, he copied them onto a floppy disk that he had brought with him for perusal back at Zushi. Then he started up the e-mail software and quickly browsed through the incoming and outgoing messages before copying them onto the same disk.

Mitchell popped his head around the door. "Anything?"

"No, nothing. You?"

"Nothing but damn garbage. This guy is a real slob."

Stockton sat back in the chair and pulled out his cell phone. "I think I'll give Tim a buzz. Maybe he has a couple of bright ideas."

The phone rang twice in Zushi before Crawford answered.

"Tim. It's Frank. I am in this guy Suzuki's machine, but I can't find anything of interest. If you had something to hide, where would you put it?"

Crawford thought for a moment. "I'd probably upload it to my on-line account or hide it in an FTP server. Does he have on-line capabilities?"

"Yes. I've already got his e-mail messages."

"Broadband or modem?"

Stockton looked under the desk for a BB router, and not finding one, checked the desktop icons. He immediately located the dial-up shortcut and spoke back into the telephone. "Modem," he said.

"Right, click on the dial-up icon and see if his password is set to be remembered by the computer."

Stockton double-clicked on the icon and checked the settings. "No, it's not. He enters it each time he goes on-line."

"Damn!" The line went silent while Crawford considered the situation. A few moments later, he said, "Right, listen. I can probably hack together some sort of auto-complete program that will log every one of his keystrokes and send it to us automatically whenever he transmits a piece of e-mail. But that will mean you will have to go back in again to plant the program in his machine. Is that acceptable?"

"I guess so."

"Okay. In the meantime, I need copies of a few files. Are you ready?"

Stockton located each file that Crawford instructed him to find, then copied them across to the floppy disk that already contained Suzuki's mail messages. When he had finished, he powered down the computer and called to Mitchell.

They left the apartment as quietly has they had entered and caught a taxi at the station to take them back into Tokyo. Stockton telephoned Hiroko, who had missed the second appointment with Suzuki, and instructed her to meet them at the entrance to Tokyo Station. Two hours later, they were back in the apartment in Zushi drinking a well-earned beer.

Chapter Thirteen

Japan (Zushi)

A refreshing, early-morning breeze blew through the apartment as Stockton, Mitchell, Crawford, and Hiroko pondered on the contents of the message from Geneva. The temperature was already up in the early nineties despite its being only six o'clock in the morning, but all of them were satisfied to leave the air-conditioning off and have the sea breezes waft through the rooms.

"Do you really think it could be Hirata, Don?" Stockton asked.

"Sure, why not? In fact, I hope it is. I didn't like him from the first, and I would be more than happy to tear his head off and ram it up his ass."

"Yeah, well, rather him than me. How do you think we should go ahead with it? Do you know of any suitable place, Tim?"

Crawford took the proffered sheet of paper and read

through it again. Marceillac had proposed to inform Hirata of a bogus address and have Stockton and Mitchell watch it from a distance. If it was burned, they knew who their mole was. Marceillac had asked them to provide the address.

"You'll have to give me a bit of time. I'm sure I can come up with something," Crawford said.

"What if it is a double cross?" They all looked at Hiroko with interest. "What if you provide them with an address and, while you are waiting around the corner, someone creeps up behind you and shoots you in the back? You said there was a possibility that the leak came from Geneva."

Stockton and Mitchell looked at each other. Nobody had thought of that.

Mitchell leaned over and patted her hand. "You're becoming a regular private detective, aren't you?" She smiled back, pleased.

"Well, I guess it's worth thinking about," said Stockton, "Tim, try and find a place where we can also watch our backs."

"You want to go through with it, then?"

"Sure, why not. It's too good a chance to miss."

Crawford pulled a road map of Kanagawa prefecture down from a shelf and laid it on the table before him. He sat back and closed his eyes for a moment in thought. He needed somewhere that would provide more than one clean route of escape. He racked his brain for any place he had been in the past that would provide a clear view of a house—any house—as well as allow the area behind to be kept under surveillance. Maybe a park or something. He knew of several parks, but they would make it too easy for a few potential assailants to spread out and block off all routes of escape. What he needed was a densely wooded hill overlooking a residential area. Well, Kanagawa had no shortage of hills. The image of a shrine built onto the side of a hill floated into his head. Surely he had visited a shrine somewhere near Ofuna one New Year's Eve with some friends. If he remembered rightly, that had overlooked several houses, and the precincts of the shrine were well wooded. He bent forward and traced his finger over the map until he found the place he was thinking of. Kasuga Shrine in Sakae ward.

He looked up. "I have a potential. It is a small shrine located on a hill. From what I can remember, it has one main entrance, but you can wander through the woods in any direction and get back onto the road. The back of the shrine overlooks a residential cul-de-sac, which would be perfect for the target address."

"Do you know the address?" asked Mitchell.

"No, but I can easily find that out today. I'll drive down there and check it all out while you lot are up in Tokyo. If it's no good, I'll think of another. We can phone Geneva later and set it all up for tonight."

"Sounds good to me. Are you two ready?"

Mitchell nodded and looked over at Hiroko. She looked especially beautiful today, he thought. Her faded jeans and white T-shirt emphasized her petite figure and made her seem like a child pretending to be a grown-up.

"Just let me get my bag and I will be with you," she said, hurrying into the bedroom.

Mitchell watched her go and suppressed another tide of anger that was rising within him. True to her word, Hiroko was back to normal during the day, but he had stayed awake the night before and heard her gentle sobs as she had mourned for Murata. If they found out that Hirata was responsible, Mitchell was going to pay him a visit and introduce him to the meaning of real agony.

He clenched his fists at the thought and a grim smile appeared on his face.

Japan (Tokyo)

Noriyuki Suzuki left his apartment at eight-fifteen and headed toward Kita-Senju Station. He did not notice the girl in her midtwenties drop into step some ten meters behind him, and would not have seen the two foreigners watching her go if he had looked, for they were well concealed behind a removal van.

Stockton and Mitchell waited until he had turned the corner before crossing the road and walking up the steps to Suzuki's apartment for the second time in twelve hours. Attempting to break in during daylight was a calculated risk that they had decided to take. If anybody questioned them, they would say that they were friends of Suzuki and had been given a key to collect some books he had promised them. The art of the exercise was to avoid looking suspicious, which was more difficult than both of them had imagined. Mitchell, in particular, had great difficulty chatting normally as they climbed the stairs, and it took supreme physical strength to stop his eyes from darting everywhere to see if they were being observed.

They reached the door to the apartment and pulled out the key on the end of the string. They could hear voices in the apartment next door, but nobody came out to challenge them. At least they did not have to worry about Suzuki himself returning. Hiroko would phone them if he began to retrace his steps for a forgotten document or some other item.

The apartment was as untidy and squalid in daylight as it was under artificial light. It amazed both men that anybody would voluntarily live in such a mess.

"I pity any poor, unsuspecting girl who marries this sewer rat," said Mitchell with feeling. "How the hell can he live amongst this shit?"

Stockton grunted a reply and turned on the personal computer. "Let's hope this works," he said, holding up a CD-ROM that contained Crawford's hurriedly coded program.

Once the computer was up and running, Stockton checked the incoming and outgoing e-mail once again to see if any new messages existed, but apart from a single message containing a lengthy discourse on the ability of JEF United and the Kashima Antlers—professional soccer teams in the J-League—that had been received the night before, Suzuki and his e-mail friend seemed to have little in common and did not discuss work.

Stockton inserted the CD-ROM into the drive and swiftly copied the program across to the directory that Crawford had stipulated. Then he rebooted the computer and checked the task manager to make sure the program was running properly. It was.

"That should do it," he said, removing the CD-ROM and switching off the computer. "We should receive a copy of Suzuki's password the next time he sends an e-mail."

"We still don't know if he uploads anything to his account," pointed out Mitchell. "It could turn out to be nothing."

Stockton looked across at Mitchell reprovingly. "Now, come on, Don. Don't be such a pessimist. Look on the bright side for a change."

"Yeah, right," he said, kicking moodily at a pile of soiled clothing left on the floor.

Japan (Tokyo)

The loud noise brought Tsutomu Hirata out of a deep sleep, and his hand automatically fumbled around for the light switch. He screwed his eyes tightly closed as the penetrating light chased all shadows under the bed. The noise continued unabated until he reached a hand out toward the bedside table and grabbed the telephone receiver. "*Hai, Hirata desu,*" he slurred.

"Tsutomu. Hewes, here! Sorry to wake you up so early in the morning. What time is it, anyway?"

Hirata squinted across at his alarm clock. "Just after two, Jasper. What's the trouble?"

"Well, actually, I want to expand on our conversation of the other day. We think that Stockton's apartment was burned and are convinced that the leak is in your office, despite your official statement that Murata was involved with the mob. Did you really believe that yourself?"

"Well, to tell the truth . . ." Hirata was wide awake now. He had suspected that this conversation would evolve sometime in the future, but he had not expected it at two o'clock in the morning. "I and a few of my colleagues had our reservations, but we were more or less forced to take this stance because of the guns. A law-abiding police officer does not walk about town with

230

two illegal weapons. I am sure you can understand that, Jasper."

Hirata pushed himself up until he was seated with his back against the headboard. Unlike many Japanese of his age, he did not like to sleep on futons. In fact, his entire house leaned toward Western culture. He had spent only two years in England as an exchange student in his teens, but this experience had instilled in him a love for a culture that, he conceded, was slightly more practical than his own. The Japanese culture liked to center around tradition, but Western cultures had managed to maintain tradition within a framework of comfort.

"I can see your point, Tsutomu," replied Hewes. "But you surely can't suspect Murata of running guns while being mixed up in this business."

"Excuse me, Jasper, but my opinion must reflect the opinion of my government. My personal feelings do not enter the equation. May I ask the reason for this call?"

"Oh, yes. Mustn't get carried away, must we? I am phoning to let you know that Stockton contacted me. He and Mitchell are furious about Murata's death, and I am of the opinion that they will need your help to clear this affair up. They don't know that I am in touch with you, but I would appreciate it if you would contact them and work something out. I suggested that they leave the country immediately, but they won't listen to me. They are determined to get to the bottom of this."

"Well, I could try," said Hirata warily. "Do you have their telephone number?"

"Just their address. The telephone has not yet been connected. Do you have a pen?"

Hirata opened the drawer to his bedside cabinet and withdrew a small pad of paper and a pen. "Go ahead."

Hewes gave him the address he had received that day from Stockton. Hirata wrote it down.

"I'll let you have their telephone number as soon as I get it," Hewes continued. "I hope you can manage to sort this problem out between you. It certainly has gone far enough."

"Well, I'll try, Jasper. I'll let you know what happens."

Hirata said his good-byes and slowly hung up the receiver, a deep frown on his face. What should he do with this piece of information? If he passed it across to Sakaguchi and this place was raided, it would point the finger right at him. He was sure that he had managed to avoid suspicion so far—Hewes confiding in him seemed to confirm this—but acting on this new development would incriminate him as effectively as if he walked into the office with "Guilty" stamped across his forehead in gothic script. Unless . . .

He jumped out of bed and padded across to the spare room he used as a study. It contained a desk, a computer, several small cabinets, and one wall full of books. He switched on the light and opened the bottom drawer of his desk. He rummaged around until he came up with a small plastic cylinder the size of a thumbnail with two small wires protruding from the back. He closed the drawer and left the room. Back in his bedroom, he took a clean handkerchief from the wardrobe and began to thoroughly wipe the cylinder until any fingerprints it might have concealed were completely removed.

With the cylinder still wrapped in the handkerchief, he moved back over to the bed and removed the back of the telephone with the screwdriver attachment of a Swiss army knife that he kept in the bedside cabinet. When the workings of the telephone were exposed, he inserted the cylinder and wrapped the protruding wires around two soldered points.

He wiped out the inside of the telephone with the same handkerchief and assembled it again. Satisfied that he could now prove that his telephone was being tapped, he picked up the receiver and punched out Sakaguchi's number.

Japan (Yokohama)

Mitchell adjusted his position on the dry ground and looked across at Stockton, who was checking out the controls on the digital Handicam Crawford had lent them. "How long do you think we'll have to wait?"

"Could be hours yet," said Stockton. "Hewes was to phone Hirata at two o'clock, and it could take several hours for a raid to be mounted." He flashed the penlight onto the face of his watch. "It's nearly three now."

Mitchell turned his attention back to the row of four terraced houses one hundred meters below him. They had been encamped in this position for an hour, and he was beginning to tire of the darkness, the hard ground, and the mosquitoes. The eerie cry of a strange animal also made him nervous. Stockton had told him that it was a *tanuki*, a raccoon dog indigenous to Japan and to which folklore had attributed magical powers, but it sounded like something much more sinister to him.

Stockton hit the speed-dial button on his cell phone and it was answered immediately. "Anything?" he asked.

The voice of Crawford answered. "Nothing. All is peaceful."

"Well, don't forget. Let us know if anybody even walks past."

Crawford was parked just along the road from the main entrance to Kasuga Shrine and was keeping the area under surveillance. Murata's Pajero was parked several hundred meters around the corner, in an area to which Stockton and Mitchell could make a hasty retreat if anything untoward occurred.

The grounds of the shrine were perfect as a lookout point. A small green fence marked the boundaries of the precinct, but even a child would have no trouble climbing over it, so it was not looked upon as a hindrance. Stockton and Mitchell had decided upon a small clump of trees as a base to watch occurrences, as it not only protected them from prying eyes, it was also located in such a position that they could run out in any direction and eventually get back to the road. It could even be defended if necessary.

All they had to do now was wait.

"You know, I am beginning to like Japan."

Stockton looked up in surprise. "You? Don't make me laugh. Where would you get your corn pone over here?"

"No, I'm serious. I am also beginning to understand that there is a touch of truth in what you are always saying about Japan handling things differently. That hostage deal in the newspapers the other day, for instance. Some guy takes a cop hostage for seven hours, and a bunch of his pals attack the gunman with fire extinguishers, for God's sake. Fire extinguishers! Can you imagine that? In Chicago, the guy would have had six hundred pounds of lead drilled into him. In Japan, they tell him to drop his gun or else they'll put his fire out!"

"Well, that was slightly unusual, I must admit. But I see your point. Maybe there is something else that has contributed to this change of heart, as well."

"Like what?"

"Like Hiroko?"

Mitchell felt himself blush in the dark. Damn! Forty-five years old and blushing at the mention of a girl he had a crush on. His son would split his sides laughing if he could see his old man now. "It's that obvious, huh?"

Stockton realized that his friend was more serious about Hiroko than he had expected. "Sort of. Hiroko has certainly noticed it. Are you thinking of plighting your troth?"

"Not yet. I want to wait until the forty-nine-day period of mourning is up before mentioning it."

"Wow, you are learning something about Japan, aren't you? Where'd you hear about that?"

"Just something Hiroko mentioned. But I feel like such a louse. Jesus, Akio's body is still warm, and here am I trying to muscle in on his act." Mitchell picked up a dead leaf and shredded it slowly. "Goddamn country is screwing me up completely. I'm glad there is a trade surplus. At least I've got something to bitch about!"

"There's no trade surplus, Don. A figment of the American government's imagination."

"Oh, bullshit! Look at the figures, for God's sake!"

"Oh, sure, look at the totals and you'll find a difference, but remember that America has twice the population of Japan. If you divide Japan's trade figures into the total population of America and then do the same for America's trade figures, you'll probably find that Japanese people are spending more on American goods per capita than the other way round."

Mitchell threw the shredded leaf at the ground. "Great! So there's no trade surplus, huh?"

"Nope, sorry."

Mitchell sighed deeply and looked around him. He thought he could detect a faint smudge of light on the horizon—the harbinger of dawn. The woods were still wrapped in darkness and shadows, but the narrow street with its peaceful houses was clearly visible below in the glow of the streetlamps. He could make out several of the houses with their windows open, something he had not seen in America since his childhood. An open window in Chicago was an invitation to the scum of the streets to come and help themselves to anything they wanted.

Stockton's cell phone beeped quietly, drawing Mitchell's attention back to the present. Stockton answered it and listened for a moment. "It's probably nothing, but let me know if anybody else turns up," he said before breaking the connection.

"Some guy out walking his dog." Stockton explained to Mitchell.

"I wish they'd hurry up if they're coming. My ass is going to . . ." Mitchell stopped midsentence and looked across at Stockton. The sound of an engine was approaching, maybe two.

Stockton passed the Handicam across to Mitchell, who brought it up to his eye and turned it on. They had decided to use the eyepiece for filming in case the light emitted from the small screen gave away their position. A small Band-Aid also concealed the red indicator light. Two black cars slowly turned into the cul-de-sac and came to a stop just before the row of terraced houses. Mitchell zoomed in on the cars and managed to get a clear shot of the number plate on the first car. Eight men dressed in dark colors got out of the cars and left the doors open as they walked up the street, checking the number of each house.

Stockton pulled out his cell phone and punched in one-one-zero for the emergency services. He asked for the police, gave them the address of the house below his position, and advised them that a robbery was in progress. He hung up without providing his name.

The eight men located the house in question at the end of the row. One of the men stood out in the street as if overseeing the raid, but said nothing. He lit a cigarette and watched the men move into position. Three of the men climbed over a white fence and disappeared from view around the back of the house. Three of the remaining four men pulled handguns from holsters and took up positions behind the last man, who crouched in front of the door and went to work on the lock.

"They seem professional enough," whispered Mitchell as he watched the lock of the door being picked skillfully through the lens of the camera. "And not a single word spoken. Nice discipline."

The man working on the lock suddenly stood up and nodded to the men behind him. They moved closer, with their pistols at the ready.

"See if you can get a close-up of the guy in the street," Stockton said, "He is obviously the leader."

"I'll get him in a minute. They're about to go in."

One of the men leaned forward and quietly opened the door. It snagged up against a door chain. He placed one foot against the wall beside the door and put all of his weight behind a gigantic tug. The splitting noise as the chain fitting was wrenched from the wood was clearly audible to Stockton and Mitchell, and the three men rushed inside before the residents could have a chance to react to the commotion.

"I've just realized something," Mitchell said. "Japanese doors open outwards. In Chicago, you kick a door in, not pull it open. This way seems better."

"Keep your voice down!" said Stockton in a hoarse whisper. "Japan is earthquake territory. It's easier to kick the door out from the inside if you get trapped. Most of the doors are made of metal, as well. They hold up better in a quake."

"Sneaky," Mitchell said.

Shouts could be heard coming from the inside of the house, but there was no visible action. The muscles of Stockton's shoulders were bunched in tension—awaiting gunfire. Crawford had been worried over the fact that using a bogus address could get some people killed, but Stockton had overruled him, saying that the raiders would discover their mistake without resorting to violence. But he had been worried. The guys going in would be stressed out with the unknown territory, and it would take only a loudmouthed householder demanding an explanation to bring about an unhappy ending. The fact that no shots had been heard so far was a good sign, but he could not shake the feeling of anxiety.

With nothing but an open door to aim his camera at, Mitchell panned around to the man standing in the street. He calmly smoked his cigarette and leaned his weight on one hip in an extremely arrogant fashion. Mitchell cursed under his breath. This, conceivably, was the guy who had killed Murata, and the very sight of him brought a sour taste to Mitchell's mouth. He zoomed in onto his face but was able to get only a three-quarter profile from the rear. "Go on, you bastard. Turn around!" whispered Mitchell in frustration. A fresh scar was visible down the man's cheek, but apart from that he doubted if the film would provide a positive identification.

"They're coming!" Stockton said, tapping Mitchell lightly on the arm. He grabbed the cell phone from the ground before him and hit Crawford's quick-dial number.

The faint sound of a police siren could be heard in the distance. It grew gradually louder until the man standing in the street suddenly began to look around in panic.

"Gotcha!" hissed Mitchell in glee as the man provided a full frontal view of his face to the camera. "Say cheese, sucker!"

"Tim, it's Frank. The police are on their way. You had better move out right away. We're right behind you." Stockton rammed the telephone into his back pocket and struck Mitchell on the arm. "Come on, Don. Let's get out of here!"

"Just a moment. This is great! That dumbshit has just realized his driver is somewhere else and his car is pointing in the wrong direction. Crawford chose this place well."

Stockton looked down at the agony of decision the man in the street was going through. The sirens were loud enough to indicate that the police cars would be upon him before he could get his men out of the house, and he would never have the time to rush down to the cars and U-turn one of them into an escape. He frantically turned his eyes up toward the hill that concealed Stockton and Mitchell, and noting that this was his only route of escape, ran over to the edge of the steep hill and began to scrabble up with the use of handfuls of grass.

"Quick, Don. Let's get out of here, man!"

Mitchell needed no further urging. He switched off the camera, slung it over his shoulder, and followed Stockton through the undergrowth in a direction that took them away from the man who was unknowingly climbing up to meet them.

They had to make a small detour to avoid a patch of open ground, but even keeping to the brush line, they made it down to the road in just over three minutes. They emerged from the undergrowth approximately two hundred meters behind their car. Once on the road, they decided it would be better to walk at normal speed to avoid looking suspicious. With the confusion of the police raid in full swing on the other side of the hill, the last thing they wanted was for their vehicle registration number to be reported to the police by an observant local. Avoiding the mob alone was giving them enough trouble.

Five minutes later, they were driving along the Kamakura Kaido. With no traffic on the roads, it was only a thirty-minute drive back to Zushi. Mitchell phoned both Crawford and Hiroko from the cell phone to let them know that he and Stockton had escaped safely.

"Anything happen?" asked Hiroko.

Mitchell smiled grimly to himself. "A little, I guess. But I'll tell you this. If you have any relations in the undertaking trade, give them Hirata's address. I can guarantee them business."

Japan (Tokyo)

Sakaguchi remained calm as Narita reported on the events of the night. He could see Narita flinching beneath his glance, like a whipped puppy patiently awaiting another kick from his master, and knew the man was near breaking point. If he pushed him too far, Narita might deem it necessary to take drastic measures to avoid his wrath. Although he hated to admit it, Sakaguchi needed Narita more than Narita needed him. Now that his precariously built pack of computer cards seemed to be poised on the brink of collapse, Sakaguchi's mind was frantically searching for a method of saving his own skin. That method, he had decided, would be Narita. A loyal servant well-versed in the code of the Yakuza, Narita would accept responsibility for all crimes without ever mentioning Sakaguchi's name. Narita was therefore more valuable to him alive than dead.

"Relax, Narita. This is not your fault. Are you sure the two *keto* were not in the house?"

"Not completely, *oyabun*. I watched our men being arrested from the top of a hill, but the only other people to exit the house were a couple in their pajamas. They could have been hiding inside, but I doubt it. The men were in there for several minutes and had plenty of time to find them."

"So we were set up, right?"

"I would say yes, *oyabun*."

Sakaguchi tapped his fingertips on the table. The tenacity of the two foreigners had amazed him. He would never have thought it possible that they would have the ingenuity to manipulate him so effectively from afar. Every step he had taken, they had been one step behind. They had discovered that the ECB was being tapped. They had slipped through his fingers in the Tamachi raid, albeit with a sacrifice on their side. They had removed the man Crawford and his family from circulation, effectively eradicating the only lead to them. And now they had somehow managed to feed him a false address that had resulted in the arrest of seven of his men. Damn, it was driving him crazy. He didn't even know how close they were to exposing him. How much did they know? He congratulated himself once again on closing down Intersystems's operations. At least they wouldn't get much information if they got that far. Unless that fool Tokoro blabbed, of course. But no. He may be a fool, but he knew that such an action would result in his immediate execution.

Where the hell were they getting their information? It was almost as if they had a spy working for them. . . .

Light dawned on Sakaguchi's face and he looked across at Narita. "And who would you say had set us up, Narita?"

"The only person I can think of is Hirata, *oyabun*."

"Hmm, I was just thinking the same thing myself. So Hirata is trying to get his revenge, is he? I think we shall have to interview Mr. Hirata and find out how much he has told the *gaijin* scum. We might need a small incentive to loosen his tongue, however."

Sakaguchi looked back at Narita and a smirk of pure evil spread across his features.

"Narita," he said softly. "Bring me Hirata's daughter."

Chapter Fourteen

Japan (Zushi)

Three messages from Noriyuki Suzuki awaited Crawford when he checked his e-mail account the following morning, indicating that Suzuki had been on-line the night before. He excitedly copied the three attached files across to a directory and checked them one by one. The program he had hacked together deleted each file as it was sent to prevent it from becoming progressively larger with each sending, thereby alerting Suzuki as the transmission time increased, so the contents of each file were different. The only problem was, unless he could persuade Stockton to make a return visit and erase the program, Crawford was destined to receive details on every one of Suzuki's keystrokes for the rest of eternity.

Or until the authorities separated him from his keyboard and threw him in jail, thought Crawford wryly.

It took only a few moments for Crawford to pin

down Suzuki's password. It was located close to the beginning of the first file, which meant that Suzuki had gone on-line almost immediately after starting up the computer—probably to check his e-mail. Crawford already had the parameters and access number for his provider, garnered from the files he had asked Stockton to copy on his first visit to the apartment. He was set to roll.

He waited until the clock displayed nine o'clock before using Suzuki's ID and password to access his account in order to ensure that Suzuki was not using it himself. He had to wait until Stockton got off the phone with Marceillac—who was being treated to another early-morning call and being briefed on the events of the night—as the apartment had only one phone line. The moment Stockton was finished, he fired up the software preset with Suzuki's parameters and established a connection onto the Internet.

Logging into the mail server, he noted that the subject lines of five messages were displayed—four of which had been set for nonautomatic download, meaning that they would stay indefinitely within the server and not be downloaded with other mail during the normal collection procedure.

"It seems as if we were right," Crawford shouted across to the others, who quickly gathered around him. "He has sent four compressed files to himself. You see his own ID under the sender label?"

"What about the other one?" Mitchell and Stockton took up positions directly behind Crawford and peered eagerly over his shoulder.

"That's from his e-mail chum. I recognize the ID."

"How do you know they are compressed files?" asked Mitchell.

Crawford pointed to four file names under the heading of "Subject." "You see these four file names? Well, this is the area where the title of the message appears, but Suzuki has used it to remind himself of the file names. Each file ends in the three-letter ZIP, which is the default log extension for the compression software. Anyway, let's download them and see what they contain."

One by one Crawford downloaded the files and then deleted them from the server.

"Why are you deleting them?" asked Mitchell, puzzled. "He'll know somebody's been into his account if you don't leave them there."

"Once a file has been downloaded, an asterisk is planted beside it to indicate that it has been 'read.' I'll have to upload each file again so that he won't notice. That is, of course," Crawford continued, "as long as he doesn't check the date of upload. There is no way I can disguise that."

They waited patiently while Crawford covered his tracks by uploading all four of the files and setting the nonautomatic download flags. He didn't bother touching the other e-mail message; they had already determined that the sender had nothing to do with the case. When he had finished, he terminated the connection and quickly "melted" the files into their original condition.

When the files were decompressed he began to check their contents. The first file contained a short but interesting virus program of which he was obviously proud.

The software was designed to kick in on April 29, the late Showa emperor's birthday, search through all .txt and .doc files, and exchange the phrase *"Tenno Banzai"*—or "Long Live the Emperor"—for every letter E, S, and T that it found. The sentence "Thank you for your letter of September 9" would subsequently be modified to "Tenno Banzaihank you for your lTenno BanzaiTenno BanzaiTenno BanzaiTenno Banzair of Tenno BanzaiTenno BanzaipTenno BanzaiTenno BanzaimbTenno Banzair 9Tenno Banzaih."

The second file contained a total of seven original files, but all were of a personal nature regarding insurance policies, a detailed list of serial numbers for various appliances, his résumé, and other mundane data.

They hit pay dirt on the third file.

Crawford moved his face closer to the screen. "Boy, if this is what I think it is, we'd better get a printout." He hit the Print button and the small desktop printer began to spew out the contents of the file.

Stockton grabbed the first page as it was ejected from the printer. "Oh, oh! I've just found Hirata's name. And here is Hiroshi Nagai, the author. Jesus, will you look at some of these names! Here's Hajime Nojima! And here's Akira Morita. Damn!"

"Who are they?" Mitchell asked.

"Nojima is one of Japan's most forthright politicians. He was the Minister of State for the National Land Agency when the Liberal Democratic Party was in power, but he now lobbies for the Shinshinto Party. A highly respected statesman."

"And Morita?"

"He started off his career as a stand-up comedian, believe it or not, but now has a seat in the house."

Stockton collected the printout from the machine when it had stopped and brought it over to the table. Crawford started the second file printing and came over to join them.

Stockton spread the list out on the table and they all pored over it. The list contained the names of one hundred and twenty-seven people, the organizations that they worked for or were linked to, and a code number. They easily found the names of the three people on their original list who had disappeared mysteriously, and they were aghast at some of the other names and corporations that were listed.

Hiroko sat next to Mitchell and explained to him the importance of some of the names: the chairman of one of Japan's largest real-estate agencies; the president of a large automobile manufacturer; a famous movie director; a well-known newscaster; the administrative vice minister of health and welfare—the list went on and on.

"But this is incredible!" said Crawford in awe. "If this really is mob-controlled, they've got the whole of the country in their hands. The implications are staggering!"

"What do you think these code numbers are?" asked Stockton, indicating a seven-digit number beside each entry.

"Just control numbers, I guess. Probably nothing of importance."

The printer went silent. Crawford collected the printout and scanned it as he walked back to the table. "Ah-ha! I've found our code numbers."

He laid the pages out on the table and stood back while they glanced over them.

"Oh, my!" said Hiroko.

"What is it?" Mitchell asked, looking at the pages of Chinese characters. "What does it say?"

"Well, good old Suzuki! He has saved somebody a hell of a lot of work."

"What is it?" Mitchell repeated.

"Wait till the press get hold of this," said Crawford with a grin. "There will be no more live baseball on TV for the next few months." Sports programs were always the first to be scratched when a big news story came out in the open. Every channel produced tedious news specials where famous celebrities would discuss established and imaginary items related to the case ad nauseaum.

"Will somebody tell me what it is, for Chrissakes?" shouted Mitchell in frustration.

Hiroko placed a hand on his arm. "They are summaries of how each person on the first list is implicated with the crimes. A complete report on all activities related to these people. It seems that Hirata purchased his present position as director general of the ECB with false data being planted against the two people who were contenders for the same job. One was framed as a compulsive gambler, and the other as a wife beater given to uncontrollable periods of violence."

Stockton noticed that Hiroko had not removed her hand from Mitchell's arm and winked at him. "The whole lot, Don. We've cracked it! There is enough evidence here to stick every one of these people behind bars for years. The only thing we don't know is who is behind it. My guess is still the mob, but that doesn't tell us who."

"Then we haven't cracked it," Mitchell said. "We don't even know who to hand this over to."

Crawford shook his head. "You're wrong, Don. If we

can get this into the hands of the correct authorities, any one of the people on this list could point them in the right direction. Our job is finished."

"No!" Mitchell's stubbornness came as a surprise to everybody. "I want the people who killed Akio. There is no way I am going to let a bunch of politicians wheedle their way out of this and leave Akio's death unsolved. We find the culprits!"

An uncomfortable silence surrounded the table as Mitchell stared defiantly at Stockton and Crawford in turn. Hiroko squeezed Mitchell's arm in encouragement. His outburst had reminded her of his promise in her apartment on the night of Murata's death. He had promised to make the murderers pay, and he obviously intended to honor his words.

"Are you sure that is wise, Don?" asked Stockton warily. "After all, we have no weapons and don't even know who the enemy is. The authorities would have a better chance of success."

"The authorities would screw it up. If, as you say, this is going to cause a national outcry, the cops are going to be under severe pressure and are likely to take the easy way out by making an example of the people on this list." He banged his hand down on the printout. "I've seen it a thousand times, Frank. The big guys always get away. They employ expensive lawyers whose duty it is to discover mistakes in procedure, and then get their clients off on technicalities. It's the way of the world. The smaller guy always gets to take the drop."

"Aren't you being a little overdramatic?" Crawford asked.

Mitchell turned on him, his eyes flashing. "Aren't you being a little shitheaded? We are not talking Agatha

Christie here, chum. The bad guy is not going to stand up in front of the fireplace and admit his crimes and motives simply because a little fat guy with a mustache has placed his hand on his collar. We've got to get him ourselves just to make sure that somebody does. Does that make any sense to you?"

Crawford looked away petulantly and refilled his coffee cup.

"Come on, Frank. What do you say, man? Surely we owe it to Akio."

Stockton scratched his head and sighed. "Us getting killed is not going to help Akio, Don. But . . . !" he continued, preventing Mitchell's interruption, ". . . I am inclined to agree. To a certain extent, anyway. I suggest that we give ourselves a deadline. It is going to take us several days to correlate all of the information we have so far. I think we have to document everything that has occurred from the moment we met Armin in Geneva and then send it to the IOCC and see what they decide to do with it. In the meantime, we can try and find out who is behind it all."

Mitchell thought about the offer and nodded his head slowly.

"Tim and Hiroko can start work on translating Suzuki's files, and you and I can spend the rest of the day writing out everything that has happened. From tomorrow we will be free to continue the chase while Tim and Hiroko sort out all of the information into a cohesive report."

"Okay, I'm happy with that. We should get a bit more information from Geneva when Hewes challenges Hirata. Hopefully, enough to give us a start."

Stockton passed his eyes between Crawford and Hiroko. "Everybody agree?"

Both nodded their heads.

Hiroko pecked Mitchell on the cheek. "Thanks, Don," she said quietly. "Akio would have appreciated that."

Switzerland (Geneva)

Marceillac arrived at the office at eight-thirty and immediately checked the top of his desk for messages and his terminal for e-mail. There was nothing waiting. He was buzzing with an internal electricity that he was having difficulty controlling. He knew that Hirata was the mole, but was powerless to do anything alone. "Damn Hewes," he thought vindictively. "Why the hell can't he arrive at the office on time?"

He knew that he had at least two and a half hours before Hewes would put in an appearance, and he wondered if he could settle down to anything constructive while he waited out this period. Damn, damn, damn! Things were at last reaching a head, and he had to waste precious time while his boss ambled into the office at his own convenience.

Sylvie Keppler arrived just before nine o'clock, and he breathed a sigh of relief. At least he could share his knowledge with somebody. Maybe they could work out a plan of action to present to Hewes when he arrived. Anything to keep busy.

"Sylvie, my angel!" Marceillac helped her off with her coat and reached around to kiss her on the cheek. "The love of my life, my princess. I have news and simply must share it. Let's borrow Hewes's office."

Sylvie was immediately serious. "Was it raided? Quick, tell me!"

"It was. We have our man."

Marceillac grabbed hold of Sylvie's arm and led her down the corridor to Hewes's office. He swung open the door with a flourish, and stopped dead as he noticed that Jasper Hewes sat at his desk. The surprise was mutual. Very few people effected such a flamboyant entrance to the office when Hewes was in residence.

"Armin, my boy! Where's the fire?"

Marceillac stood speechless for a moment, then shook his head and stammered out a reply. "I'm . . . I'm . . . Excuse me, sir. I had no idea that you were . . ."

"I arrived early. I was worried, you understand. You have news?" Hewes left his desk and crossed his office quickly. "Tell me, Armin. Do you have news?"

"Yes, sir. It was raided."

"Damn and blast!" Hewes sat down on the couch and waved Marceillac and Keppler into their normal chairs. "I was hoping we were wrong. I was praying we were wrong. . . . But we were not, right?"

"I'm sorry, sir. Stockton phoned me early this morning and told me the house was raided by a group of men who he supposes were connected to the mob. He telephoned the police during the raid, and anything up to seven of them were probably arrested. He filmed the entire raid and will send us the tape soon."

"So. Hirata is the turncoat? What a terrible waste. What a damn stupid waste of an excellent man. How could he do such a thing?"

Hewes suddenly seemed smaller. His frame was sunk into the couch and he looked like an old man. He felt betrayed by a man whom he had trusted. A man who had been on equal standing. A man who had fought for the same ideals. A man who had, by joining the police force, dedicated himself to uphold the law in an unspoken promise more binding than the Hippocratic oath.

Hewes remembered back to the time when he was a constable walking the beat for the Thames Valley Police. His inspector, a man he had feared even more than his father, had once told him that there was no criminal worse than a bent copper. "Your normal criminal," he had said, "will encourage the hate of the victim, but will still be loved by his mother. A bent bobby, on the other hand, will encourage the hate of the whole world, including his mother."

Hewes had remembered those words.

"Right!" he said, slapping the arm of the sofa. "Down to business!"

He walked across to his desk, picked up the telephone, and dialed Hirata's home number, a look of determination on his face.

"Hirata? This is Hewes in Geneva. Why in hell did you do it?"

"Good morning, Jasper. Do what?" Hirata's voice sounded dull and void of all interest.

"There is no need for you denying it. We know all about your involvement in this despicable business. It was you who provided the address that resulted in Murata's death. How could you betray our trust in this way?"

Hirata paused for a moment and an audible sigh floated across the line. "Jasper, I cannot apologize, for I have done an awful thing. My life is in your hands."

"What? Not even an excuse?" Hewes was baffled. He had expected at least token resistance. "You're not even going to try to lie your way out of this?"

"Jasper, my daughter was kidnapped tonight by the people I have been cooperating with." Hirata's voice was flat and displayed no emotion. "Although you may look upon this as an excuse, most of my recent crimes have been the result of trying to protect my daughter from the hands of these people. Unfortunately, they now suspect me of being in your employ, and have kidnapped my daughter in revenge."

"The raid? They think you provided the false address?" Hewes tried to suppress a feeling of pity that was arising within him. "You were being blackmailed?"

"Yes. Although I was at fault by placing myself in this position in the first place. I am not squeaky clean, as I understand the saying goes."

Hewes rubbed his face with his hand. "Oh, Christ, what have you gotten yourself into? I hope you realize where my duty lies, Tsutomu. I have to report this to the director general of the National Police Agency."

"Of course I understand that, Jasper. But I am going to press upon your goodwill and ask you to give me twenty-four hours before you do that."

"My goodwill? How dare you even imply that I am willing to display any form of goodwill after what you have done!"

"Jasper, my daughter is in terrible danger. You must let me have the chance to rescue her."

"I am sorry, Tsutomu. That is not possible. You will have to leave it up to the authorities."

The line went silent for a moment as Hirata digested Hewes's words. Hewes could hear the gentle sound of Hirata breathing.

"Jasper, please don't be offended, but I want to make a deal."

"What? A deal . . . ?" Hewes looked over to Marceillac and Keppler and raised his eyes in exasperation. "I hardly think that you are in a position to make a deal."

"My proposal is simple. I shall create a document addressed to the director general of the NPA in which I shall outline every event of this case from the very beginning, including names, addresses, dates, and motives. Everything! In return for this, you will not contact anybody until this same time tomorrow morning."

"And if I refuse?"

"Then I shall go into hiding until I have prepared my attack on Sakaguchi."

"Sakaguchi?"

"Yes, the leader of the Sakaguchi-gumi. The underworld group responsible for all this."

Hewes scribbled the name down on the edge of his blotter. "That could be dangerous, Tsutomu."

"I know. I am prepared to expend my own life in return for my daughter's. I will go ahead with this whatever your decision, but the only difference is that you will have no evidence if you do not agree."

"You are placing me in a very difficult situation, Tsutomu. I don't think I can allow it."

A note of pleading slipped into Hirata's voice. "Jasper, I implore you to let me do this. I have to save my daughter. If a group of policemen raid the place, there is no knowing what will happen to her. Please do not make my daughter pay for my mistakes."

Hewes closed his eyes and his head sank lower to the desk. There was no mistaking the determination in Hirata's voice, and he was tempted to allow him his twenty-four hours. Surely an additional day would not change matters much, and if Hirata did sign a full confession, it would save a lot of time in the long run.

"All right, Tsutomu. You have twenty-four hours. But under one condition."

"Go on," prompted Hirata.

"I want you to give me a number where Stockton and Mitchell can contact you. Maybe they have some information that would be useful to you."

The line went silent for a few moments. "I don't think that is necessary, Jasper. I have all the information I need."

"Then no deal," Hewes said.

"Jasper, you are making things difficult. They might create problems for me that I don't need. I must save all of my concentration for the rescue of my daughter. I cannot be hindered."

"It's your choice. Deal or no deal?"

Hirata sighed deeply. "Very well. We have a deal." He provided the number of his cell phone and Hewes wrote it down.

"And, Jasper," Hirata continued, "although I am unable to condone my actions, I want you to know that I have great respect for you and—"

Hewes slammed the receiver down onto its cradle.

"So we were right?" asked Sylvie. "He didn't even try to deny it?"

Hewes raised a hand and massaged the back of his neck. He was feeling more tired than he had in a long time. "No. His daughter has been kidnapped. Apparently, they were blackmailing him and using his daughter's life as a bargaining chip."

"Shall I send a message to Stockton?" asked Marceillac.

Hewes leaned forward and wrote out a small message on a slip of paper giving details of the Sakaguchi-gumi and Hirata's telephone number. He walked over to the sofa and laid the piece of paper in front of Marceillac. "These are the only details I have, but please also tell him that Hirata is planning a solo raid on Sakaguchi within the next twenty-four hours."

Chapter Fifteen

Japan (Zushi)

Crawford moved across to the printer and tore off the message from Geneva. He read through it while ambling across to the kitchen table, where Stockton and Mitchell were busy writing out all items of the case as they remembered them. "Hirata is guilty as stands," he said, holding the piece of paper out to Stockton.

Stockton read the message and passed it over to Mitchell, who read it and returned it thoughtfully to Crawford.

"Ever heard of the Sakaguchi-gumi, Tim?"

Crawford pulled up a chair and sat down. "No, but that means nothing. Organized crime is not really my favorite subject. Maybe you should ask Hiroko when she gets back." Hiroko was out shopping for food.

Mitchell yawned, stretched, and walked into the living room. He and Stockton had spent hours writing down everything they could remember, and his back ached from bending over a thick pad of paper. They had decided to write out everything separately in case one had overlooked a point of importance, and the task was beginning to lose its appeal. Mitchell himself had filled out more than thirty pages of script, and he knew that Stockton had exceeded forty pages. He hoped it was all worth it.

Mitchell picked up the telephone, jabbed in the number he had just memorized from the e-mail message, and perched himself on the edge of the desk, awaiting an answer.

Back in the kitchen, Stockton and Crawford were discussing whether it was worthwhile checking out a few databases to see if there was anything registered on the Sakaguchi-gumi when Mitchell's voice, raised in anger, interrupted them.

"You're a dead man, Hirata! I'm coming for you!"

Stockton jumped to his feet and sent his chair crashing into the sink unit. He moved swiftly around the table and rushed into the living room just as the front door opened and Hiroko, carrying two white plastic supermarket bags, walked into the apartment. She immediately noted the tension in the room and looked over to Mitchell, whose face was red with rage as he shouted down the telephone.

"Bastard! Murdering bastard! I'm gonna make you suffer so bad you'll pray for death, you son of a bitch!"

"Don, that's not going to help!" shouted Stockton, moving toward Mitchell, who glared at him with contempt.

"I don't want to hear your apologies, you little shit! Save them for your maker!"

Stockton leapt forward to grab the telephone away from Mitchell, but Mitchell was quicker. He thrust out his arm in a lightning jab, and Stockton collapsed onto the sofa, holding his chest in pain. Crawford began to edge around to the back of the desk, but Mitchell pointed at him meaningfully and clenched his hand into a threatening fist. Crawford self-consciously returned to the sofa, where Stockton was cursing under his breath and preparing himself for a second charge.

Before Stockton could launch himself, Hiroko dropped her bags and hurried across to Mitchell, placing herself between him and Stockton. "Don!" she said softly, placing a gentle hand on his arm. "Give the phone to Frank." Mitchell looked at her in amazement. She leaned forward and laid her head on his shoulder, her arms going around his neck. "Please, Don. Let Frank have the phone."

Mitchell's shoulders slumped and he reached up to stroke the back of Hiroko's neck. He removed the receiver from his ear and held it out to Stockton, muttering a soft apology as if in a daze.

Stockton accepted the phone and winked at Mitchell, rubbing his bruised chest ruefully. "Forget it, man." He hooked two fingers behind the main unit of the telephone and walked over to the sofa with it.

"Hirata? Stockton here. I'm afraid you have made our friend extremely angry. Now, this will have to be very good, or you'll have two of us on your case. Start speaking!"

Stockton listened to Hirata's toneless voice as he related his story of blackmailing and the kidnapping of his daughter. He interrupted when Hirata was outlining his plan to go in alone and rescue his daughter. "You'll never do it. You'll need backup. We can help."

"I thank you for the offer, Mr. Stockton," Hirata said, "but I must do this alone. I have caused too much trouble for other people already. I will solve this myself or die trying."

"That's stupid! At least take an army of police officers to back you up. I'm sure you can arrange that."

"I'm afraid that is impossible. The wheels of Japanese bureaucracy turn slowly. I would be obliged to obtain a search warrant and fill out countless forms in order to do as you say. Too many questions would be asked. No, it is something I must do alone."

Stockton looked across at Mitchell and Hiroko and felt a brief twinge of elation to see that things finally seemed to be working out for them. Mitchell was still sitting on the desk with his arms around Hiroko, who was standing in front of him whispering gently into his ear. Stockton caught Mitchell's eye and smiled. Mitchell managed an embarrassed grin and looked away.

"Then you must let us back you up," Stockton continued. "Don't get me wrong, Hirata. I don't give a shit if you get your head blown off, but I want you to die in atonement for your crimes. Not out of stupidity."

"I appreciate your candor, Mr. Stockton, but I am adamant. I will not place other people in danger. I am going to hang up now and switch off my telephone. I am facing death tonight—win or lose—and wish to prepare myself for it. This is the last time we will speak, and the final thing I would like to say to you is, sorry."

"Hirata . . . ?" Stockton shook the phone and listened

again. "Damn!" he said, replacing the receiver. "The bastard hung up!"

Japan (Tokyo)

Tsutomu Hirata switched off the power to his cell phone and tossed it into the wastepaper basket beside his desk before returning his attention to the sheet of paper laid before him. He reread the first paragraph and wondered if it contained the right tone. He did not want it to seem as if he was making excuses for his conduct, but he also wanted to avoid a sense of arrogance that was inherent with simply laying down the facts. Not that it really mattered. By the time the letter was read, Hirata would no longer be in existence.

That was strange. No longer in existence. It seemed impossible. How could he be here now, but not tomorrow? The concept of death was too deep to imagine, too ambiguous for comprehension. What would become of his thoughts, his memories, his talent for languages, his knowledge? Would he be allowed to keep them while he floated around in a different dimension, separated from the real world by a simple lack of perception? Would they be taken from him and passed across to an as yet unborn infant? Or would they simply disappear into thin air, like breath off a mirror?

Did it matter?

He decided to leave the first paragraph as it was.

He took a sip of green tea and looked about his office with interest—as if seeing it for the first time. He had never noticed that the top of the white walls were decorated with a pale lime-green stripe that ran around the entire room. He had never thought of his office as a room before, for that matter. It had always been a place that contained his desk and the other tools of his trade. His eyes settled on the photograph of himself, his wife, and his daughter that adorned the top of his desk. It had been taken only six months before his wife's death—a mere three years ago—and he was surprised to notice that he had aged considerably. It was like looking at a photograph of himself taken some twenty years previously.

They all looked so happy in the photograph, especially his daughter, Machiko. What had become of the proud family that had asked a passing stranger to take the photograph of them during a three-day trip to the Island of Sado? He felt the tears of self-pity prickle behind his eyes, and placed the photograph back on his desk. He would not allow himself the luxury of crying.

He picked up his fountain pen and began to write.

He wrote solidly for five hours, occasionally checking his diary to ensure accurate dates. He wrote about being approached by a man who introduced himself as Akira Matsumoto, a man who stated that he represented a conglomerate who had decided that Hirata himself should become the general director of the about-to-be-established Electronic Crime Bureau. He wrote about being flattered and seriously considering the appointment for the first time. He wrote about paying the five million yen that Matsumoto described as "running costs." And he wrote about the subsequent blackmail.

He wrote continuously without pausing for lunch or liquid refreshment. He wrote down every name, date, and event; every address, time, and place; every fact, every supposition, and every assumption.

The only thing he did not write was the fact that Jasper Hewes of the IOCC in Geneva had allowed him twenty-four hours to rescue his daughter. Some things were better not revealed.

It was past four o'clock when he finally stamped the bottom of the affidavit with his personal name seal—his *hanko*. Ensuring that the red ink from the stamp was dry, he folded the thirty-six pages, inserted them into a buff envelope, and addressed it to the director general of the National Police Agency. He placed the envelope in the top left-hand drawer of his desk.

He still had several hours to go before he intended leaving the office, so he reached into his briefcase and pulled out a handgun. He would spend the time cleaning and oiling it.

Japan (Zushi)

"Well, I disagree!" Mitchell paced the carpet in front of the open window, a look of deep thought on his face. "I say we should let the bastard get his head blown off."

Stockton sighed and took a gulp of beer from the can. "But why, Don? You were the one who wanted to snatch Hirata's head off and shit in his neck. Why the sudden change of heart?"

Mitchell stopped pacing and glared at Stockton. "Because he is worthless and he will die anyway! If this Sakaguchi doesn't get him, he'll eat the bullet himself. You told me that, for God's sake! Why should we place ourselves in danger to save his scrawny ass?"

Stockton slapped his leg in exasperation. "You pigheaded bloody yank! If Hirata gets topped, we lose our link to Sakaguchi. Can't you understand that? If you want the guy who did in Akio, then we have to make sure that Hirata's alive to testify in court. Sakaguchi is bound to have covered himself from here to kingdom come. These guys are sneaky! Hirata is not our enemy at the moment, Sakaguchi is! Oh, Jesus, what's the use?" He kicked the leg of the desk and walked out into the kitchen to get another beer.

Mitchell resumed his pacing and waited for Stockton to reemerge from the kitchen before saying, "The message from Geneva said that Hirata was going to nail Sakaguchi in a signed confession. That's good enough! Hirata is the one responsible for Akio's death. I want him dead, and there's no way I'm putting my ass on the line to save him."

Stockton threw his arms up to the ceiling, spilling some beer down his arm. "Talk is cheap, Don. What if he doesn't?"

Crawford cleared his throat. "I think Frank's got a point, Don. You're going to lose everything you've worked for. The idea of the exercise was not to put Hirata out of action, but to nail the bastards who started all this."

Mitchell turned on Crawford. "Well, after you, Tim," he said patronizingly. "Maybe you'd like to take my place. Only remember, there are going to be a lot of bad men with guns taking aim at your balls. Have you got the stomach for that? Are you willing to get your dick shot off so that a scumbag like Hirata can keep breathing?"

Crawford said nothing and looked at the floor.

"Oh, for God's sake, shut up!"

The outburst took everybody by surprise. All three

men turned their attention to Hiroko, who was sitting at the kitchen table with her head in her hands.

"Why can't you stop fighting for just a few moments? You're like kids in kindergarten, you really are!" She looked up and stared at each man in turn. "Discuss the problem and come to a decision like normal adults, please. Forget the macho stuff and just get the job done."

Stockton looked slyly across at Mitchell. He wanted to gauge Mitchell's reaction before he threw down the olive branch, but was inclined to agree with Hiroko. Confrontation was going to get them nowhere fast.

Mitchell stormed off into the kitchen, and Hiroko looked up in alarm.

They all heard the door of the refrigerator bang shut and avoided each other's eyes. Nobody had yet seen Mitchell throw a tantrum because he couldn't get his own way, but it appeared as if there was a first time for everything.

Mitchell reappeared at the door of the kitchen, four cans of beer grasped in his big hands. An embarrassed grin spread over his face, and he said, "Beam me up, Scotty!"

Stockton was the first to react. "Damn you, Mitchell, you have got the weirdest sense of humor." He began to laugh, and the others joined in. "Where did you get this sense of timing? Priceless!"

Mitchell distributed the beer, and they banged the cans together as if in celebration. Mitchell proposed the toast.

"Well, children, I apologize for being a pigheaded Yank. From here on in we have to live off our wits— except Stockton, here, who has shit for brains . . ."

Stockton booed and stamped lightly on Mitchell's foot. "Bloody useless Yank! Can't even get the words right." His face suddenly lost its smile. "Do I take it you're in?"

Mitchell clanged his half-empty can against Stockton's. "I'm in. But don't blame me if I shoot the wrong guy."

Japan (Tokyo)

The slap resounded around the wooden-floored room, and Machiko Hirata's head snapped back with the force of it. Her long black hair stuck to the perspiration that covered most of her face, but she had neither the means nor the will to brush it back. She was thankful for the slap—at least, thankful that it was not another punch. Her split lip could not take another punch. The sharp pain whenever her tooth touched the raw wound was excruciating and prevented her from slipping into welcome unconsciousness.

She knew the pig inflicting this pain upon her was enjoying every moment of it. He stood back to view his handiwork after every blow, probably simply to get a good look at her underwear. Her legs would no longer obey her mental commands to stay together, and the short skirt she wore would not conceal much.

But modesty was the last of her problems.

She heard the door open and saw the man with the scar on his face out of the corner of her eye. He walked slowly toward her with a wide grin spread over his features.

"So it seems that your father has decided that you are dispensable, my dear. I am sure you have a greater awareness of the length of your captivity than I have, but your father still fails to arrive. And you seemed to take such pains over assuring me that he was a nice man. Such a shame."

Machiko fought against the pain and sucked on the wound in her mouth. She felt the top of her tongue run with metallic-tasting blood, and spat it at the man standing before her. The glob of red spit flew from her mouth and hit him on the neck, quickly running down the inside of his shirt.

"Bitch!" he screamed, instinctively lashing out with his hand.

The blow caught her on the side of the head and stars swam before her eyes. The agony was immediately followed up by a sharp pain at the back of her head as he grabbed a handful of hair and yanked her backward until the front two legs of the chair to which she was tied no longer touched the floor.

"You have just assured yourself a painful death," he snarled, his face not twenty centimeters from hers. He wiped the spit from his neck and rubbed it roughly into her face, smearing it across her nose and cheeks. "But not yet. Your father will arrive sooner or later, and we cannot deny you the opportunity of witnessing his slow and agonizing demise first, now, can we?"

Machiko Hirata's head slumped onto her chest as Narita released her hair. He began to laugh as he walked over to the door.

"Hayashi," he said with his hand on the doorknob, addressing her torturer, "enjoy yourself, but try to keep her conscious."

With another explosive laugh, Narita left the room.

Japan (Zushi)

Crawford and Stockton were alone in the apartment, collecting together all of the evidence they had for sending to Geneva. Mitchell and Hiroko had gone shopping for some items they would require that night. It had taken Hiroko several hours to type out the transcripts of Mitchell and Stockton's reports, but the work was finally finished. Crawford created a brief index of all the material they had available and named each file in sequence. His index, which he would send in the cover note, read:

DAT_0001.TXT	Overall summary
DAT_0002.TXT	Report by Frank Stockton
DAT_0003.TXT	Report by Don Mitchell
DAT_0004.TXT	Outline of Intersystems, Inc., taken from the Teikoku Databank
DAT_0005.TXT	Original name list of suspected people involved (Taken from Suzuki's account)
DAT_0006.TXT	English translation of DAT_0005.txt
DAT_0007.TXT	Original list of suspected crimes (Taken from Suzuki's account)
DAT_0008.TXT	English translation of DAT_0007.txt

Crawford passed the eight files and the cover note across to his sending directory and also burned them onto a CD-ROM, which he handed to Stockton. He powered up the communication software and began to send each file on-line to Geneva.

Stockton inserted the disk into a plastic case and placed it in the small cardboard box beside the videotape of the raid on the house behind Kasuga Shrine. Having ensured that the contents were well padded with newspaper, he used Scotch tape to seal the box and wrote the address of the IOCC in Geneva on the top with a thick marker pen.

Japan (Zushi)

Hiroko parked the car alongside the marine sports shop and entered its cool interior together with Mitchell. The shop, located on the Shonan coastal road, catered mostly to surfers and sailors, but it also had a comprehensive selection of underwater diving gear.

The two shop assistants—both dressed in cutoff jeans and white T-shirts to show off their deep tans—allowed them to browse through the rows of equipment without hindrance. They walked to the back of the shop and began to inspect the diving gear set out on several racks. Mitchell selected two lethal-looking diving knives with black rubber scabbards. He drew one from its sheath and tested the edge. "Damn thing couldn't even cut bait," he muttered. "They'll need sharpening when we get back."

"What about this, Don?" asked Hiroko. She held up a small underwater spear gun that could be operated with one hand. It was shaped like a crossbow and was fitted to a black rubber glove that enabled it to be worn on the back of the hand. Three small bolts, about fifteen centimeters in length, protruded from holes at the back of the contraption and laid parallel to the arm, where they were both out of the way but accessible. Mitchell slipped the glove onto his right hand and cocked the rubber sling without a bolt. He pulled the trigger mechanism over the top of his wrist until it lay comfortably in his hand, took aim down the length of his arm, and pulled the lever. The solid *thwack* sound that it generated caused one of the shop assistants to look up in their direction, but he returned to his magazine when he realized they were not breaking anything.

"Cute," said Mitchell, inspecting the spear gun closely. "Wouldn't cause much damage at a distance, but perfect for close-up work."

He selected two of the spear guns and continued his search along the racks. He didn't want to be weighed down with too much equipment, but both he and Stockton knew that it would be sheer lunacy to approach Sakaguchi unarmed.

He found some flares over by the yachting equipment and added four to his small stock of goods. They were small, waterproofed canisters that ignited automatically when a small plastic tab was pulled off the top.

"We'll need some sunglasses with these flares. Do they have any?"

Hiroko glanced around the shop and located a rotary stand of sunglasses on the counter near the register. Mitchell selected two pairs of wraparound frames with rubber cords attached to allow them to be hung around the neck.

Their shopping spree complete, they paid the bill and walked back out to the car, hand in hand.

Switzerland (Geneva)

Marceillac spread the pile of printed paper out on the coffee table and sat back as Hewes flipped through it incredulously. He glanced at Sylvie, sitting next to him, and smiled. She returned the smile and squeezed his arm affectionately. At last it appeared that the fat lady was standing in the wings awaiting the start of her recital.

"But this is incredible!" Hewes said in delight. "They've got everything. Not only do we now know who did it, we know why, how, when, and with whom. This list of people here," he picked up the translation of the naming list from Suzuki's on-line account, "do we call them criminals or victims?" He chuckled to himself. "A touch of both, if you ask me, but whatever happens they will have to pay for their stupidity."

Marceillac cleared his throat. "The cover note says that the only item outstanding is a firm link with the Sakaguchi-gumi. They said they will try to sort that out within today."

"Send them a message and tell them not to bother," Hewes said, "Hirata will provide that link. That reminds me—did Stockton contact Hirata?"

"The message didn't say, sir. It was very brief and businesslike."

Hewes nodded and turned back to the paper in front of him. "Well, I'd say that we have a long night's work ahead of us. I would like to correlate all of this information into a single report to send it off to the NPA as quickly as possible. Would you two mind a bit of overtime?"

Marceillac and Keppler shook their heads.

"Good!" Hewes looked up at the clock on the wall. "I think we shall need some sustenance to see us through." He flipped open his address book and traced his finger down until it came across the Uchino Restaurant. He dialed the number and ordered three *Makunouchi Bento* boxes to be delivered to his office.

Hewes looked across at Marceillac and Keppler and said with a grin, "This might be the last time I have the stomach for Japanese food, and I don't want to waste the opportunity."

Chapter Sixteen

Japan (Tokyo)

The grounds of Sakaguchi's house were large in comparison to most houses in Tokyo, and were surrounded by a two-meter-high wall. The front gate had double doors arched over with a small tiled roof for decorative purposes. The doors stood open, revealing a gravel drive surrounded by masses of architectured trees and bushes. Plenty of cover.

Hirata checked his belt for the pistol and crept inside, immediately concealing himself behind some bushes to the right. From his hiding place he could hear the voices of the two guards who stood in front of the house. He had noticed the guards on his first dry run past the front gates, but they were relaxed and obviously not expecting trouble. He was still left with the problem of getting into the house, however, and was hoping for a slice of luck once he was inside the grounds. Very few Japanese houses had air-conditioning in every room, so he was confident of finding a door or window left open to fight against the stifling heat of summer.

Hirata moved quietly through the bushes until he reached the eastern wall and began to follow it along. The earth beneath his feet was soft composite, but he had to beware of twigs and dried leaves. He took every step with care, tentatively placing each foot gently into position before leaning his full weight onto it. Once he came up against a tree growing so close to the wall that he had to detour around it, but apart from that the going was smooth. The darkness was both a blessing and something to curse. It hid his movements from the guards, but it also prevented him from seeing where he placed his feet.

A twig crunched beneath a foot and he stopped, his breath held while he strained his ears to see if the guards had noticed. He remained in the same position for thirty seconds, but the guards continued to chat in low voices. His shirt was soaked with sweat beneath his jacket, and he swore at his stupidity in not wearing more applicable clothes. He had come straight from the office, and clothing had been the last thing on his mind.

He drew level with the front of the house and realized that he would have to brave an area of open ground where a concrete path dissected the undergrowth and ran to a small door set in the wall. The two guards were now only eight meters from his position, and there was a definite element of risk. Fortunately, the two men were not serious in their attempts at security. They merely shuffled their feet at the front door to the house and carried on a sporadic conversation. The area Hirata was in was several tones darker than the halogen-lighted driveway in which the guards kicked their feet, so the chances were they would not notice him as long as he made no jerky movements.

Hirata waited until the men were speaking and gently eased his way around the bush in which he was hiding. He wished it were a little later in the season. The crickets were making a certain amount of noise, but another week and the whole garden would be ringing with the deafening screech of cicadas. He could drive a tank through the garden without anybody hearing him then; but now he had to be content with the thin sound of crickets and the occasional tree frog. He looked across at the other side of the path. It mocked him with its very proximity.

He stood revealed at the edge of the path. If the guards looked over now, they would see him. He watched them carefully and waited until both were looking in the other direction before launching himself across the two-meter space. He made the distance remarkably well, considering his age, but he had not bargained for the opposite side of the strip of concrete being raised a few centimeters above the level of the path. The tip of his shoe landed on the raised section, but the forward momentum of his body caused it to slip off and hit the concrete with a resounding slap.

Realizing that the damage had been done, Hirata launched himself into the bushes and rolled over as he hit the soft earth. He quickly regained his feet and squeezed himself behind the trunk of a tree, reaching into his belt for his pistol.

Damn! He had really screwed up now. He heard one of the guards screaming for backup, and his narrow line of vision showed the other guard squinting into the blackness as he looked for the source of the noise. The guard slowly approached the clump of undergrowth in which Hirata was concealed, a cocked weapon held before him. Hirata raised his pistol and drew a bead on the middle of his chest. He didn't want to use the weapon, for he knew that it would not only rouse the entire house but also betray his position.

He looked over to the side of the house, not five meters away from him. Somewhere inside his daughter was being held captive. Had he ruined his only chance of rescuing her? Would he have been inside now if he had worn more suitable clothing with a pair of sneakers, instead of hard-soled walking shoes?

He could not give up so easily. His capture did not bear thinking about. He had to go on the offensive or leave his daughter to her fate. He could no longer shrink from his responsibilities. It was time to be strong.

The guard continued to close on him, but Hirata was no longer worried about detection. He returned his gun to his belt and reached into the pocket of his jacket for the stun gun he had brought along. A black wedge of plastic with two prongs leading from one end, the weapon could generate ten thousand volts of electricity between the tips of its prongs and disable any man foolish enough to place himself between them. His finger found the button to operate the device, and he brought it up to shoulder level. Then he moved a foot out and shook the bottom of a bush off to his right-hand side.

The guard stopped and peered into the darkness. He had obviously heard the noise and swiftly pointed his gun at the depths of the bush. He looked over his shoulder to see where his partner was, but the other

guard was still standing at the door to the house awaiting somebody to cover his position. The guard moved
forward a few steps.

He was now close enough for Hirata to hear his
breath wheezing in his throat. Too many cigarettes, the
humid air, and a huge chunk of stress were giving him
slight respiratory troubles. Hirata watched him approach and waited until he was within an arm's length
before placing all of his weight on his right leg and
thrusting himself out from behind the left side of the
tree, his finger pressed hard to the button of the stun
gun. The guard reacted to the movement almost immediately, but he was too late to prevent the electric charge
from coming into contact with his neck. Hirata could
hear his teeth chatter as he took the charge and shook
from head to toe, before collapsing in a heap into the
bushes.

Hirata was now committed. The noise of the guard
falling must have been heard all over the garden, so before the other guards could come running, he exchanged the stun gun for his pistol and stepped out
from behind the tree. He dashed across to the side of
the house, slamming up against it with his back, and
sidestepped his way up toward the corner. Three guards
came running together, but one stayed back so he could
monitor the bushes and the front of the house.

Hirata moved quickly. He lowered his shoulder and
charged into the first of the guards, knocking him
sprawling onto the concrete path. He then grabbed the
other around the neck before he could react. The third
guard swiftly brought his weapon up to shoulder height
in a double-handed grip, but realized immediately that
he had no target.

"Drop your weapon!" Hirata hissed into his hostage's ear. "Now!"

The man dropped his gun and raised his hands, choking on the tightness of Hirata's arm across his windpipe.

Hirata pointed the gun alternately at the man on the ground and the third guard. "You, get up!" he growled at the man who lay on the ground. "Throw your gun over here!"

The man swore under his breath and slowly got to his feet, leaving his weapon lying on the ground. He watched the barrel of Hirata's gun pointed at him and reluctantly kicked the gun over toward him.

"Now you!" Hirata swiveled the gun around to the third man and pushed his hostage away from him in the same action. The man crouched, laid his gun gently on the floor, and regained his feet with his hands above his head. "Kick it over here!" The man obliged with a soft oath.

Hirata covered all three men with his gun while he deliberately kicked each pistol deep into the undergrowth. Then he gestured with the barrel of the gun for the third man to move over toward the two other guards.

When the men were standing in a line with their backs to the wall, Hirata began to back around to the front of the house. He glanced behind himself quickly to ensure there were no other guards and, satisfied, kept his weapon trained on the three men. He backed up slowly until his foot found the step into the house. The three men followed him around at a constant distance of about four meters, each with hate and a desire for revenge displayed openly on their faces.

Hirata toyed with the idea of shooting them. The

concept tempted him dearly, but he didn't know how many other guards there were left within the house. The noise of gunfire would bring them all running. But could he afford to allow them to go and collect their weapons from the underbrush and raise the alarm the moment they were out of range of his gun sight? His revised plan called for locating his daughter and holding Sakaguchi hostage while they made their escape. His gun held only ten bullets—nine in the magazine and one preloaded into the chamber—and he didn't want to waste them on unarmed men. In either case the element of surprise would be lost, so he decided to save his bullets and backed farther into the house.

He was unprepared for the attack and screamed in agony as the metal vase crashed into his arm, snapping it cleanly in two. The gun clattered to the tiles of the *genkan* among the shoes as he collapsed onto the floor, cradling his shattered arm to his body. He had never known such pain. It streaked up his arm and burst within his head as if the attack had been on his brain, not a limb. He heard the three guards rush forward and felt hands grabbing at his feet to remove his shoes.

Hirata screamed as he was pulled roughly to his feet. He could feel the bones in his arm rubbing against each other with each tiny movement, and was only barely conscious of the fourth man, who had hidden behind the door in ambush for him.

They dragged him down a corridor, knocked on a door, and threw him unceremoniously inside. The pain flared up again, but the scream no longer seemed to come from his own mouth. He knew that shock was trying to protect him by sending him into unconsciousness, but the rough handling kept bringing him back from the edge of blissful sleep.

He felt himself lifted up into a hard-backed chair, and he nearly passed out as his hand was wrenched from his grip and tied to the arms of the chair. His head lolled involuntarily to the right, as if the angle could somehow relieve the pain, and he blinked in his misery.

"Ah, we have a visitor for you, Machiko-chan."

Hirata's head snapped up. His beloved daughter's name coming from that hated mouth made him forget his pain and take in his surroundings.

"You bastard! What have you done to her?" cried Hirata emotionally, straining at the ropes. "Oh, my God! No! No!"

Machiko Hirata sat tied to a chair two meters in front of Hirata. Her head was slumped onto her chest, but the dried blood and bruises on her face were easily visible through her sweat-drenched hair. Her white blouse and yellow skirt were spotted with drips of blood.

"You barbarian! You animal! I'll kill you for this!"

Hirata rocked in his chair and fought the ropes that constrained his body, but the pain of his arm was too much and he eventually subsided into stillness, his body racked with sobs.

"We've been waiting for you, Hirata. Glad you could finally make it."

Hirata raised his head toward the voice and saw Sakaguchi sitting cross-legged on a cushion beside a small table. He was wearing a dark gray *yukata* and sipping contentedly from a glass that contained clear liquid and ice. Narita, in shirtsleeves, sat opposite him with a similar glass. He looked over to his daughter again and saw a large man standing expressionless behind her.

"How dare you lay your filthy fingers on my daughter, you bastard! I'll kill you for this!"

"Tut tut. I hardly believe you are in a position to issue threats, Hirata. Can I get you a drink? Oh, no, maybe not. I don't think your arm could support the glass." Sakaguchi burst into loud, explosive laughter. Narita grinned and sipped on his drink.

Hirata gritted his teeth in pain and fury.

"Maybe we should wake Machiko-chan up and let her know her father is here. What do you say, Hirata?"

Hirata looked away from Sakaguchi and cursed.

Sakaguchi got to his feet and took a liter bottle of mineral water from a table at the back of the room. He unscrewed the top as he approached Hirata's daughter. "She has provided us with great amusement while we awaited your arrival, you know. She still doesn't believe that you would voluntarily become involved with people like us. Such loyalty. It becomes a man of your position to have such a daughter, Hirata. I hope you are proud."

Sakaguchi upended the bottle above her head and the water chugged out, soaking her hair and clothes. She began to stir, and her tongue thirstily lapped up the water that ran near her mouth.

"Machiko?" Hirata said softly. "Machiko?"

Her head slowly came up until she was looking at her father with confused eyes. "Father?" she whispered in a voice that sounded like gravel. "Is it you, Father?"

Hirata broke down in tears, his apologies to his daughter distorted by the sobs that prevented him from clear speech.

"Touching," said Sakaguchi, tossing the empty bottle to Narita. "And now, Hirata. Tell me. How much do the *gaijin* know?"

Hirata ignored the question and stared in disbelief at his daughter's injuries. One eye was nearly closed and already blackening, and an angry purple bruise spread out from a split and bloody lip. The rest of her face was red and swollen, and he knew that it was only a matter of time before it became a similar hue.

Sakaguchi nodded to the man standing behind Machiko. He acknowledged the nod, reached his hands around Machiko's shoulders, and ripped open her blouse. She screamed in terror as the knife came over and cut the narrow piece of material holding her bra together beneath her breasts.

"Oh, no! Oh, no! Oh, no! What are you going to do?" Hirata's voice was near hysteria as he saw his daughter's small breasts exposed to everyone in the room. He recognized the fact that he was hyperventilating but could do nothing to stop it. His voice was nearly an octave higher than normal, and he had trouble catching his breath.

Sakaguchi smiled in approval. "Must I repeat my question, Hirata?"

"No. Please stop. I'll say anything you want. Please. Cover her up. I'll do anything!"

"So tell me how much the two *keto* know."

"I don't know. Really, you must believe me. I have not been in contact with them."

Sakaguchi walked slowly over to Hirata and stood domineeringly in front of him. "I suggest you tell me, Hirata," he said. "Your daughter has already been through enough misery today. I'm sure she doesn't want to witness the death of her father, too."

Machiko gasped and struggled against her bonds, now fully awake and as feisty as ever. "Leave him alone, you bastard!" she screamed. "Don't you dare touch him!"

Sakaguchi turned around and nodded to the man standing behind her again. He walked around the chair and raised an open palm into the air.

"Stop!" shouted Hirata, but his voice was cut off by the sound of a loud slap. Machiko's head jerked to one side, but she was determined not to show any weakness. She gritted her teeth, shook her hair from her eyes, and looked defiantly back at her tormentor.

Hirata physically jumped at the sound of the slap, letting out a grunt of pain as his broken arm met the resistance of the rope confining him to his chair. He screwed his eyes shut in pain, and when he opened them again, Sakaguchi's face was just inches from his own.

"Would it interest you to know, Hirata, that the moment you are dead you will be followed into hell by your loving daughter here?"

Hirata shook his head from side to side. "Please, please, please," he said, his voice lower now. "You must let her go. She has done nothing. Kill me if you must, but please let her go. . . ."

"And what purpose would that serve? No, I don't think so. It was your betrayal that resulted in her being here. Surely you don't think that we can just let her leave and go to the authorities, now, do you?"

"But she knows nothing."

"That's where you are wrong, Hirata. She knows too much. She must die."

"No, please . . ."

"But that needn't concern you too much. You won't be around to see it. So I'll ask my question once again: How much do the *gaijin* know?"

"I told you, I don't know—"

Sakaguchi raised a fist and brought it down heavily on Hirata's arm. Hirata screamed as the pain visited every nerve end in his body. Tears flowed from his eyes and dripped from his chin. Somewhere in the midst of his misery his brain registered his daughter's voice shouting expletives. The voice brought him back to his senses, and he turned his eyes up to Sakaguchi. "I was not in contact with the *gaijin*," he croaked, his throat raw from screaming. "I was set up by Geneva. I had no idea what was going on—"

"Wrong answer!"

Sakaguchi's clenched fist landed forcibly on his broken arm once again. Hirata's scream echoed around the room, competing against his daughters shouts of fury, until it subsided into an unearthly moan. He could feel himself slipping into unconsciousness but tried valiantly to fight against it. He had to stay awake. His daughter's life depended on it. But the pain had affected him so greatly that his brain was attempting to shut down his faculty for comprehension. Gentle groans of misery emitted from his throat, fascinating him as they echoed around in his head. He tried to concentrate on the noise, mesmerized by the comforting vibration it set up within him. The cold liquid splashed into his face shocked him back to reality, and he looked up into Sakaguchi's cruel eyes. He tried to make sense of the words coming from Sakaguchi's mouth and had to shake his head to clear it.

". . . have many more bones in your body that we can work on. Are you ready to answer my questions yet?"

Hirata blinked away the final cobwebs of mugginess and nodded his head slowly.

"Fine. Now, how much do the *gaijin* know?"

"I . . . I have not been in contact with them . . . so do not know exactly. . . . But . . . " he added hurriedly as Sakaguchi raised his fist again, ". . . Geneva knows about my involvement and must have informed them." Hirata's head lolled against his chest and his words faltered. Sakaguchi placed his head closer to hear them.

"And what about the false address in Yokohama? Why did you set us up for that?"

"I did not know. Geneva fooled me."

Sakaguchi sighed deeply and returned to his cushion, shaking his head sadly. Narita poured him another drink to replace the one he had thrown in Hirata's face.

"I'm sorry, Hirata, but I find that difficult to believe. You must have been working for them all along. How else could they have gotten the information?" He took a sip of his drink. "It is sad that your daughter must bear witness to this, but you have brought it on yourself." He looked across to the torturer and nodded his head toward Hirata.

The man withdrew a knife from his belt, tested the edge with grim satisfaction, and walked across to Hirata's chair.

Machiko lashed against her bonds, trying to release a foot that would trip the monster before he moved out of range. "Leave him alone! Please, oh please, leave him alone," she cried, her voice trailing off to racking sobs.

Gripping the wrist of Hirata's broken arm, the torturer laid his hand out along the arm of the chair and placed the knife over the little finger before looking up to Sakaguchi for further instructions.

"Nooooo!" screamed Hirata. "It's true. I give you my word! Please, you must believe me."

Sakaguchi looked across at Machiko, her body shaking in fear and rage. "I'm very sorry you have to see this, my dear. But don't worry yourself too much. Dead men don't need fingers."

He looked back to the torturer and nodded his head.

Chapter Seventeen

Japan (Tokyo)

Stockton walked quickly back along the street and climbed into the Pajero. "Damn!" he said when the door was closed. "They've got Hirata. Now we've got two people to rescue."

"Yeah," Mitchell said from the backseat. "Just as long as you know where my priorities lie."

"Maybe we should just call the police," suggested Hiroko, her hands resting on the steering wheel. "It's just too dangerous."

"It's tempting, but the sirens would simply alert Sakaguchi and give him a chance to escape. No, we'll have to go in. Are you okay with that, Don?"

Mitchell grunted agreement, and they began to work out their plan of attack. Hiroko's role was to wait until Stockton and Mitchell got into position on the outside of the east wall, throw two ignited flares over the wall at five-second intervals, and then drive like crazy until she was at least six blocks away. She would then wait until receiving a phone call. If no call was received within thirty minutes, she was to phone the police.

Stockton and Mitchell were dressed in dark clothing with rubber-soled training shoes, and both had the sharpened camping knives strapped to their belts. Hiroko started the engine of the car and slowly pulled off to circle the block, while Stockton and Mitchell pulled the glove parts of the spear guns over their right hands and hung the sunglasses over their necks with the rubber cords.

"Just in case," Stockton said, holding up the two remaining flares. Mitchell grabbed one and pushed it into the pocket of his trousers.

Hiroko stopped the car before they had circled around to the position where Stockton and Mitchell were to get out. Stockton looked across at her in surprise. She swung around in her seat until she could look both men in the face, and Stockton noticed the dampness in her eyes. "You have to come back," she said quietly, a small catch in her throat. "You know that, don't you? You must come back."

Mitchell stretched his arm over the seat and took Hiroko's hand. He squeezed gently and said, "We'll be back, Hiroko. You ain't getting rid of me that easily. I promise."

She nodded unhappily and craned her neck over to receive Mitchell's kiss.

Stockton turned to the front and began to mutter to hide his embarrassment. "Bloody typical! Why is it that the sodding Yanks always get the girl? Here I am, a fine, upstanding Englishman who is at least fifty times more handsome than the Yank, and what happens? The bloody Yank walks off with the girl. . . ."

A wet noise coming from behind Stockton's head signaled the end of the kiss. "Eat your heart out, limey!" Mitchell said, chuckling.

Hiroko leaned over and planted a kiss on Stockton's cheek. "And one for you, too," she said. Before Stockton could complain about the size of his kiss in comparison to Mitchell's, she put the car in gear and moved off.

She pulled over a few minutes later, and both men jumped out with a final promise to see her soon. She drove around to the front of the garden brushing tears from her cheeks.

The first flare caught the guards by surprise. The three guards who had been held up at gunpoint by Hirata were laughing at the discomfort of the fourth guard, who had been hit with the electric charge and was now sitting on the wooden steps that led up to the house rubbing the back of his neck, when the bright orange flare sailed across the wall and landed about ten meters in front of them. Their hands went instinctively for their guns, but they stared at the sizzling flare long enough to completely ruin their night vision. They consequently failed to see two strange figures wearing wraparound sunglasses jump over the wall by the side of the house and crouch down behind a bush.

The second flare sparked them into action. It landed a few meters closer to the men, and they scattered to take up positions at equal distances apart to protect the front of the house from attack. One of the men shouted through the front door for backup. The sound of tires screeching as they tried to gain a grip on the asphalt outside of the main gate caused two of the men to run up the length of the garden and out into the street. They just managed to catch sight of a four-wheel-drive vehicle speeding around the corner out of sight, but the effects of the flares made it impossible for them to discern the color, make, or registration number of the vehicle.

Stockton and Mitchell waited until the second flare landed before rushing across to the shadow of the house. They waited for a moment to make sure they had not been seen, then began to work their way along the side of the house looking for an open window or door.

There were several windows along the length of the house, but all were closed. Near the rear of the house they came across the only open window, but it was too far off the ground and had bars across it. Stockton mouthed "Kitchen" to Mitchell and gestured for him to go around the back of the house. Luck smiled on them halfway along.

The sound of a television alerted them to the proximity of an open window, and they grinned at each other in the dark as they noticed that it was a French window with three steps leading up into the house. Stockton held a finger to his lips and they crept silently up to it. The sliding door was completely open but covered with an *amido*—a mosquito net to keep the creatures of the night outside where they belonged. The curtains were closed and shifted slightly in the light breeze. Mitchell moved across to the far side of the steps and crouched down beside them. Then he pointed to the spear gun on Stockton's wrist and indicated that he was going to open the mosquito net.

Stockton withdrew a bolt from the back of the crossbow and cocked the mechanism. Then he moved back slightly and knelt on one knee directly in front of the door, his right arm steadied on a location that he hoped would be just below head height. They had decided to go for throat shots with the spear guns, as they had no intention of taking prisoners. Mitchell slipped his knife from its scabbard and held it poised in case Stockton missed his mark. Stockton would have no time to reload, and he wanted to be ready.

Stockton nodded at Mitchell, who began to apply pressure to the mosquito net. An eerie scraping sound was emitted as the frame slid reluctantly along its rails. Mitchell kept his eye on the curtain, awaiting the slightest of movements. He heard a sound from inside, and the noise of the television was cut off. He continued with the pressure, eliciting a curse from inside, and heard soft footsteps approaching.

The moment the fingers curled around the edge of the curtain, Mitchell put all of his weight into opening the mosquito net and wrenched it all of the way back to allow Stockton an unhindered shot. The noise of this and the sight of Stockton crouching directly in front of him caused the man to jump when he opened the curtain, but before his surprise could be formed into words, Stockton's bolt slapped into his throat and he disappeared from sight with a muffled gurgle. Mitchell was on his feet before the man fell, and rushed into the room with his knife held before him. He rolled over to avoid any bullets that would presumably be aimed at body level, and came up onto one knee with his knife ready to throw.

Apart from the man lying prone on the floor, the room was empty.

Stockton's head appeared in the open window, and Mitchell nodded the all clear. He entered and crouched over the man lying on the floor, where Mitchell joined him.

"Nice shooting," whispered Mitchell. The bolt had embedded itself deeply into the throat, with only about five centimeters protruding. A thin line of blood ran down the left-hand side of the man's neck. His fingers were still jerking in their death throes, and a few bubbles leaked from the entry point of the bolt.

Stockton looked around the room. It was obviously used as a recreation room by Sakaguchi's henchmen and contained a sofa set in front of a television, a dining table with eight chairs, a drinks cabinet containing numerous bottles of spirits, a refrigerator, and a bookcase that overflowed with pornographic magazines and videotapes.

"Shall we stick him outside?" asked Stockton. There was no place in the room capable of concealing a full-grown man. Mitchell nodded, and they took hold of an arm and a leg each.

The bubbles had finally stopped escaping from the wound when they dropped the man in the shadows of the house and returned to the room. They closed the curtains—leaving the mosquito net open in case they needed to make a hurried departure—and moved over to the door. Mitchell gently opened the door and looked out into a deserted corridor. Motioning Stockton to remain where he was, he softly padded down the corridor to the left and peered cautiously around the corner. Then he tiptoed back and continued past Stockton's location to the other corner. A moment later, he was back in the room with the door closed.

"It seems as if this corridor runs around a block of four rooms in the central part of the house," he said quietly, his heart pounding in his chest. "The left-hand side is deserted, but there is a single guard standing outside a room on the right-hand side. It is my guess that Hirata is being held in that room." Stockton nodded and began to construct a mental picture of the house within his mind. "There is also a staircase that runs up to the second floor down on the right-hand side. Shall we clean house from top to bottom?"

They had no idea of exactly how many guards were within the house, so they had decided to work their way through the entire premises, eliminating as many people as possible before trying to find Hirata and his daughter. They slipped quietly out of the room and moved along the corridor to the staircase. The stairs were partly visible to the guard standing outside the room, but by pressing themselves to the rail on the right, they managed to gain the upper floor without being seen.

The decorations on the second floor were less luxurious than those on the first floor, leading the men to believe that it contained the guards' bedrooms. The door to each room was made of cheap wood and contained a small frosted-glass window set in the center. From where they stood, a light was apparent in only one of the rooms.

Stockton pointed to the door and Mitchell nodded. They moved forward silently and took up positions on either side of it. Mitchell placed his ear close to the door, but shook his head when he failed to hear any noise. Shrugging, he took hold of the doorknob and turned it slowly. A slight click was heard as the lock disengaged, and Mitchell threw the door open and rushed inside, Stockton in his wake.

The man lay on his bed in a single pair of boxer shorts. He dropped his magazine and rolled off onto the floor in a fluid motion, his hand scrabbling for a heavy flashlight standing on the cabinet beside his bed to use as a weapon. Mitchell pounced on him before he could get a firm grip on it, and forced him flat onto the floor with a hand clamped tightly across his mouth. The man wriggled like an eel, and Mitchell cursed when a knee hit him soundly in the back of the head. Stockton rushed over and grabbed the man's legs to stop them from banging on the floor and raising the alarm, although Mitchell thought the action was to prevent him from being kicked and mumbled a quick "Thanks."

The man's skinny body was no match for the weight of Mitchell, and a moment later he was pinned down, squirming fruitlessly against the American's superior strength. The man's eyes opened wide when he saw the camping knife raised above him and tensed his body for the unavoidable blow, as if muscle alone could deflect the point of the instrument. Mitchell drove the knife deep into the man's chest and moved it backward and forward to inflict as much damage on the heart as possible before pulling it out again. Blood flooded from the wound and spurted up over Mitchell's face and shirt as the heart frantically tried to ignore the injury and continued pumping. Mitchell maintained the pressure on the man's mouth as the strength of the blood being pumped uselessly outside of the body began to diminish. He stayed in that position until the blood flow trickled away to nothing and the man's eyes glazed over, the figure of a fury-crazed *gaijin* imprinted on his retina.

Mitchell felt slightly nauseous but reminded himself of Akio. He had never killed a man as viciously before, and was not proud of the act, but how much mercy had scum like this shown Murata? Or Hisamitsu, for that matter? He felt Stockton lay a hand on his shoulder and snapped back to reality. He took one last look at the death mask before him, smiled grimly at Stockton, and got to his feet. Stockton grabbed the man's legs and swung them under the metal-framed bed. Then he pushed the upper torso until the whole body was concealed from sight. They switched the light off as they left the room.

They slowly checked each room on the second level, but found no other people. Stockton checked his watch and realized that nearly fifteen minutes had passed since Hiroko had dropped them off. They would never make the thirty-minute deadline. They ducked into a vacant room and quickly telephoned her to extend their time by an additional thirty minutes, assuring her that things were moving according to plan.

The guard was still on duty outside of the room on the first floor as they crept down the stairs and turned left along the corridor. They circled the central block of rooms until they arrived at the main entrance, and came across two more guards in the front hall, one seated beside a huge glass display case that contained an antique hand-carved figure of a Buddha, and the other leaning against a wall with his hands in his pockets.

Stockton tapped Mitchell on the shoulder and gestured for him to back up. He gently opened the door of the first room he came to and slipped inside with his knife held before him. Mitchell followed him in. It was dark in the room, but the slice of light from the corridor shining through the centimeter-wide crack in the door enabled Mitchell to make out Stockton's features.

"They are too far away," said Stockton in a hoarse whisper. "The bolts could go in any direction from that distance. We have to lure them closer."

"We could rush them with the knives."

"That might give them the chance to raise the alarm. We have to take them out silently."

Mitchell nodded. They hastily worked out a rough plan, and Stockton palmed a small glass ashtray from a table in the room. They loaded their spear guns and crouched in position. Stockton opened the door a little wider and sent the ashtray skidding along the corridor like a hockey puck.

The scraping noise caused both guards to look over toward the ashtray. The one seated jumped to his feet and swiftly pulled a gun from the holster in his belt. They cautiously moved toward the ashtray and peered myopically along the corridor. The scratching noise caught their attention immediately, and they looked at each other and shrugged. They were both still jumpy from the flare incident, but burglars did not advertise their presence by rolling ashtrays along corridors and then scratching the woodwork. There must be a reasonable explanation. The noise was coming from the *oyabun*'s office. He had probably kicked the ashtray outside in a flash of temper. Such occurrences were not unknown. The men replaced their guns in their holsters and walked up to the door. Their boss would not take kindly to having guns pointed at him, but they thought it prudent to check out the source of the noise anyway.

Mitchell and Stockton tensed as a gentle knock came at the door. Mitchell was crouched on the floor to the left of the door and Stockton was standing beside the doorjamb. Mitchell scratched his knife along the wooden floorboards once more.

The door was pushed open slightly, and a voice said, *"Oyabun?"* It opened a little wider, and Mitchell released the bolt. The *thwack* sounded loud in the silence. Stockton swiftly leaned around the door and grabbed the man by the arm before he could topple backward and pulled him into the room, where he collapsed in a heap at Mitchell's feet. In the same movement, he reached out for the second man's shirtfront and tugged as hard as he could. He both heard and felt the material rip, but the momentum was enough to bring the man stumbling into the room, where he tripped over his dead colleague and went sprawling onto the floor. Stockton was on him immediately. He grabbed an arm and spun him over so that he was facing the ceiling, then put the full weight of his body behind his knee and landed heavily on the man's chest, snapping at least one rib. The breath rushed out of the man, but his valiant efforts at drawing the next breath were foiled by Stockton's hand clamping over his mouth and nose. The knife flashed in the semidarkness, and Stockton felt, rather than saw, the warm blood spurting all over him from the fatal throat wound. A bubbling, hissing noise emitted from the man's throat as he struggled frantically to feed his lungs with the air they craved. Stockton closed his eyes and hung on tightly, as if riding a horse. The body began to convulse violently, and Stockton distributed his weight more evenly to restrict its movements.

It took more than four minutes before the body was completely still, but it seemed like an hour to Stockton. He was exhausted, both mentally and physically, when he finally got to his feet and received a reassuring slap on the back from Mitchell. He began to fantasize on a cool shower and a schooner of iced beer, but forced the image out of his mind as Mitchell peeped warily through the crack in the door. Four down, and God knows how many to go. He had to keep his concentration. His life, and Mitchell's life, depended on it.

They searched the rooms on the eastern side of the house but discovered no more guards. They calculated that another three—possibly four—guards remained outside, but they did not want to risk any more confrontations than were necessary. That left the guard standing outside the room on the western side.

They split up and moved quietly in opposite directions along the corridor, Mitchell going around the front of the house and Stockton around the back. Mitchell peered around the corner and waited until he spotted Stockton looking around the far corner before stepping out into full view and walking along the corridor with a big grin on his face.

The guard caught a movement out of the corner of his eye and turned toward it. His mouth dropped open in amazement as Mitchell waved at him genially and continued to walk toward him. The guard blinked to clear his head, but there was no doubt about it. A huge *gaijin*—smeared from head to foot in blood with a pair of fluorescent sunglasses suspended around his neck on a bright yellow cord and a strange contraption strapped to his wrist—was greeting him as if they were long-lost friends. His hand moved to the holster at his side, but before it got there his head exploded in pain and smashed with a sickening thud against the door he was guarding.

Stockton was proud of his flying kick. He had studied the martial art of *Shorinji Kenpo* in his youth, but had not had the chance—nor the necessity—to use it in years. No doubt his sensei would have scolded him for bad form, but you could not argue with results. His foot had caught the guard squarely on the ear, snapping his head over and smashing it into the door. He looked down at his victim and decided that the angle of the snapped neck meant he would not have to use his knife for the coup de grâce.

He looked across at Mitchell, who nodded his head in grudging approval.

Chapter Eighteen

Japan (Tokyo)

"Go and see what that was, Narita." The crash on the door had startled Sakaguchi. The room was soundproofed, but the bang had been audible to everyone.

Narita got to his feet and walked over to the door. He placed an eye to the spy hole drilled in the door but could see nothing but the far wall of the corridor. Shrugging, he turned the knob and swung the door open.

The bolt hit him under the chin, penetrated his lower jaw and tongue, and came to rest embedded in the roof of his mouth. He screamed in agony as a large foot hit him in the chest and sent him staggering back into the room, where he slid to the floor with his hands scrabbling at his face.

Sakaguchi watched in amazement as the two *gaijin* charged into the room like gruesome blood-drenched barbarians of a past age, each roaring and waving lethal-looking knives before them. He reached around to get the gun concealed in the folds of his *obi* just as the torturer launched himself at the two men with a shouted curse.

Stockton sensed that there were several people in the room, but had no time to take a head count. A large man with a bloodstained knife in his hand came running at him like an express train, and he had to skip nimbly out of the way to avoid getting stuck on its point. Mitchell grabbed the man's hand and brought his knee forcibly up into his stomach. He hardly flinched. He was a man of great strength, and his fury was pushing him to even greater limits of power. He shook Mitchell off like a Labrador ridding itself of fleas, and brought the point of the knife up to chest level.

Mitchell managed to avoid the first thrust, but Stockton realized that he was going to have to fell this man immediately. He was not going to lie still for five minutes while he asphyxiated over a slit throat, and as long as he had that blade in his hand, he would be intent on taking both Mitchell and Stockton into the realms of hell with him. The second thrust jagged on Mitchell's shirt but failed to penetrate his flesh. Stockton moved fast. He stepped around until he was standing almost next to the man, and brought his knife around in a wide arc until it smashed into his face, finding little resistance as it forced its way through his eye and into the brain beyond. A mixture of ocular fluid and blood burst from the wound and sprayed over Stockton's hand, making him release the knife handle in disgust. The man collapsed in a heap on the ground, twitching spasmodically.

The shot rang loudly throughout the room, and before Stockton could react, Mitchell slumped down onto one knee and then toppled over onto the ground with his hand clamped to his left side. Torn between rushing to his friend's aid and tackling Sakaguchi, the owner of the gun, Stockton's mind was made up for him as another shot cracked out and a projectile whistled by his ear. He jumped over the prone body of the torturer and came in low just as Sakaguchi was taking aim for a third shot. Stockton swung his hand up and hit Sakaguchi's hand a fraction of a second before he pulled the trigger, and the shot buried itself harmlessly in the ceiling. He grabbed hold of the hand holding the gun and brought it down with all his strength on the edge of the table. The gun skidded away and came to a halt beside the torturer's leg.

Mitchell saw the gun sliding toward him and forced himself to ignore the pain in his side while he reached out for it. The sound of the reports had alerted the guards in the garden, and he could hear the sound of running footsteps nearing the room. He had to reach the gun. There was no way he and Stockton could hold out against three armed guards in their present position. His side felt as if it were about to explode with pain when his finger brushed the edge of the trigger guard. A little extra exertion and he managed to hook a finger inside it. He had to rush—the footsteps were getting closer. He wriggled over until he was lying on his front and held the gun out before him in a two-handed grip, awaiting the arrival of the guards.

The guards, obviously not expecting an ambush, ran into the opening of the door, and Mitchell squeezed off a shot. The guard at the front crumpled in a heap on the floor, but the other two, realizing just how exposed they were, dived out of range behind the door. Mitchell scrabbled across the floor and just caught sight of them disappearing around the side of the corner by the staircase that led up to the second floor. A shot rang out and a bullet embedded itself in the wood one meter above Mitchell's head with a sharp thunk.

Mitchell pulled his head back inside the door and fumbled in his pocket for the flare. He ripped the plastic igniter off the top and threw the flare out into the passage in the direction of the two guards. Another bullet careened off the side of the wall, and Mitchell made a loud groaning sound as if he had been hit. He pulled on his sunglasses and edged toward the door, where he watched the writhing smoke stretch its fingers out in all directions. One area of the smoke began to get darker, and Mitchell took aim with the gun. The shadow danced and jigged with the movement of the smoke, but steadily began to take on human form. Mitchell pulled the trigger, and the shadow fell to the ground with a scream. Only one left.

Sakaguchi had more strength than Stockton would have credited him with. Stockton was on top of Sakaguchi, but both of his wrists were being held in viselike grips, preventing him from exploiting his advantage. They rolled about the floor, Sakaguchi exerting all of his energy to push Stockton off him, and Stockton straining to remain in position. The gunfire behind him had Stockton's back cringing in anticipation of a bullet. He had no idea who had possession of the gun, but he fervently prayed that it was Mitchell. The fact that he had not yet been shot seemed to back up the idea that his prayers had been answered, but he wanted to get back to Mitchell as quickly as possible and see how bad his friend's wound was.

"Over here! Guide him over here."

Stockton looked up at the voice and saw Hirata tied to a chair not one meter away, his face thin with heavy black clouds under his eyes. He had noticed the two people tied to chairs when he charged into the room, but had not had time to take in details. Hirata began to rock his chair backward and forward, and Stockton got the idea.

He lunged down with his forehead and head-butted Sakaguchi on the bridge of the nose. Sakaguchi grunted in pain but did not release his hold on Stockton's wrists. Stockton butted him again, this time connecting with his teeth. Sakaguchi's face streamed blood, but his grip remained as strong as ever. Stockton stretched out a leg and managed to find the edge of the table with his foot. He gathered his strength and pushed off as hard as he could. Both he and Sakaguchi moved about sixty centimeters closer to Hirata's chair.

Hirata mentally measured the distance and decided that the back of the chair would connect with Sakaguchi's head perfectly. He began to put more power into the rocking, until the chair teetered on the edge of its balance.

Sakaguchi saw what was happening and swore through his broken mouth. Stockton raised his head as far back as he could without allowing Sakaguchi to wriggle away and waited for the chair to fall.

The chair finally exceeded the limit that gravity was able to hold it upright and slowly toppled over. Sakaguchi screamed as Hirata's bulk loomed over him, and began to struggle wildly. The wooden chair hit him on the side of the forehead with a clunk, and Sakaguchi stopped struggling. Stockton didn't even bother to check if he was alive or dead. He muttered a quick "Thanks" to Hirata and rushed over to Mitchell, who was lying on his belly with the gun held before him in both hands, aiming out into the corridor.

Stockton crouched beside him and searched for a bullet hole. "Don, where are you hit? Is it bad?"

Mitchell looked up and caught sight of Stockton's sweat-stained, mussed hair and blood-smeared face. "Jeez, you look like shit," he said with a giggle. "That's why you never get the girls, limey. You gotta take care of appearances."

"You're no centerfold yourself, you ugly bastard. Where are you hit?"

"Just a scratch on the side, I think. It hurts like hell, but not too serious, as far as I can make out. Did you get all the baddies?"

"Yeah. You?"

"There's one left outside, but he's gone to ground and won't show his ass."

"I'll get the bastard."

Stockton stood up and began to survey the area for a weapon. He saw a pistol sticking out from underneath a guard who was lying in a pool of blood just outside of the door, and leaned over to get it. "You keep him covered from here. I'll go round the back way."

Stockton stepped out the door and sprinted down the corridor, the smoke from the flare swirling around him like a vortex. He ran past the front entrance and turned left up the eastern corridor, slowing down only when he got to the corner. He peered slowly around it and could make out the figure of the last guard crouching down by the side of the staircase, his gun pointing down the corridor toward Mitchell.

The distance of twenty meters would more or less guarantee a miss from the short-barreled pistol, so Stockton decided to brave exposure and hope the guard didn't notice him until he was closer. He held the gun before him and stepped out into the corridor, feeling ridiculously like a cowboy walking toward a showdown at high noon. He aimed the gun at the chest of the guard and slowly walked toward him.

He was ten meters from the guard when his presence was detected. Unfortunately for the guard, he had threaded his arms through the banisters of the staircase to add stability to his aim and was unable to untangle himself to get off a shot. Stockton swiftly recognized his advantage and ran the next few meters. He began to fire. Only three of the five bullets hit the guard, but he was dead when Stockton reached him.

"Everything okay?" Mitchell's voice pierced through the smoke, heavy with anxiety.

"Fine," Stockton shouted back. He walked over to the burnt-out flare and began to stamp out the small flames that were tentatively leaping from the wooden floorboards. The fire extinguished, he walked over to the room and was able to take in detail for the first time.

Mitchell was on his feet pointing a gun at Sakaguchi, who had regained consciousness and was sitting groggily against a wall with his legs splayed out before him, his face a mass of contusions and drying blood. Stockton avoided looking at the horrendous sight of the man with the knife handle protruding from his eye, and cast his glance over to the other of Sakaguchi's henchmen, who was moaning steadily on the floor with his eyes wide open. The man's face had drained of color and his irises were small pinpricks as he went into deep shock, the black bolt buried in his chin looking strangely out of place against a background of white flesh.

"My daughter. Please help her. She must have medical attention." Stockton looked over to Hirata and felt a surge of pity for the man. He was no longer the confident boss of a governmental bureau, issuing orders with supreme authority. He was a broken man, pathetically lying on his side tied to a chair and pleading for attention with tears in his eyes.

"You got your knife, Don?"

Mitchell handed him the knife without taking his eyes off Sakaguchi, and Stockton cut Hirata's ropes. With a shock, he realized that the small finger on Hirata's right hand ended in a bloody stump one centimeter above the knuckle.

The moment he was free, Hirata hurried across to his daughter's side and placed his good arm around her shoulder, grimacing at his own pain and the pain of his daughter. "What have they done to you? Oh, what have they done to you?" he repeated in Japanese, the tears running freely down his face.

"Oh, Father," she sobbed, leaning her face against his shoulder, "They hurt you so badly. Why did they do this to you? Why do they hate you so much?"

Stockton walked around the back of Machiko's chair and cut her ropes. The tingling sensation as the circulation returned to her hands made her whimper as she wrapped both arms around her father's neck. Stockton crouched in front of her and caught sight of her face for the first time. "My God!" he exclaimed in shock. "The bastards! Don. Take a look at this."

Mitchell backpedaled until he was level with Stockton and glanced down at Hirata's daughter. His eyes flew open as he saw her bruised face and split lip, and when he caught sight of her exposed breasts, fury flashed in his eyes. He grabbed Hirata by his good arm and tugged him to his feet, raising the gun until it was pointing at his chest. "You are the cause of this, you son of a bitch!"

"No!" shouted Machiko, but Stockton placed a hand on her shoulder and raised a finger to his lips. Her English was not good enough to understand the words being spoken, but Mitchell's body language spoke louder than words. She looked plaintively at Stockton, and he smiled at her. "Don't worry," he whispered. "Everything will be all right."

Hirata faced Mitchell defiantly, his good hand cradling his shattered arm. "I accept the punishment. You may shoot me, but please take my jacket first to cover my daughter. And then promise me you will get her to a hospital."

"Don," said Stockton softly, "this girl has been through enough. Let the courts decide his punishment."

Mitchell said nothing, but the gun did not waver.

"We have to get her to a doctor, Don. And you too, for that matter," Stockton pleaded. "We don't have time for retribution."

"Damn!" shouted Mitchell. "Damn! Damn! Damn!" He lowered the gun and gestured for Hirata to remove his jacket, his anger and frustration apparent in his contorted face.

Stockton pulled his cell phone from his pocket and phoned Hiroko.

"It's Frank. Bring the car round to the front of the house. It's all over, but we have a girl we must get to the hospital. Phone the police and tell them they will find the director general of the Electronic Crime Bureau at this address, standing guard over the leader of the Sakaguchi-gumi. Tell them to hurry and to bring a dozen body bags. Yes, we really are fine. Don, too."

"I guess you'll need this." Mitchell reversed the gun and held it by the barrel. He passed it across to Hirata, who stared at it in amazement. "Well, go on, then. Take it before I change my mind." Hirata reached out his good hand and accepted the pistol.

Stockton draped Hirata's jacket over Machiko's shoulders and whispered words of encouragement in her ear. He looked up at Hirata. "She'll be fine. Don't worry. It looks a lot worse than it is."

Hirata cleared his throat. "I thank you both. I am sure you don't wish to hear my apologies, but at least accept my gratitude. If it were not for you, my daughter would probably have been . . ." His words faded out to nothingness.

Mitchell took the last bolt from the rear of his spear gun and loaded it into the breech. Stockton glanced up at him suspiciously, but Mitchell avoided his eyes.

"Hirata, you are a goddamn bastard, and I hope you rot in hell."

Hirata's eyes flickered apprehensively between the miniature crossbow and Mitchell's face. He felt the weight of the gun in his hand but made no attempt to raise it.

"But you now have a job to do, and I want to make sure you do it properly," continued Mitchell. "When the police arrive, I want you to tell them everything.

Can you do that? I don't want to hear about you holding anything back to save your own sonavabitching ass. Do I make myself clear?"

Hirata nodded.

"Your first job is to hold on to this slime bag until the cops get here. Are you capable of that?"

Hirata nodded again. Sakaguchi looked wearily up from the floor and sneered at the men. He did not know what they were saying, but it obviously concerned him.

"You don't think he looks a little too perky? I mean, if he suddenly jumped you, do you think you could fight him off with one cranky arm?"

A smile appeared on Stockton's face. He had caught the drift of Mitchell's monologue. Hirata looked at Mitchell in confusion.

"Well, I think you might need a little help to keep him sitting on the floor there. Now, what could we use? Ropes maybe? What about a few staples? Do you have any staples, Frank?"

Frank went through the charade of searching his pockets. "Not a one, Don."

"Well, what have we here?" Mitchell looked at the spear gun as if seeing it for the first time. "I wonder if this would be of any use?"

His face suddenly grim, Mitchell took swift aim at Sakaguchi's groin and pulled the trigger.

The bolt passed through the edge of Sakaguchi's penis, chipped a lump of flesh from his groin, and completely penetrated his scrotum before thudding to a halt deep within the wooden floor. Sakaguchi screamed in shocked agony, his face screwed up like a newborn baby's.

"Now, that's better," said Mitchell conversationally. "Riveted to his seat, you might say."

Without looking back, Mitchell and Stockton helped Machiko to her feet and led her from the room.

Chapter Nineteen

Japan (Tokyo)

At twenty-three minutes past nine o'clock in the morning, a coach containing twenty-six policemen and six plainclothed detectives pulled up in front of Intersystems, Inc. Three patrol cars parked immediately behind it, and within moments the entrance to the gray building had been secured to prevent people leaving or entering.

Masashi Yanagida's heart nearly stopped beating when the front door opened and a middle-aged policeman dressed in riot gear shouted for everybody to stop working and replace telephones. The room began to fill up with policemen, and he abandoned his idea of sneaking away to the elevators.

A plainclothed detective pushed through the policemen and began to walk toward the elevator bank with determination. Other detectives followed. Yanagida saw one policeman open the metal door to the telephone distribution board and flick a breaker switch. He felt a small sense of relief. He was obliged to warn his boss of the impending raid, but that was now impossible. He wanted to do as little as possible to attract attention to himself.

His staff was goggle-eyed at the raid, looking around with open mouths and exclamations of outrage. He heard a few of the more senior staff demand the meaning of this, but nobody was listening. One of his salesmen leapt a full twenty centimeters out of his seat when a policeman slammed his riot stick on his desk for being slow in hanging up the phone. It would have been comical had he not suddenly discovered an urgent need to visit the toilet.

Inspector Saburo Kawaguchi, the detective in charge of the raid, made his way up to the third floor with five policemen in tow. The arrest of Osamu Tokoro took a mere three minutes, and the remainder of the staff on the third floor was herded down to the first floor, with the exception of two secretaries who were to be present when the search for incriminating evidence was started. Japanese law demands that a third person be present when searches are carried out in the capacity of "*tachi-ai*."

Having completed his duties on the third floor, Inspector Kawaguchi moved down to the second floor, where ten policemen were trying to induce the occupants of the locked room to open up. Two policewomen stood off to one side. They had gained access to the inner cubicle with the use of a security card taken from a manager, but the second door could only be opened from within. Kawaguchi threaded himself past his men and peered through the window into the room. People were frantically rushing around moving documents off their desks to more neutral areas, and two women were stuffing papers into a pair of shredding machines off to the right.

"Break it down," Kawaguchi said.

Two policemen in riot helmets moved to the front and applied crowbars to the hinges of the door. Loud cracking reports echoed around the small room as the wood gave in to the excessive pressure. The movement inside the room became more frenzied as the policemen moved back and kicked twice at the door. The top hinge relinquished its hold and the door toppled inside at a drunken angle. One additional kick severed the bottom hinge, and the policemen rushed inside.

The occupants were rounded up and placed in a meeting room with two policemen to stand guard over them. Some of the women were crying, and several of the men were shaking uncontrollably. The policemen on guard had little idea of the crimes these people had committed, but they instinctively knew that sympathy should not be wasted on them. Innocent people, in their experience, did not grizzle and tremble with fear; they demanded to be informed what was going on.

Kawaguchi walked over to the computer console room and tried the door. It was locked. He looked through the window and saw a screen on one of the monitors scrolling through lines of code. He cupped his hands and placed them against the window to reduce reflection. The word "Deleted" prefixed by strange code words—or file names, had he known better—were rolling out on screen, and he realized that the machine was in the process of committing electronic suicide.

He grabbed the nearest chair, raised it over his head, and smashed it into the pane of glass in the door. It shattered impressively, and Kawaguchi leaned his hand through the space it had created and opened the door from the inside.

Kawaguchi knew absolutely nothing about computers, but as far as he was concerned, that was to his advantage. He didn't even consider touching the keyboard, but went straight to the main power switch on the main tower and flicked it off. The hum of the machine began to wind down until it was silent.

Satisfied, he looked around for any other pilot lights that might indicate evidence being destroyed, but found none. He returned to the main room.

A desk had been cleared for his use at the back of the room, and a can of iced coffee had been placed thoughtfully upon it for his consumption. He took out a notebook and began to jot down a few notes to prepare himself for the following interviews.

"Excuse me, sir." Kawaguchi looked up and saw a plainclothed detective standing beside him.

"Yes, Sergeant? What is it?"

The detective handed him a two-page computer printout. "This is a list of all people authorized to use this room. We took it from the security system that guards the first entrance. All of the people on this list are cardholders."

"Well, that certainly makes things easier." Kawaguchi checked an item in his notebook and ran his finger down the computer printout. "First of all, I want you to send me this young lady. Reiko Uchida. And send along the two policewomen with her. Then I want to see Noriyuki Suzuki. After arranging that, issue warrants on everybody on this list and order transport to take them to the station. We can interview them at our own convenience. I also want a list of all people who are not on this list. I'll speak to them here. Okay?"

"Yes, sir!"

The detective moved off, and Kawaguchi awaited the arrival of Uchida.

Four minutes later, Reiko Uchida, accompanied on either side by a policewoman, walked toward Kawaguchi's desk and was waved into a seat.

Kawaguchi looked up at her without smiling and then referred to his notebook. "Reiko Uchida," he intoned, "I arrest you for your part in the murder of Shigeo Kitazawa in Madrid on the seventh of April, this year."

Uchida's face drained of color and she looked about her helplessly, as if expecting somebody to pop up from behind a desk with a "Candid Camera" placard.

"You will also be charged with breaking into and entering the premises of the Sunset Travel Bureau on the third of April with intent to destroy property. You are not obliged to say anything now, but it is my duty to advise you that you will be placed in custody until the case against you has been prepared and passed across to the public prosecutor. You have the right under the constitution to legal counsel. Get her out of here!"

Kawaguchi did not even bother watching as Uchida was silently led away by the two policewomen. He flipped to another page to see on which charges he was to arrest Suzuki.

By the time Uchida reached the front entrance of Intersystems, Inc., she was wearing handcuffs concealed beneath a blue cardigan and had a beige coat draped over her head. The area outside was packed with spectators, television cameras, and reporters, and policemen had formed a human chain to pass the boxes of confiscated documents to a waiting truck. Uchida was led to a police car and guided into the backseat. Reporters and cameramen fought each other for the best position to see into the back of the car as it pulled away, its revolving lights competing against the flash guns of the many cameras.

United Kingdom (Sunderland)

John Wills checked the passports and tucked them into a small pouch belted around his waist. His wife was still messing around with an open suitcase and wondering what medicine to take.

"That's enough, Rita, for Pete's sake! They'll get us for drug smuggling if you put any more medicine in there."

"But foreign food doesn't agree with us English. You know that. You spent nearly a full week on the toilet when we went to Majorca."

"Yeah, yeah. But hurry it up, will you? The taxi will be here soon."

Rita Wills finally decided to include the Andrew's Liver Salts after all, and closed the suitcase. She secured it with a worn leather belt while her husband went off to the kitchen to check that the gas and water had been turned off properly, and placed it with the other case.

Two weeks on the Island of Rhodes. A dream come true. Rita was still a little concerned over where her husband had gotten the money for the trip, but he had tapped the side of his nose conspiratorially and she had given up asking. John was a good man and wouldn't get mixed up in anything naughty. She was sure of that. The redundancy pay he had received from Yamada Motors had been used as a down payment on a new house, so it couldn't be that. He must have won it on the horses. Or maybe even the dogs.

She was glad she had married a computer specialist. So few of the people laid off by the car factory had managed to get other jobs, but her John had sailed straight into another position at a factory making industrial air-conditioners and air-purifying systems. "Not luck, luv. Skill!" John had said when she had commented on his good fortune. "Most computer people move up to the big cities and work in smelly offices. There's nobody around here who knows computers."

John Wills returned from the kitchen. "About time, too," he said, observing the locked suitcases. "Let's get them out to the front door. The taxi will be here any moment."

The sound of a car pulling up outside entered the room.

"Here it is now. You ready, luv?"

Rita nodded, and they picked up a suitcase each, reaching the hall just as the front doorbell rang.

"Coming. Hold your horses," Wills said. He opened the door and stepped back as he saw two policemen standing on the doorstep.

"John Wills?" asked one of them.

Wills nodded, his throat suddenly dry.

"I have a warrant for your arrest. Would you please accompany me to the station?"

Christopher Belton

France (Paris)

Thiery Glaude was not at home when the three gendarmes knocked on the door of his apartment located nearby Saint-Mande-Tourelle Station. The landlord informed them that he was away on vacation, and they left.

The following afternoon, they returned with a search warrant. The landlord unlocked the door to the apartment and stood by while the three gendarmes spent two hours sifting through the contents of drawers and cupboards. They finally left the landlord scratching his head in confusion, a receipt for a single box of documents and two personal computers gripped tightly in his hand.

Glaude did not return to his apartment for three weeks. The landlord was given instructions to contact the police the moment he arrived home, but despite this, they were too late. Glaude had grabbed his passport and run upon realizing that his computers were in the possession of the police. He had no idea what had tipped the police off to his activities, but if they had his hard disks it no longer mattered.

Glaude was a professional hacker. He even advertised his services on the Internet. He prided himself on being able to get into any computer in the world, and had made a lucrative living by breaking through the security systems of hundreds of computers in order to obtain information for his somewhat dubious clients. Industrial espionage was the most common task for which he was contracted, but he had also been known to dabble in military secrets. And he knew how much mercy he would receive from a French court of law on a charge of treason.

So he had run.

He was traced as far as the Swiss border, where his passport had been inspected aboard a TGV running between the Gare de Lyon in Paris and the Gare de Cornavin in Geneva, but from there he seemed to have dropped off the face of the earth.

The man responsible for amending the data in the computer of Coppens Industrial Construction S.A., losing the company not only a valuable dam-construction project in Zaire but also several other large contracts on the African continent, was never apprehended, although a body matching his description was discovered in an apartment in Amsterdam three months later—apparently the victim of an arms deal that had gone wrong.

Japan (Odawara)

Tim Crawford drove through the hills of Odawara in a light and breezy mood. He had not seen his wife and children for nearly a week, and he was joyfully anticipating the reunion. The pressures he had been under had been lifted from his shoulders, and a strange form of euphoria had spread its way throughout his body, making him feel slightly drunk but in total control of his limbs.

He had visited the office that morning and been relieved to discover the main computer up and running and his staff coping well with his absence. One or two reproving looks had been directed at him for taking an extended period of leave without giving prior notice, but after the events of the week, the menace that these looks generated was almost laughable.

The glint of an aircraft high in the sky caught his attention. Although logic informed him that this was the domestic Tokyo-to-Osaka flight, he gave it a brief salute in case it contained Stockton, Mitchell, and Hiroko, who were due to have taken off some twenty minutes earlier on their flight to Geneva. He reached a hand over to the passenger seat and patted the cardboard box that rested there. True to his word, Stockton had arranged for a case of single-malt Scotch whisky to be delivered to his office in payment for Crawford examining—or attempting to examine—the ECB master tapes.

Jason and Erika were jumping up and down by the door when he turned into the driveway. They must have heard his car coming up the road. His heart jumped slightly to see them healthy, bronzed, and full of high spirits.

"Daddy! Daddy! Look what I've got!" Jason waved a clear plastic case with a blue lid at him.

"Whoa! Don't I get a hug first?"

The children threw themselves into his arms and he held them closely, not ever wanting to let go again. His wife appeared at the door and walked over to him, placing an arm around his neck and kissing him lightly on the cheek. He had expected a little more than that, considering that he was a national hero. But of course, his wife knew nothing of his involvement in the free-for-all taking place in the press and on television. He had telephoned her the day before to simply say that all threats had been exaggerated and there was no danger at all. Her relief had been profound.

"Daddy, look! I've got three stag beetles!"

Crawford took the proffered case and inspected the

contents. Three shiny black beetles longer than his son's index finger sat on a thick stump of wood. "Wow, they're smashing, Jason. Did you catch them yourself?"

"Yes. Me and granddad got up early every morning and found them in the woods. But two died."

"He's gross, Daddy. Don't take any notice of him or his nasty beetles." Erika stood pouting beside Crawford. "He lets them out of the cage at night and they crawl all over the floor. Ughh!" she finished with a shudder.

"It's ages before lunch, Tim," Yoko said. "Do you want something to eat now?"

Crawford looked over at his wife and smiled. The domestic conversations had brought him back down to earth. The anticlimax was delicious in the sense that it reminded him that he was a family man, not some he-man rushing off to protect the world from unforeseen dangers. He was just a normal man with a normal family. And that suited him just fine.

"No, thanks," he said, putting an arm around her waist. "But I could kill a beer. I have a thirst I wouldn't exchange for thirty minutes in the buff with your sister. Better make that two. I'll take one in for Dad."

Armed with two cans of iced beer, Crawford slid open the door to his father-in-law's room. Hidemitsu Murayama was sitting at the low table, reading one of the several newspapers spread out before him.

"Ah, Tim-san. You're early."

"Not much traffic on the roads this time of day."

Crawford took a seat opposite Murayama and passed across the beer can. "A bit early, but cheers anyway," he said.

"Cheers."

They sat in silence for a moment while they savored the cool beer. Crawford looked out at the garden and immediately felt a sense of relaxation wash over him.

"I take it that this . . . ?" Murayama indicated the newspapers laid out across the top of the table.

Crawford nodded.

"Then where are the names of you and your friends from the United Nations?"

"The Japanese government has decided to hush up our involvement. They would be a laughingstock if it were discovered that foreigners were the first people to discover the link between the mob and so many government agencies. They would also be forced to prosecute us, and that would bring too many facts out into the open. There are already cries for the government to step down, but most of these are halfhearted, as the opposition parties had an equal number of infiltrations. They have subsequently decided to privately commend us for our good work and let the matter rest there."

"The government asked you to keep quiet?" Murayama's eyes reached up into his forehead in amazement. "The Japanese government?"

"Yes. I received a telephone call from the prime minister himself. I have even been compensated for my inconvenience. Three million yen."

"But that's astounding!"

"Not really. There is a lot of information not released that would send the press into a feeding frenzy."

"Such as?"

"Armed foreigners operating on Japanese soil. Government agencies bugged. High-level politicians feeding the mob information. You name it."

Murayama wiped a handkerchief across his forehead.

"Were you one of these armed foreigners?"

"No. I was what you might call an administrator. Strictly no rough stuff."

"And what of this Hirata? Are the reports on him correct?" Hirata was still in the hospital, suffering from a nonfatal, self-inflicted gunshot wound to the head.

"Yes, although he was not responsible for the deaths in Sakaguchi's house. My friends from the UN helped out there."

Murayama lapsed into silence while he digested this information. He finished his beer and suggested Crawford go to get some more.

When Crawford returned from the kitchen with the refills, he noticed that his father-in-law had collected the newspapers together in a neat pile and laid them on the floor behind him out of sight. A visual full-stop to the conversation.

They cracked open the beers and drank in silence.

"I suppose you will be going back home this afternoon," said Murayama after a few minutes.

"Yes. Back to normality, for a change. I hate to imagine how much work there is on my desk."

Murayama nodded pensively. He looked out at the garden and heaved a heavy sigh. "The insects enjoy my garden more than I, Tim-san. I think I must begin to charge them rent. Although I doubt if they would pay."

Crawford laughed dutifully.

"You know, Tim-san," said Murayama, rolling the cool can across his forehead to combat the heat, "your Japanese is improving."

Chapter Twenty

Switzerland (Geneva)

Armin Marceillac and Sylvie Keppler met the flight into Geneva's Cointrin Airport and drove Stockton, Mitchell, and Hiroko to the IOCC office on the Chemin des Colombettes, where Jasper Hewes was waiting for them in his office. Two bottles of champagne stood chilling in a bucket of ice on the coffee table.

"Welcome, welcome, welcome, my friends," enthused Hewes as they were ushered through the door. He walked swiftly across the carpet and grasped everybody's hand in turn, his face turning sad only when he reached Hiroko. "Oh, my poor child. I am so sorry about Mr. Murata. I would have done anything to prevent such an untimely, er, death. How can you ever forgive us?"

Hiroko smiled wanly and accepted the apologies. She

felt slightly out of place—as if she had been called into the headmaster's office for praise she did not deserve—and was not completely sure of how to conduct herself. Her Japanese upbringing prevailed in the end. She bowed gravely and accepted Hewes's proffered hand graciously.

Don Mitchell watched her closely. He knew of Hewes's involvement in Murata's death, and had wondered himself how he would react to this reunion. Meeting the instigator—albeit unwitting—of his friend's demise had caused him to ponder on the possibility of his losing control and striking out. This possibility had concerned him all the way from the airport, but he recognized that his feelings were dictated by Hiroko's demeanor, and her forgiving attitude meant that he would be able to stay under control. He also noticed that he was looking forward to a swig of cool champagne. His mouth was dry and the wound on his side was itching.

The greetings dispensed with, Hewes turned to Marceillac. "Armin, the honors, please."

Marceillac removed a bottle from the ice bucket and skillfully popped the cork without loss of the precious liquid. Sylvie Keppler lined up the champagne flutes and passed them out as they were filled.

"To justice and a damn fine job!" Hewes raised his glass, and they each clinked their glasses against it in turn.

The toast completed, they all sat down—Stockton, Mitchell, and Hiroko on the couch, Marceillac and Keppler on the armchairs, and Hewes on his desk chair, which he had rolled over to the head of the coffee table.

"I understand that you are moving to America, Miss

Ito," said Hewes when their glasses had been topped up. "A very beautiful country. I am sure you will enjoy it."

"I'm sure I will, Mr. Hewes. I am looking forward to it very much. But I think it will take some time to get Don out of his bachelor habits. He is a very stubborn man." Hiroko looked fondly at Mitchell and placed a hand on his thigh. Mitchell took a hasty drink of champagne to hide his embarrassment.

"Oh, my God," said Stockton, grinning in delight. "He's gone all shy on us. Where's that big, brash Yank that I have come to know and love?"

Mitchell ignored him and turned his attention to Marceillac. "I guess we haven't really thanked you for all your help, Armin," he said. "Sorry for all those early-morning calls, and thanks for everything."

It was Marceillac's turn to blush. "My pleasure," he said. "Glad you got out alive. It certainly developed into something none of us imagined. What made you suspect that it was Hirata?"

"We didn't know for sure until we saw the results of the raid on the bogus house in Yokohama. We knew it had to be somebody near the top to be able to set up the logistics for modifying the computer master tapes and manipulate the press so effectively, but the only other item of information we had to go on was the fact that he forbade us from leaving the office without his authorization, which seemed a bit strange, considering the amount of trouble and expense the Japanese government had expended in getting us over there in the first place."

"How is Hirata's daughter, by the way?" asked Stockton, finishing off his champagne. Marceillac reached for the second bottle.

A frown creased Hewes's face. "Physically, fully recovered. Mentally . . . Well . . ." He shrugged helplessly.

Stockton nodded somberly. "And Hirata himself?"

"Stable," said Hewes. "It will be some time before he is released from hospital, but I don't think he is in any rush. It seems preferable to his next address."

"I can't believe that," Mitchell said, screwing up his face at the memory of the two days he had spent in the hospital while the gunshot wound in his side had been tended to. "The food is awful! I got a bowl of rice and a thin soup with seaweed in it for every meal, including breakfast, and the main course was a tiny portion of either cold meat or fish with a few vegetables. It was enough to kill anybody. God knows how I survived."

"You survived because it was a healthy diet," said Hiroko, slapping his leg.

"Well, I agree with Don." Stockton had had two experiences of hospitals in Japan. Once for an appendix removal, and once for observation when he had fallen off his motorbike in high school. "I think hospital food is the sole reason for the high suicide rate in Japan."

"And how is your injury, Don?" asked Sylvie.

"Fine, but it itches like crazy. A clean entry and a clean exit. I was lucky, I guess."

The small talk continued for a while until Hewes retrieved a buff folder from his desk.

"Well, here is the official update. Anybody interested?"

They all indicated that they were, and Hewes began to speak.

"First of all, the Japanese government has asked me to extend their unofficial gratitude to you all. They have managed to avoid a major embarrassment and have even come out of this smelling of roses. Several editorials have praised the National Police Agency for finally taking a heavy line with organized crime, something the press have been screaming for since the mid-eighties. It also mentions here that the sum of three million yen for each of you has been allocated in lieu of compensation. Sorry, lads, but I'll have to check to make sure it is ethical for you to receive these sums. Miss Ito, of course, is not subject to this and can receive the compensation tomorrow if she will let me have her bank account number, which I will pass on to Tokyo."

"Well, well," said Stockton. "The Japanese government goes soft. They must be grateful."

"They certainly are. No less than fourteen different agencies had been infiltrated, not to mention some very large institutions and corporations with close ties to the government. The implications are staggering. The very idea of the Yakuza controlling Japan would not only have destroyed Japan's overseas economy but would have caused riots at home. Fifty years of progress could have been wiped out in the blink of an eye, pushing Japan into a corner that it would never have been able to get out of."

"I understood that the motive was blackmail, not control." Mitchell held his glass out while Sylvie filled it up.

"Strangely enough, that is correct. The Sakaguchi-gumi is—or was, I should say—a small group on the fringes of the underground crime world, and lacked the vision to see beyond a regular income. From what has been gathered, however, Sakaguchi was obliged to report his activities to the larger controlling groups, and it would have only been a matter of time before the extent of his operations was fully understood and taken over forcibly. You people arrived on the scene in the nick of time, it seems. Hence the gratitude of the Japanese government."

"How did they select their victims?" asked Mitchell.

"I think Armin can answer that one. Armin?"

Marceillac shifted in his seat. "Well, it appears that Sakaguchi employed four computer-literate information collectors whose job it was to read all of the gossip magazines and newspapers and check out various online bulletin boards for people who were slightly down on their luck. They would research anybody unfortunate enough—and wealthy enough—to fall within their net, and work out a reasonable price that could be afforded on a monthly basis. If this sum seemed worth their while, they would then draw up plans to reverse the victim's luck. One of Sakaguchi's other men would approach the target and pretend to be the representative of a consortium, the interests of which followed a similar direction to the victim. A sum was received up front to put the plan into action and belay suspicions, and all computer-related specifications were drawn up by these men and passed across to Intersystems, Inc., who carried out the actual development and installation. Once the plans were activated, the targets were blackmailed. A very simple and effective MO."

"So what about the Korean bank scam? The reconciliation system. Who was the target there?"

"That was the first nonblackmail case they had attempted. The success of the other computer jobs went to their heads slightly, and the concept of making a onetime killing was evolved by one of Intersystems's managers, a man named Yanagida. It appears that they had already paid out more than one million U.S. dollars in bribes to get their hands on the documentation for the system's development. Fortunately, a great deal of the paperwork for this was left in the office in Kamata, and most of the source members for the revisions they had devised were found in one of the computers, despite a last-minute attempt to destroy them. Four people in Seoul have subsequently been arrested in connection with this."

"So far a total of two hundred and thirty-seven people have been arrested," continued Hewes, taking over from Marceillac. "This figure includes not only the culprits and so-called victims in Japan, but people who were used for varying purposes all over the world. The Japanese police also discovered the three people on the list you compiled for questioning. They had been removed forcefully, as you had assumed. One of them, the president of a pharmaceutical company, was found dead. He had been placed in the charge of a quack doctor who screwed up and overdosed him. The other two have since been arrested."

"So what happens now?" asked Stockton.

"Nothing. As far as we are concerned, that is the end of it. We have provided a report of all occurrences to the NPA in Tokyo, based on the evidence you managed to gather, but they have decided not to admit to your involvement. You will therefore not be asked to provide witness, and can go about your lives as if nothing happened."

"How long do we have to stay in Geneva?"

"That is up to you. If you feel like a break, stay as

long as you want. I'll square it with London and Chicago. Let me know when you wish to leave and I'll have your air tickets arranged."

Stockton turned to Mitchell. "What do you say, Don? Fancy a few days' break before heading back to the hamburgers and corn pone?"

Mitchell rubbed his chin and looked at Hiroko. "Sounds pretty good to me. How about you?"

Before Hiroko could answer, Sylvie said, "If Mr. Hewes will allow Armin and me to have some time off, we will be pleased to show you our country. I know of a beautiful hotel in Grindelwald on the slopes of the Jungfraujoch. They serve wonderful food and delicious wine."

"That's an excellent idea!" said Hewes. "Consider it a practice run for the real honeymoon, eh?"

Stockton looked up quickly. "What? Oh, no. You're not telling me that . . ." He waved his hand between Marceillac and Keppler. Hewes nodded proudly, as if he were the father of the bride. "Oh, Jesus, I don't believe this." He buried his face in his hands. "I've got to play chaperone to two couples who will probably be holding hands and kissing at every opportunity?"

Mitchell slapped him on the back. "Serves you right, Brit, for being so damned ugly!"

Stockton raised his eyes to the ceiling as if in prayer. "Beam me up, Scotty," he said.

ISOLATION
CHRISTOPHER BELTON

It was specially designed to kill. It's a biologically engineered bacterium that at its onset produces symptoms similar to the flu. But this is no flu. This bacterium spreads a form of meningitis that is particularly contagious—and over 80% fatal within four days. Now the disease is spreading like wildfire. There is no known cure. Only death.

Peter Bryant is an American working at the Tokyo-based pharmaceutical company that developed the deadly bacterium. Bryant becomes caught between two governments and enmeshed in a web of secrecy and murder. With the Japanese government teetering on the brink of collapse and the lives of millions hanging in the balance, only Bryant can uncover the truth. But can he do it in time?

THE FIFTH INTERNATIONALE

JACK KING

Stan Penskie is an FBI agent working as the legal attaché of the American Embassy in Warsaw. Robert Sito, an officer of the Polish Secret Service and an old friend of Stan's, needs to talk to him right away. He's found some pretty incredible information regarding various intelligence agencies around the world. But Robert never has a chance to go into detail . . . before he is killed.

Stan knows it's up to him to find the killer and uncover the truth. But as Stan digs deeper, more people are murdered and Stan himself becomes the primary target. Can one man battle a clandestine organization comprised of the most powerful people in the world? Can one man expose the hidden agenda of . . . *The Fifth Internationale*?

JOEL ROSS
EYE FOR AN EYE

Suzanne "Scorch" Amerce was an honor student before her sister was murdered by a female street gang. Scorch hit the streets on a rampage that almost annihilated the gang, but it got her arrested and sent away. That was eight years ago. Now Scorch has escaped. The leader of the gang is still alive and Scorch wants to change that.

The one man who might be able to find Scorch and stop her bloodthirsty hunt is Eric, her prison therapist. Will he be able to stand by and let Scorch exact her deadly vengeance? Or will he risk his life to side with the detective who needs so badly to bring Scorch back in? Either way, lives hang in the balance. And Eric knows he has to decide soon. . . .

ABDUCTED

BRIAN PINKERTON

Just a second. That was all it took. In that second Anita Sherwood sees the face of the young boy in the window of the bus as it stops at the curb—and she knows it is her son. The son who had been kidnapped two years before. The son who had never been found and who had been declared legally dead.

But now her son is alive. Anita knows it in her heart. She is certain that the boy is her son, but how can she get anyone to believe her? She'd given the police leads before that ended up going nowhere, so they're not exactly eager to waste much time on another dead end on a dead case. It's going to be up to Anita, and she'll stop at nothing to get her son back.

BODY PARTS
VICKI STIEFEL

They call it the Grief Shop. It's the Office of the Chief Medical Examiner for Massachusetts, and Tally Whyte is the director of its Grief Assistance Program. She lives with death every day, counseling families of homicide victims. But now death is striking close to home. In fact, the next death Tally deals with may be her own.

Boston is in the grip of a serial killer known as the Harvester, due to his fondness for keeping bloody souvenirs of his victims. But many of those victims are people that Tally knew, through her work or as friends. Tally realizes there's a connection, a link that only she can find. But she'd better find it fast. The Harvester is getting closer.

THE CRIMINALIST
WILLIAM RELLING JR.

Detective Rachel Siegel is a twelve-year veteran of the San Patricio Sheriff's Department. But she's never seen anything like the handiwork of the Pied Piper, the vicious serial killer who's been terrifying that part of California for months. Because she's the best at what she does, it's now her job to catch this maniac—but she has very personal reasons, too, for wanting him stopped

Kenneth Bennett works for the Department of Neuropsychiatry at St. Louis's Washington University. There's something special about the Pied Piper case that draws Bennett almost against his will to the west coast. He has no choice but to help Siegel in her frantic search—even if it gets both of them killed in the process.